The

WET NURSE'S
TALE

The

WET NURSE'S

TALE

Erica Eisdorfer

G. P. PUTNAM'S SONS

New York

G. P. PUTNAM'S SONS
Publishers Since 1838
Published by the Penguin Group
Penguin Group (USA) Inc., 375 Hudson Street, New York, New York 10014, USA •
Penguin Group (Canada), 90 Eglinton Avenue East, Suite 700, Toronto, Ontario M4P 2Y3,
Canada (a division of Pearson Canada Inc.) • Penguin Books Ltd, 80 Strand, London
WC2R 0RL, England • Penguin Ireland, 25 St Stephen's Green, Dublin 2, Ireland
(a division of Penguin Books Ltd) • Penguin Group (Australia), 250 Camberwell Road,
Camberwell, Victoria 3124, Australia (a division of Pearson Australia Group Pty Ltd) •
Penguin Books India Pvt Ltd, 11 Community Centre, Panchsheel Park,
New Delhi–110 017, India • Penguin Group (NZ), 67 Apollo Drive, Rosedale,
North Shore 0632, New Zealand (a division of Pearson New Zealand Ltd) •
Penguin Books (South Africa) (Pty) Ltd, 24 Sturdee Avenue,
Rosebank, Johannesburg 2196, South Africa

Penguin Books Ltd, Registered Offices: 80 Strand, London WC2R 0RL, England

ISBN-13: 978-0-399-15576-5

- Printed in the United States of America

Book design by Meighan Cavanaugh

This is a work of fiction. Names, characters, places, and incidents either are the product of
the author's imagination or are used fictitiously, and any resemblance to actual persons,
living or dead, businesses, companies, events, or locales is entirely coincidental.

While the author has made every effort to provide accurate telephone numbers
and Internet addresses at the time of publication, neither the publisher nor the author
assumes any responsibility for errors, or for changes that occur after publication.
Further, the publisher does not have any control over and does not assume
any responsibility for author or third-party websites or their content.

To Sophie & Charlotte

"... the moral state of the nurse is to be taken into account ..."

—FROM *Mrs Beeton's Book of Household Management,* 1861

The

WET NURSE'S

TALE

One

There was snow on the ground when my time came. I'd expected pain but, Reader! How could this be! I bellowed, I know I did.

"It's like shitting a pumpkin, it is," I cried.

"Shut up, if you can, girl," said Dinah, the midwife, "for you're hurting my ears and you'll be fine in the end. I'm feared your baby'll be deaf with the noise you're making."

"I'll never be fine in my end again," I panted, which made her laugh herself, but then the pains started back up and so did my shrieks.

When it was all over, I cried for my mother, to think what the poor thing suffered for all of us. And then I did what I'd seen my mother do for my whole childhood, and that was to open my shift for the baby and let it nurse.

~✿~

My mother told me that at first, she didn't take in other people's children because she wasn't a cow now, was she? But when Father wasn't

ERICA EISDORFER

drunk, he'd become frustrated at his wife's constant greatness and he'd hit her. One day she took someone else's child to nurse along with her own and she was paid for it, more than she ever made plaiting straw for hats or for selling eggs. And so she gave that money to him as a little extra and he drank it away and was a lamb for a week. She seemed to have milk for both her own and another, so why waste it, said she.

"Mother," I said to her once, when I was small, "will I nurse a babe as you do?"

"Well, my dear," said she, "you'll need more than that to do it," and she pointed at my own flat front and then laughed and hugged me to her so the baby in her arms gave a great squawk and then a belch. I recall her words for twasn't long before I began to grow, and when I stopped, well, I could nurse the whole of England now, is how I can say it best.

My name is Susan Rose. Here I sit in a lady's house with a lady's babe at my breast, and it's where I've been before though the house was different and the baby too. I've got what rich ladies need right here in front of me and I learned to do what I do by example. It's my mother's milk that washed me up on this shore. It has got me to places far from my own mother, and it has got me close to those I should have avoided and it has got me far from my own hopes, but I dream still. Nursing's good for dreaming, for it takes a good deal of sitting still.

In this house, the Chandlers' it is, I nurse a pair of little ones. I'm feeding one now and there's another awaiting in the cradle across the room: I can hear it mewling for me already and if it wouldn't disturb this wee one, almost asleep now, I'd get up from my chair, with him still suckling away, the dear, and fetch the next one. But it would. This one's a persnickety little mite, and doesn't like to be jostled once his eyes begin to droop. The girl's different. It's as if she's already accustomed to waiting for her brother's leavings and to catching sleep where she can. Of the two of them, I'd bet on her.

My mistress is the shrew, Mrs. Chandler. She hates those babies for losing her her figure, and she bids her maid lace her as tight as she can bear it, which sours her temper yet more. She bedecks the babies in cheap lace that scratches so they squall when she's showing them and so who could wonder why they fret? Yesterday, her mother tried to say something to her about it but she'd have none of it. "Mother," she said all high about herself, "this is Chantilly and it's from Paris and that's all there is to it." Mrs. Haver, as the lady's mother is called even by her son-in-law, catched my eye for a second but I looked away. I don't want to lose my position even though twins are hard.

Mr. Chandler loves his wife and that's a nice thing I can say. He's a barrister and young but quite ugly though he'll get better, I think. I notice things like this—how something appears now and what I think it'll look like later on. That's the thing of gazing at babies. It makes you right good at predicting. She's still angry at him for filling her in the first place, is how I see it, and she hasn't yet let him touch her, at least it doesn't seem thus, from the way he gazes at her as if he could eat her. She'll give in to him, I suppose, sooner or later, when she wants some bauble, or when natural urges strike her, which they will, once she stops hurting down below. Her bosom is still almost as big as my own, but those bladders will burst soon: that's how we put it, my mum and I, though it's not a very pretty image and I hope you'll forgive me for it.

Mrs. Chandler's house is not as clean as I could like. There's often grease on my cup and on the handle of my fork. And just yesterday, I saw one of the housemaids flirting with the farrier's boy for a whole half an hour and then give short shrift to the linen. I see a lot through that window, as I sit still at my duty. I do love a window. In my first position, I had no window, just a closet off a larger room, and to pass the time I sang. I know a lot of songs and for that I thank my mother, who sang to the ten of us every day over her own duties.

Yesterday, Mr. Chandler brought his own mother up to see the babes. The boy was at the breast and the girl asleep in her cradle. The lady stood very straight and looked at the baby in the cradle without a smile and then came up to look at the one at my breast. She sniffed like there was a dirty nappy though there wasn't. Then she fixed her eye on me, and if I'd been a shrinker, I'd have felt like a mouse in a field with a hawk overhead.

"And how do they do, Nurse?" she asked me.

"Rightly enough, ma'am," I says. "The girl's thirstier than the boy, but the boy cries off the breast."

"Well, see that you don't spoil him," she said just as if we hadn't been getting along fine without her for this week. "It's good for him to cry. How long has he been on just now?"

"He's not really suckling right now, ma'am," I said, "he's more dozing, the pet."

"Well, take him off, then."

We're used to obeying straightaway, of course, but I'd been alone for all the day without a word to no one and forgot myself and so before I thought I said, "Oh, but this one needs the breast to help him . . ."

Well, didn't she near rip that baby out of my arms, though his little mouth was still working at being roused by the talking, and there was my dug out and me hurrying to cover it and the baby wailing and Mrs. Chandler that was Mr. Chandler's mother briskly putting him in his cradle, none too gently.

And where was Mrs. Chandler the wife, all this time? Just looking out the window as if maybe there was a horse downed in the street.

"There," said the old Mrs. Chandler, "that's how we do it in town." And then to me, "Mind your place, girl." And didn't she just blow out of the room like a high wind with Mr. Chandler and Mrs. Chandler his wife right behind her. I waited for a moment, and then I walked outside my door like to stretch. When I heard nothing and saw nothing, I went back into the room and picked them both up and put them in my lap and rocked them til they slept again.

Later that night, Mrs. Chandler, and by her I mean the mother of the babies, this time, came up to my room to pretend to look at them, swishing around like, dipping a look into the cradle and then right back out.

"He's asleep, I see," about the one in the cradle, said she as if she didn't much care, but neither did she leave. Instead, she walked around the room with her candle held high, not looking at the babies, though there wasn't much else to see, was there? I asked myself what she could want, though I thought I knew, pretty well. Ladies'll ask things of us milky-cows they couldn't bear to broach with one of their own, see.

"Mistress," I said to get her started, "this is a nice little family you have here now, isn't it."

"Yes," she said, though she glared at me for talking first, "but it's all I want for a while. It was difficult . . ."

"Aah," I said. "Did you have a hard time of it, poor thing?"

Her face changed for just a flit. "Yes," she said, "I thought I'd die . . ." but then, afore the sentence was even yet finished her lip got hard again. "That's all I want for a while," she repeated, and this time she looked at me like she wanted something, and right now.

I looked down at the head of the mite at my breast. "I've heard about lemons," I said low, almost whispering.

"Lemons?" she said.

"Cut 'em in half, mash the pulp soft," said I, carefully not looking at her, "and then, you know . . ."

It took her just one second, but then she understood. She didn't thank me, nor did she cast another glance at the little boy in the cradle before she left.

❧

My own mother is a little wisp of a thing, and for all that, she bore thirteen children, ten of whom lived to see two numbers in their years. I had a brother who died of being kicked to death by a horse, and I had a sister who died on the childbed with her first. Losing Ada was terrible on my mother and partly because she catched the baby herself, but it died too. My mother has seen many babies come into this world but never, she said, never had she seen as much blood as there was with Ada. It ruined the mattress, and soaked the floor under the bed, so that it had to be cut out and replaced. I loved my sister. Childbirth is a dangerous business and that's why it's such a joy when all goes well.

When we were young, our father was not a bad man. He would use what he made to pay the rent and buy us food and shoes, and he'd carry us about on his shoulders. The bottle led him astray, though, and he became a harder man than he might've otherwise been, though perhaps he'd have turned bad in any case. Tis hard to know for sure. At any rate, twas my mother kept us fed long after there was any of us at the breast.

And thus it was that there was always an extra babe in the cradle by the hearth, whereas my own brothers and sisters might sleep in a plain box like a kitten. Indeed, we older ones, especially us girls, made the paying babies our special pets as they had finer things than did we. I recall a sweet little lass all the way from Leeds, with the softest lawn bonnets you might wish for, and a funny little fellow whose own mother brought him to mine and wept when she laid him in her arms.

"Oh, Mrs. Rose," the lady cried, "he's the only one I've put out to nurse and I do regret it deeply, but it must be so. Please, watch him with care and by all means, do not let him fall into the fire!"

"I'll watch him like he was mine," soothed my mother, but it did not help the poor lady to hear it and she wept as her husband helped her into the coach. She left us with many prayers that we would love him, as well as a pudding of some sort, and I ate very much of it.

꙳

I was always a good girl. I am neither the youngest nor the eldest of the children in my family but stuck right in the middle, right between John, who grooms for Mr. Bonney at the Great House in Leighton, and Ada, who died. When I was very little, our father worked his own fields and did a bit of this and that on the side. But when it was no longer enough to keep us, he went to the Great House and worked there: in the stables and gardening about and also some in the fields hisself. He is a big man with a full head of black hair and the bluest eyes you could ever hope to see. I inherited his blue eyes but also his stout posture, my misfortune. Ada stood more like my mother, like a reed in the wind, she was. Once, when my brother Georgie teased me for the wideness of my leg, I grabbed him and nearly broke his nose before he screamed for his brothers to help him. Now, as I think of slim Ada in the ground with her babe in her arms, I understand what my body's for. My bosom is as deep as all the oceans and my hips as wide as the fields and now, with no brothers around me to laugh, I sometimes feel pride, though I know it's a sin.

When I walked into the Great House for the first time, the cook told me to close my mouth else I'd draw flies into it. I was that amazed. On her afternoon off, my sister Mary, who worked in the kitchen there, had told of the carpets and the silver and lace on the underdrawers. What I did not expect and Mary, the goose, did not recall to us, was the pictures on the wall. As I scrubbed the floor or did my scullery chores, ofttimes I'd sit back on my haunches and gaze up at a field with horses so real it looked like they'd pull a cart up a hill, or a lady with her hair dressed in the old way, with that same round eye as my mistress had, looking back down at me. When, one night, I praised the pictures to Mary, she swore I was making it all up. I thought not to tell her she was stupid; she seems to feel her witlessness and also, to be charitable, they've not exactly given her a grand tour of the house. She's mostly peeling potatoes under the eye of the cook.

One day, as I polished the banister of the main staircase with a cloth finer than anything I've ever had against my own skin, I chanced to see a picture I'd never before spied. I polished my way close to it. The picture was small in size, really no larger than one of their table napkins that I'd ironed just that morning, unfolded. Twas a picture of a young woman with a baby, a fat baby, with cheeks as red as the lady's sash. It was a dear picture, and though I know my place, I wondered how my mother might have felt about it if she had a picture of one of her poor dead ones, just to help her remember their little faces.

"That's the thing of it, Susan," she'd sobbed to me when little Nancy had just died not two days old, born too soon, "their features are so muddy yet, they're hard to stick in my mind."

Gazing away, I didn't even hear the footsteps masked as they were by the rug's pile. There was a sigh, I whirled.

"Beg pardon, sir," said I, and bent right over my work once again. Invisibleness, Susan, that's the key, I told myself, and, looking down, I scrubbed at that banister, til I saw his boot in my way. I knew he'd seen me looking. There wasn't any hiding it. What was I to do but bob my curtsy? I hoped to keep my place and not be sent home in shame.

"You were looking at that picture?" he told me.

"Yes, sir, I'm sorry, sir. I . . ." and then I trailed my sentence off. I had no excuse for looking, I knew. I wondered what could be the harm of it, but I know my place.

"The lady's my mother. The baby's myself."

I looked up at him in surprise. Why, Susan, I told myself, what's he telling you things for?

He was not a pretty young man, Freddie Bonney, his beard all in patches and a nose like a box, too stout and a dandy in any case. I'd washed his underdrawers just that morning and wrinkled my nose: they were stitched small enough, but stank for all that.

I knew better than to give him any reply but I couldn't help it that I smiled a bit; he gazed at the picture just as I had done, but with a wrinkle in his face, as if he were trying to find the unsightly thing he'd become in that innocent smile in the paint.

Here's the thing of it: I knew his feelings for I'd felt 'em. I've told you: I'm plump and red myself, but as a lass I was as sprightly and sweet a thing as ever you could hope to see. And I sometimes wonder where she went, that girl, especially when I look down at my hands all wrinkled and red from the soap, or my legs, with their black hairs.

The master of the house was Freddie's father, James Bonney. Mr. Bonney hunted a great deal, even in the roughest weather, and we servants would run to pack hampers and linens for the master's picnics, as he called them. Once I heard a guest of his, a gentleman down from London, say to his lady, "Surely he doesn't expect us to shoot in this weather?" She looked over at me clearing away their breakfast and nudged him none too kindly with her sharp little elbow. That let me know they'd not had money long: the ones born into it forever never cared what they said in front of us.

Mistress Bonney was planted on a settee, and if she could have never raised herself from her seat, she never would have. She'd been pretty, which you could see easily enough: her blond hair still curled and her step was small, but myself, I never preferred that weak look. I liked the young girls of the house, Freddie's sisters, who laughed and ran, though their mother begged them to act like ladies. They did as they pleased though, and rode horses fast and stayed late at their entertainments, both summer and winter, escorted most often by a cousin of theirs, Miss Anne, when she could keep pace with them. I'm not sure Miss Anne was any older than Miss Maria Bonney and Miss Eliza, but her pursed lips and plain dress gave her situation away and some of the servants treated her slightly shabby. Not me. I felt for her, though for all that, she never cast a kind eye upon me.

As much as my master loved Miss Maria and Miss Eliza is as much as he disliked his own son. Twas too bad, really, because it wasn't Master Freddie's fault that he wasn't born to the horse and that he couldn't care a fig about a fox or a dove. He took after his mother: he liked a warm place, he liked a comfortable chair. She fed him sweetmeats when Mr. Bonney wasn't looking.

Very early one morning, the master and Master Freddie walked into the breakfast room whilst I still set the fire, and by their leave, I continued with my work. The master snorted and then I heard him say in a voice that curled my toes in my shoes for fear I'd hear it aimed at me one day, "Don't trouble yourself, Frederick. Your sisters will be happy to accompany me." He laid hard on that word, "sisters." Freddie said, "But, Father, I've been looking forward to it. I'm all dressed and ready, as you see." I snuck a peek and caught the father look at the son all up and down. It is true that Master Freddie had chosen a strange, large plaid for his hunting clothes, but I knew from hearing his valet talk as he pressed the suit that it was perfectly in style.

"What's that you're wearing, for God's sake?" said the master. "This is not a fashion ball, this is a hunt, man." Freddie's face fell—I did not dare to peep but I could guess it. The door opened and his sisters swept in. "We're ready, we're ready," they cried and then, "Oh, Freddie, what a look!" Father and daughters laughed together. Master Freddie said nothing. I finished my chore and curtsied and left them.

Later that morning I went to clean the grate in the morning room. I knocked softly and waited; Mrs. Bonney often did her lying down in there. I heard nothing and so I walked in and then stopped short. There was Mrs. Bonney on her chaise, but sitting up for once, and there was Master Freddie, on the floor in front of her, with his head in her lap, and her stroking his hair like he was still in skirts and had bumped his knee. I watched them for a moment, how she looked down at him, how she murmured to him. I recalled to myself the portrait of the two of them together, she and he, he just a mite and she young herself. My mother had stroked my own head in that very way even up til I had left the house, especially if some one of my brothers had said a mean word.

"Ah, Susan, now," she used to say, "you should try to mind your temper. You needn't say nothing to them when they're bad to you. They're just boys. They mean no real harm." And she'd smooth my coarse hair away from my forehead and whisper, "Don't fret, lassie. You know you're worth ten of any of the others. You're my pride, Suzie, you're my darling gal."

And I'd think how lucky I was to be her favorite of all of the babes my mother'd borne. I'd feel my luck. I wasn't the prettiest, nor yet the sweetest-tongued, nor yet the one that made her laugh the loudest, but for all that, she loved me best, though she loved us all. For my whole life, that had made up for being lumpy and angry. I'd only have to go to her and she'd pet my head and my tears would dry. So when I saw Mrs. Bonney and her son, I understood, see, what it was I was looking at.

❧

Over the years, the Great House gave a right many of us Roses our employment. My brother John grooms there even now. My sister Mary worked in the kitchen for some years. I served there, in several positions. And finally my little sister Ellen, two years below me. Ellen had the prettiest look of all of us children. She had a red cheek and hair as curled as ever you could wish for and if you heard her laugh, why, you wouldn't be able to help yourself, you'd laugh back.

Ellen and I came to the Great House at the same time due to the Brown sisters, both of whom worked there and who both left for Ireland to be with their mother after their father was sent to jail for drunken behavior.

Ellen expected to work for just a year, perhaps, and save enough to marry her sweetheart, Ned Loft. They'd been in love since they were tots and were biding their time til they could save enough to rent their own cottage. Ned had always said nothing was too good for her. He wanted them to start together in a nicer house than his father's where they'd have to share a room, even as a married couple, with his old grandma. Thus, she was happy, her face all aglow at the thought of what the shillings would mean. Mary and I were glad for her, though it will not surprise you to hear that we were a bit jealous as well.

I suited a scullery job best, being strong. Ellen caught the eye of the mistress, who asked that she serve her her morning tray and be available to her when she wanted her. This excused Ellen from much of the great labor due to that she always must look presentable. So perhaps she'd polish silver with a white cloth or perhaps she'd do a bit of mending, but she wasn't allowed to iron lest it make her sweat, and her hands must stay white, so laundry was out of the question. If she hadn't been such a darling, if she'd smirked at me or teased me for the great load of work I had to do, I might have lost my temper and slapped her but instead, she knew my trials and gave me a sad little look when I'd walk past her with a dripping basket.

And certainly Ellen did not just sit on her backside. The mistress needed her constantly, it seemed, to bring a glass of lemon water or to find the lavender pillow, or to cut her toenails or, when she had a cold, rinse out her hankies by hand. "Full of green, they were," giggled Ellen, as we gossiped for the moment we were in our bedroom before we slumbered. And when the mother of the French maid Minette died, and Minette went to see her buried, the mistress required Ellen to accompany her to a ball at a house twenty miles from ours and to stay there the whole night! Oh didn't we quiz Ellen into the wee hours when she returned.

"Well, I dressed her hair, but that's simple because you know it's mostly a matter of pinning the fake stuff to what's left of the real, and I'd watched Minette do it so many times. And I helped her with her stockings and laced her corset for her and clasped her necklace. And helped her with her shoes." Then she smiled and looked as naughty as a child. "After her corset was tightened," Ellen said, "she told me to ball some stockings and tuck them into her chemise, underneath her tit."

"She's flat?" Mary whispered.

"As a wet sheet," Ellen whispered back and then we three, all of us who have plenty, laughed til the tears ran.

The trouble began when the master saw her which he would do, goddamn him to hell. There was but one thing that would take him off his horse and that was the prospect of a different sort of ride. Mary had warned us, even before we arrived, about him. She tried to be polite about it and caught me in her glance too, but it was clear to the three of us that Ellen would be the one of us he'd choose to bother. During the first months of our employment, Ellen laughed about it, she did, because looks is all he gave her, and looks don't hurt, really. And Ellen always thought the very best of people, bless her. I used to snap at her about it.

"How can you be so sunny, all the damn time," I said once, "when you watched your father be the sort of man he was?"

"Oh well, Susan," she said gently, like she felt sorry for me, like I was the ruined one instead of the wise one, which is what I really was, "the master's not so bad."

"He is, Ellen," said I. "And there's plenty like him. You have to be careful and not smile at every Tom and Dick that shows you their teeth."

But she just looked at me, with her eyes full of love for me and of course, I melted and quit scolding her and now I wish I hadn't. Though to be honest, I don't know how she could have withstood Mr. Bonney in any case. He was the master; she was a maid in his house.

She thought the mistress would help her. We'd lie in our beds, Mary and Ellen in one and me in the second, on account of they said I sweated when I slept, and she'd confess to us how he'd put his hand full on her bosom over her dress or some other such indecency. One night she was rosy and happy and when we asked why, she told us that the mistress had caught sight of one of his leers.

"Didn't she just redden," Ellen said happily. "Now that she sees it herself, it'll stop I know it."

I didn't say anything because I didn't believe it would stop, not for an instant, and what's more, Mary, who usually agreed with everything anyone said, didn't speak neither. And that scared me more than anything else.

"What do you know?" I hissed to Mary when we heard Ellen's long breaths.

"I'm not as stupid as you say, Susan," said Mary. "I know he's bad, and I know it's a boon to her not to have to worry about what's between his legs."

"To Ellie?" I said, confused.

"No, stupid. To the mistress."

I caught my breath.

The next morning, I waited for Ellen to come out of her mistress's room with the empty tray, and I pulled her into a spare bedroom.

"Just say you're sick," I told her. "Say you're sorry, you can't work here and must go home because you have woman problems or pains. Pretend to faint. Break something. Do what you must, but leave this house. You must, my love. Because he's bad and she won't help. She's the mistress. You must learn your place, dear. You must."

But she only smiled at me and hugged me around my neck and kissed my red hands.

"Don't worry yourself, Susan," she said. "Nothing will happen to me. All will be well."

But of course it was not. When the bell rang for her later that afternoon, she didn't answer it. Mary and I snatched a look at each other and for a second I could see into Mary's mind: had Ellen run? But I knew better. I don't know why I did, but I did. I've always had that talent, to understand how the thing'll be, before the facts show themselves. I knew that little Nancy would die while others were still hoping. I knew that Isaac Cray, the baker's son, would drown if he fished so far into the river. I knew that Annie Bowen, the wife of John Bowen, would die in childbirth and that the baby would live. My own mother suckled that infant, out of pity for Annie, and never got a farthing for it.

So when later that day, we looked for Ellen and then found her up in the hayloft shaking like a dying moth, with blood between her legs and two black eyes, I felt no surprise. The groom's boy took the horse for the doctor, who said she'd be all right in a day, but I knew she wouldn't.

As I laid the fire in the sitting room, I heard the mistress whisper to her niece that Ellen seemed to have been in love with one of the lower grooms and that they'd fought as lovers do. I gasped and they heard me, but I pretended like I was come over coughing. I cannot even be certain that the mistress knew that Ellen and I were sisters. There's little resemblance, and why would anyone have told her?

My father came and carried Ellen off home. Mary and I cried together all night. She came into my bed smelling of yeast from the kitchen, like she always did, and yowled til I hushed her.

"We tried to tell her, we did," she wept to me.

My teeth were gritted so hard my jaw ached. "Why did he have to beat her, the bastard," said I. "She was so mild, she would have been far too fearful to yell. He beat her for the excitement of it."

"Oh, Susan, mayn't we leave this house? May we not? Let's run."

"What, and spoil the chances for our brothers and sisters below us? Do you care to see little Bob alone in the fields all the livelong day?" This affected Mary as I knew it would. We have a cousin of our age who is quick to smile, but slow to understand, and his mother has long blamed it on those days in the fields where he was set, from sunup to sundown, with a slice of bread but without so much as a dog for company. Twas his job to scare the crows from the fields but he was a small boy, just five years, and just learning to form his thoughts into his words.

"When he were tiny," his mother would tell us, crying, "bright as a star, he were, and lovely. But the farmer will not allow the boys a mate when they work in the fields like that, not even for half an hour. My Jerry, he forgot how to form his words from having no one to use them on!"

"You do not want to see little Bob turn out like poor Jerry, do you?" I asked Mary. "No, you do not. So we are trapped here. We cannot leave this house and you know it. I'd like to kill the master though," said I, "and watch his eyes turn red with his own blood. I'd like to hear him choke like as if he had a noose around his neck. Perhaps a horse will throw him and his ribs will poke right through the flesh or perhaps . . ."

But Mary began to cry again at my words so I stopped 'em, though I thought 'em in my head all the night long.

❧

By the time Mary and I had our half-day, Ellen had already drowned herself in the farm pond near our house. When Ned heard what happened to her with the master, as he would of course, he turned his back on her. I didn't know who to hate more, the man who spoiled her or the man who betrayed her.

I wept til I screamed, til my eyes were squeezed shut and my throat was hoarse, and I ached like I'd been gored. My mother, bowed with losing another child, smoothed my hair but it helped not at all, though I cried for her not to leave me. I always loved my sisters, but besides Ada, Ellen was my favorite.

We poor ones don't get time for our mourning, though we might have a deal of it to do. The day after the funeral, my father, bleary still from the extra ale he'd drunk to help him through his tragedy, handed me a shilling as if I was a child and it would make a difference. "There's no help for it," said he, "you must go back, you and Mary." My mother wiped her eyes on her apron and waved from the door. And so, sniveling in the cold and gray, Mary and I walked back over the fields to the Great House.

MRS. CROSS'S REASON

I do admit that I am quite exhausted, though, of course, very happy. My Georgiana is so dear to me, and I did fret about her welfare during her lying-in as it is her first and she is but slight. But thanks be to God, she passed through the trials with considerable spunk and her discomfort was not above what it might have been. The baby is a dear little mite, a girl, and sleeps well. I saw her suckle and now they both sleep.

My daughter is not averse to the idea of feeding her own baby with unborrowed milk and it filled me with gladness to hear it. Her husband seems agreeable to her idea and thus she will nurse her children, or at least this child, til it can eat gruel, if indeed it does live as it ought. I believe that it may have been my example that convinced her to keep her child with her and nurse it as it needs. It is what I did myself, as much as I could, and I credit it with the excellent health of my children. Women should not be afraid of it: it is, after all, best for babies to sup from the milk of their own mothers who carried them. I give thanks to God every day for each of my six children. I never buried one. My only sadness is that I was not able to provide the same benefit for the last of my children, my Robert, as I did for his brothers and sisters. I will tell you how it happened.

My children were set as follows: Mary and then William and then Adine and then Georgiana and then Maude and last Robert. I had not one whit of trouble nursing the first four of them, though I do recall how painful the suckling was when the babes were but small and the tits not yet readied. The trouble came with Maude, my fifth.

After nursing her for some weeks—thirteen, I believe—unvexed by any problems, one morning I woke with a fever. It came from my breast, which had become hard and streaked. No compress would help. The pain was quite terrible and I am not ashamed to admit that I wept with it as I had not in any one of my lyings-in. My husband, the best and most sensible of men, called for Mr. Diggory, who prescribed what he could but the infection was such that he must finally lance the nipple. The lancing relieved the pressure but the wound was hard to heal and when it did at last, I could see scars. I gave thanks to the Heavenly Father that little Maude had set enough that my one unharmed breast sufficed to give her suck. I began to give her gruel a bit earlier than the others to be sure that she had enough and did not want. She throve.

When I found that I was again with child, I fretted very much. Would I be able to feed this one with only one good dug? When he was born and my milk came down, it was terrible: very quick did I get yet another fever and this time in my good breast. I was miserable and the baby, who had suffered from yellowness, did not do well. I feared very much that we should lose him. Mr. Diggory, who again attended me, told me that he could not guarantee that once I recovered from this breast fever, another would not follow. He suggested that we find a wet nurse. I refused at first, but after much soothing and petting, my husband convinced me to do so. Though I was much in pain, I demanded to meet the nurse. We took the baby, whom I held in my arms the whole way, to the woman, who resided in the town of Leighton. Mrs. Rose lived in a small house with a wood floor and several rooms. Her children were mostly clean and well-behaved. The children ate their dinner at table—bread and milk and turnips and even a pie—and the girls curtsied nicely. One girl was a plump little thing, which I liked to see as it told me that they all had enough to eat. I asked to see Mrs. Rose's husband and so she called for him, and though he did not smile overmuch at me, I could see that he was not of the poorest stock, which I could tell from his eye. I wept very much when I left Robert and pined for him all the months of his absence which were six. I would have him back as soon as I could and did not leave him a moment longer than there was need. When we rode up to Leighton to claim him back, we brought a present of ale and sugar and fruitcake to Mrs. Rose as a thanks for keeping him so well.

Robert is now a man and a fine one, though not as tall as his brother William, though if that is truly because of his young experience, I cannot say absolutely.

Two

Just the other day, on my half-day off from the twins, I lost myself on the wrong end of Charlotte Street and saw a sign that showed the Hebrew star with its six points and realized that I had wandered into their district. Also I saw the boys with their books. So many of them had spectacles! I longed to laugh but didn't. You ought to do what you'd have done to you is what I learned from Our Lord Jesus Christ.

I know my Bible through and through, though I can't read a word of it myself. My mother would see to it that we were all at church on Sunday so I heard the stories there. And Tim, my eldest brother, born right after Mary, learnt to read a bit at school and could make out the stories for us pretty well. There's one tale I've thought of often and that's Rebecca. When I saw those boys on Charlotte Street carrying those books like the books themselves was infants, I thought, Well, that's Rebecca's doing. She connived the smart one forward to get that blessing over the big one, she did, and if they're a shrewd race, it's her they have to thank for it.

But after all, doesn't every mother favor one more than the other? Mine loved me the best. The mistress favored Freddie, never mind what his father thought of him. Even this Mrs. Chandler, if she has any mother feeling in her at all which I haven't seen yet but still she may, will care for one more. I'll wager it's the boy if he lives; he's the prettier of the two.

~❦~

As Mary and I walked over the fields to the Great House after Ellen's burial, we held each other and cried, but knew we was bound to go back. Our younger brothers and sisters were still small, some of them. Indeed our mother still took in babies from outside to nurse, though she told me when we were home to bury Ellen that the one in the cradle would be the last. Our father, almost as useless as a pot about bringing in money, could drink it up fast enough. It was us, I told Mary, who had to send some little money back lest Mam end up in the poorhouse with all those brats.

It seemed almost too hard to go back to the Great House. There they all were, playing and gallivanting, as if our poor thing wasn't cold in the ground because of them. I blamed them all for the master's evil doings. I wished his dogs would turn on him and tear out his throat. If he walked into a room, I would have to leave it, even if I left my chore half-done, lest my stomach turn and I spew my breakfast on his shiny boots. I'd hide in the drapes outside the room and when he left it, I'd run back in and finish whatever task I was at, double quick-like, so's not to get in trouble with Mrs. Hart, the housekeeper.

The first month hurt the worst, of course, but it passed and then came my half-day and I meant to go home to my mother for it. Twas a lovely day, with a breeze and bouncing clouds and for all my heft, I am a good walker, with a firm step. Mary stayed behind to walk with her young man who, if you ask me, just wanted to feel her bosom as much as she'd let him. But really, I couldn't blame her for letting him. It was as good a way as any to take her mind off poor Ellen, wasn't it?

I walked away from that house, feeling as light as if I were one of them clouds in the sky. The fields had flowers all over and I reached down to get some. I felt like I did when I was a lass, and my mother'd let me play for an hour. The freshness of the day recalled to me one of my mother's paying babies whose mother said she'd given it over to nurse so it might have the country air in its lungs. "If she wants to pay for air, I won't say no," my mam had said. We had all of us laughed, but now that I thought on it, it seemed like the baby's mother got the ripe end of the bargain. Twas a true English day, as my dad would say, and I had the whole afternoon and need not be back til nightfall.

I climbed the hill that separated the Great House from the village where we lived and stood atop it. The breeze blew my cap off and I scrambled to get it, though the scrambling put me out of breath and made me laugh. My hair tumbled out of its bun. I must have looked a fright, but I felt big and healthy and I recalled it to me that there was joy in the world, even after it seems there'll never be gladness anymore.

The view from the top of the hill afforded no sight of any house at all; the Great House was hidden by its forest and the village wasn't yet near enough. I saw only one lone horse rider, at the bottom of the hill, small as a pinprick. The figure raised his arm to hail someone and I pretended it was I and waved back.

I came upon an old oak, the same one that John and Ada and I would climb as youngsters. It seemed the very place to rest and eat the apple I had in my pocket. Now, though I'm plump, you'd hardly believe how I can bend myself. My foot will go nearly behind my ear, if I sit on the floor and bend up my leg; that's how I'd make Ellen laugh til there were tears in her eyes. "I never saw a girl so big as you and spry," she'd say, wiping the tears away. "Just think, Susan, if your stomach wasn't in the way, you could bend yourself like a Chinee!"

As there was no one anywhere to spy me, I heaved myself up into the tree, gathered my petticoat around me and plumped myself down on a branch. There I sat in my tree, munching and spitting apple seeds on the ground. My father'd slap us if we wasted, but once a town boy stared at me and laughed, "Look at the big one eating the core as if she's a horse." So that's what I recall every time I eat an apple: my father's hand and that boy.

Twasn't long before the rider I'd seen came along up the hill. The tree was all over green leaves and I knew I'd stay hidden if I didn't shift sudden, so I sat still and moved only my jaw with chewing. Wasn't I surprised to see Master Freddie on that black horse. After those few words about the picture of the lady and her babe, he'd never talked to me again, and of course, I'd never met his eye. I'd never wanted to. I felt sorry for him, is how I felt, and that's an uncomfortable feeling for a servant to feel, is pity for her master.

He walked right over to the tree and stood with his back to the trunk of it so that if I'd have had a mind to, I could have jumped down and ridden on his shoulders the way my brothers did with each other when they swam in the pond. Truly, I was looking at the crown of his head. I was half amazed with not knowing what to do when of a sudden, he undid the front of his breeches, and before I could even clear my throat, he had his thing in his hand and was pissing, a great arc. I was so stiff with fright I dared not even look away lest he hear my eyeballs move, so I couldn't help but see his thing, though his belly was big enough to jut out.

I'd seen one before on my brothers and on animals but this was the young master and that was entirely different, of course. Oh, Susan, I said to myself, you'll lose it now, for sure, your position. Master Freddie finished his piss and I thanked God, but he didn't put it away! Instead he held it for a minute and seemed to look at it, for I know not what reason, and then I belched out of the sheer shame of it and the apple, too. It was a huge belch and he started and looked up and there I was looking straight down at him, straight into his eyes.

Neither of us said anything for a tiny second. Then I said, "Beg pardon, sir," but I wasn't sure whether it was for belching or for just being there.

Quick now, he tied his breeches back up and then looked up at me again.

"Is that you, Susan?" said he, much like he didn't believe it himself.

"Yes, sir," I said.

"Were you spying on me, Susan?" he said, angry-like, though I was there first.

"Oh no, sir," said I. "I was eating an apple, if you please, sir."

"Could not you eat your apple on terra firma then, Susan?" he said but as I did not know what he meant, I didn't answer. So he said, "Well then, you'd better come down, I suppose."

"Yes, sir," I mumbled but could not move. There was not a way I knew to climb off the tree without showing him more than he ought to want to see. He seemed to understand this and turned his back while I came down which I did without much grace, more like I fell out of the tree than anything else, in my haste to fix myself up a bit.

"You're at home in a tree, then," said he after he'd turned around. I nodded and smiled though I dared not meet his eyes.

"That's a high branch," said he, surveying it, like, and I nodded again. Generally, I am not a shy person but I know my place and more than anything I wanted to curtsy and walk away and leave him there under that oak. It seemed, though, that he wanted to speak to me.

And then, Reader, I've never been more surprised. "It is too bad about your sister," said he, and at that, my mouth fell open, I could feel it, and I stared right into his face.

"Ellen, wasn't it?" he said, not meeting my eyes but staring off in the direction of the Great House.

"Yes, sir," I said and then, because I couldn't help it, "she was a darling."

He looked at me, but this time I couldn't tell whether it was pity or maybe just he'd had enough of talking to a servant and he said, "Yes," and then looked away at the view once again. I bobbed my curtsy and I mumbled a good-bye and then I walked off, quiet-like, as if there was a polished floor for me to not click my heels on.

❧

One afternoon, not long after I'd met the young master on the hilltop, I was cleaning the grate in the mistress's own bedchamber and thinking about my dinner, when the door opened and in came my lady herself. "Oh," said she to find me there, and I bobbed and sorried and she said I might stay and complete my work. I'd only just begun but I speeded up double time so that I might leave her alone the sooner. As I scrubbed and scraped, I saw from the corner of my eye that she'd taken a seat at her little white desk to write a letter. Someone had thrown something sticky—a caramel perhaps—into the fire and part of it had melted on the hearth and I needed my scraper but I tried my best to be silent. If you were to ask me, I'd tell you that silence is half of your chores all by itself.

A knock came upon the door and the lady started. I continued to clean til she said to me, "Susan, see who it is," so I rose from my knees and opened the bedroom door wide. There stood Anne, the Bonney sisters' tall, pale cousin, daughter of the mistress's sister, whose own marriage had not been as fortunate as my lady's.

"Come in, Anne," said the mistress. "I'm writing a letter and I want you to check my spelling."

"Yes, Aunt," said Cousin Anne and drifted in, the way a tall, bony girl will. I noticed she had a new frock, when all I'd ever seen on her was her sprigged lavender and her Sunday yellow, not so good for her complexion, according to Ellen. I returned to the grate.

"I've apologized to Mrs. Presset for Freddie's bookishness. I do feel that it's a good match, you know. Just read the whole thing, will you? I find myself so distracted these days."

Anne read as my mistress rose from her desk and entered her clothes closet. "Oh my," we heard her say, "these are all so boring."

"This is fine, Aunt," called Anne. "I just corrected a word or two."

"I do need something new," said the mistress as she came out of the closet, "but I'll wait for London, I suppose. Your new dress becomes you nicely, you must remember to thank your uncle for it. Now then, let me see . . . Oh, is that not how 'friendship' is spelt? I'm such a goose. Anne, do be a darling and see to the rose gown in my cupboard there for me. Minette is bringing me some chocolate, but I find I'd like to change my clothes before I finish that letter and finish it I must. It must go out in today's post."

"Certainly, Aunt," answered Anne, walking into the closet her aunt had just left. From where I knelt I could see her in there, shifting the gowns, feeling the stuffs. I watched from the corner of my eye how she laid a lace sleeve against her arm and a silk sash to her waist. She took the rose dress off its hook and draped it over her arm to bring it out, and then, suddenly, almost as if she could not help what she did, her hand reached into a bowl on a little table and she took up a necklace. For one instant she held it up and watched the jewel at the end of it as it shone and then, quick as a cough, she put it in her pocket. She was hidden from Mrs. Bonney's eyes the whole time. There was no way for that lady to have seen her.

She came out of the closet with the rose dress over her arm and a smile on her face. "Here's the rose, Aunt. I'll help you with it. Now, the letter. It is urgent?"

"Yes," said the mistress, "and I do hate urgency. I'm sure this letter and its urgency is why I feel as if I'm all over pimples on my face. Look at this one on my lip. Do you see it? Look here."

I crept out of the room with my scullery brushes.

❧

Later that night, I finished the pots by myself. The cook had gone to bed, as had Mary, and the new girl, a horrible thing called Letty, had already slipped out of the downstairs door for who knows what sort of mischief. It was quite late. Dinner had been delayed for the master, who'd finally felled a great buck he'd spied a month before and had pursued as if . . . well, I told myself, I wouldn't start up again lest I upset myself. I couldn't stand to cry into the pots; it was too lonely a thing.

The sound of breaking glass in the cold pantry startled me and my sleeves still rolled, I went to look. Just the day before a cat had become trapped inside and spilled a jar of cream which I'd had to sop up from between the stones. Wasn't I surprised when I opened up the door! No cat did I see, but instead twas Master Freddie himself bent upon his knees, staunching a spill of milk with his handkerchief.

"Oh Lord, sir," said I. "You needn't ruin your handkerchief. Let me."

"I seem to have made a terrible mess, haven't I," said he.

"Nothing that can't be mended. Look, that's that." I squatted quick and pulled a rag from my waistband and sopped, just like he was the cat, all over again.

"Did you want some milk, then, sir, and shall I warm it for you? And some cake? I think Cook has some cake left over from tea."

"Thank you, Susan. That would be lovely."

"Shall I bring it right up, sir?"

"No," said he. "I'll have it here, I think."

He sat right there at the kitchen table while I found another can of milk and forced the stove alight again and found a suitable glass. There was a piece of pound cake that Miller had left on a plate for her breakfast, I felt sure: I cut it in half and gave it to him.

"There now, sir. Is there anything else I can get for you or shall I leave you to your thoughts?"

He seemed to smile a bit at my words. "My thoughts?" he answered.

I giggled just an ounce. "Beg your pardon, sir," I said. "It's just something my mother says to us when we're distracted-like."

Master Freddie took a bit of cake on his fork. How dainty it seemed compared to what I'd have took if I'd been eating cake. "Do I seem distracted to you?" he asked.

I could have bit my tongue. "Oh no, sir," I said quickly, looking at the stones under his feet and wishing I were in my bed. "It's just a saying. You don't seem distracted, not a bit."

He put his napkin by his plate and stood. He smiled. "How do I seem then, Susan?"

Here I didn't know what to say. I didn't dare to look at him lest I stare. I've been teased about my staring. "There, girl," said my father plenty of times, "what do you see there to make you stop like that, the man in the moon? Hurry up, or you'll wish you had."

Indeed, Master Freddie's question seemed odd to me. After all, what could he care what I should think about how he seems? It's loneliness, said a voice inside me. Now, it's a peculiar feeling, the one a servant has when she feels pity for her master. I've said it twice now and it's true. We are used to them being our betters. It's the system God made and so it must be right and thus it's strange when it's turned all topsy-turvy-like. It seems to me now and it seemed to me then that if the young master hadn't been as solitary as a single bee, he wouldn't have been sitting downstairs in his kitchen when he might've been upstairs in the parlor eating the same cake. It was uncomfortable for me—not just the pity I felt, but also the idea that if I wanted to be a good servant and keep my place and be as I should be, I should contrive to help him in some way. That's what we're to do after all, ain't it?

"I mustn't keep you from your bed, Susan," said he. But it seemed to me that he wished I'd let him. I wasn't innocent, of course, especially not after my poor Ellen's fate at the hands of his very own father, but then again I was. I was innocent. And so it fared that I felt as shocked as I could be when he put out his hand toward my cheek, just my cheek, mind you, but still. I stepped back with a suddenness that frightened the both of us. He pulled his hand back with a jerk.

"Of course," he said, low, "I do beg your pardon." He gave me a little bow, which was the first time anyone had ever done such a thing to me, and picked up his book that he'd laid on the table to drink his milk.

And then no one could have been more surprised than I when I said, "Never mind, sir. I'll stay with you, if you'd like more." And by that I meant cake, but as soon as I said it, I wondered what it might sound like and if that's all I'd really meant after all.

You may wonder to yourself how it is that I could think to offer myself to him. After all, Ellen's misery at the hands of the young master's own father still kept my teeth gritted hard enough that my jaw ached; twas not distant enough to have forgot it, nor would it ever be. But Master Freddie was not his bastard father and indeed he seemed so different—as different as I from my Ellen—that perhaps I thought twas a way to bring her back, like as when you misplace a thing and track back in your steps to find it.

When Master Freddie took me by the hand and led me back into the pantry, he treated me very kind. With his own hands, he laid a cloth on the floor for me to lie on, so it wouldn't be just the stones. He kissed me and petted me til I was ready, but nervous still, so that when he began, I couldn't but yelp though he was quite gentle. I believe anyone would think he was. When he'd finished, he laid his head on my breast and stayed quiet for a moment, though his body heaved.

"Are you quite all right?" he asked me, after a moment.

"Yes, sir," I answered.

"It sounds odd that you should call me sir," he said but as I didn't answer, he didn't say more about it.

Quietly, he pulled back on his breeches and helped me up. I felt quite sore and strange. There was a blot of blood on the cloth he'd laid down on the floor and when he saw it he said, "Oh," and I said, "Don't worry, sir. I'll tend to it."

"Good night then, Susan," said he, and then he stuttered, "Thank you," in a tone so low I hardly heard.

"Good night, sir," said I. When he had gone, I gathered up the cloth. Twas nothing important, just one of the downstairs table coverings, and there were so many. I recognized it though, as I'd washed it and ironed it just that morning.

~❧~

We met again, Master Freddie and I, late at night in the pantry and quite often. It seems strange to me now that I didn't worry myself with my sinning, but the flattery of it turned my head and ruined me and that's as near the truth as I can get to. My life had been spent with pretty sisters and brothers too, as far as that goes. It's not as if I was in the practice of mirror-gazing, and certainly I know that pride goeth before a fall, but I'm not a stupid girl and I can see what's before my nose. There was Ada's profile, as clear and lovely as if she was born fine and there was mine, like it somewhat, only as if one hundred wasps had stung me and lumped me up. There was Ellen's hair, as black and smooth as the satin my master wraps his favorite guns in, and there's mine, as black as hers but coarse enough to stay the brush every time.

Even Mary's face, most like mine for its wideness, is pleasing to look at for the way everything fits while mine, oh, well, mine isn't quite.

I'm not complaining, mind you. I know I'm a lucky girl in my own way. My eyes are as blue as a spring sky which I know for I have been told it many a time, even by my father which is where I got 'em. And my mother tells me still that though I might not be the fairest, there's somewhat about me that draws the eye and I kissed her to hear it, but then again, she's my mother ain't she, and loves me. And I daresay I have a certain knowing look to my face, like I understand what a person's thinking, because I do, often, and I know that look can be appealing to some as like to see that in a girl. I have caught a glance or two from a man, to be sure, but not so many as I couldn't count them on my hands. Mostly though, men like a sweet complexion and a downward glance and a slim waist and those I do not have, nor never will.

Indeed, I'm just trying to explain how it is that it was possible for me, always the smartest of us girls no matter how you cut the cake, to let herself get carried away and forget the future like I did. Twas simply the relief of it, you see, that someone would choose me. I felt somewhat like a queen, though if I had knowed then what it is would happen to me, I would have quick shaked off the crown and got back to work.

But I mustn't forget the truth of that matter and that's that Master Freddie is not a bad man. He took advantage, yes he did. And he was wrong to do it. If I'm to be honest though, I must confess the whole of it and that's that I let him, didn't I. I could tell: he wasn't the sort to press himself, the way his bastard father would do. I did as much of the choosing as he, is what I think. He chose me because I seemed likely. I accepted him because he seemed to need comfort and I have a big heart to go along with the rest of myself. And to be as honest as I ought to be, I must admit that I accepted him because I needed a bit of comforting myself.

As the summer waned, the master's hunting parties became more and more frequent and we were all of us run ragged. We often heard the master bellowing to my lady about the expense of all us servants, but it was the guests that required the extra help, is what we knew and what I suppose he finally caught on to. And it wasn't just the guests themselves, but their people too, their maids and their men and their grooms and whatnot. It meant that the cook needed extra help and the laundry too, but us sculleries were never thought of and we had all our extra work and more. Mary and the cook's other girls never rested from packing lunches and tending to guests, their special requests for coffee, not tea, or tea, not coffee, or for a hotter fire or for an apple before bedtime. Mrs. Hart kept us running, all the time, Letty and Sara and me and the others, what with the extra grates and boots to be scraped and chamber pots to be rinsed and Lord knows what else. The list of chores would take the day to say. I came to admire Mrs. Hart, not for her kindness to us that's sure, for she wasn't, but rather for her remembering, which was truly a wonder. I even told her as much.

"Why, Mrs. Hart," said I when she came to check on how we were coming with the reblacking of the dining hall grates, "Sir James's man marveled just this morning how you remembered that the old gentleman likes his toast very nearly burnt. He said there is no one like you at any other hall."

"And to be sure," put in Letty, "it's likely that he knows how every other hall'll treat a guest, don't he, as much as he seems to be never at his own home too much, from what I hear."

"That's enough, Letty," said Mrs. Hart. "If you didn't become so familiar quite so quickly with our visitors and their servants, you'd have less information about that that's none of your business." And that shut Letty up. But she thrust me over a pleased look which is all I'd wanted anyhow and sure enough, the very next week I was promoted up from scullery to maid, though when she told me so, she said, "And, Susan, do try to keep your apron clean or at least change it when it's soiled."

I'd been doing maid work anyhow, in addition to the scullery chores, except now it just meant I could get away from the grates. It was a lovely new life. I slept an extra quarter of an hour and I wasn't all a'sweated by six in the morning from the scraping and blacking. I'm a girl that always will put my elbow into any of my chores and I'm proud of it, but it meant that as a scullery, my nose was smudged, my apron, my hands, all of me, smudged. But as a maid: well, I might find myself in the mix with some polish or some dust, but no grates. I worked just as hard as ever I had at my cleaning, but oh, with no more grates I felt as if I could sing. And to be sure, I even had the tiniest ruffle on my cap now! No one could knock me from my cloud, not even my father, who said, on my afternoon home, that if he had riches, he'd rather see me in the laundry or such, and put a pretty girl up to be the maid. And my brothers laughed though my mother did not, but then we all thought of Ellen at once, and even my father, already in his cups, fell quiet with the memories.

The only sore spot for me was that there wasn't no one I could share my joy with and by that I suppose I mean a man. I saw how Letty led them on. I don't suppose she ever talked about anything of consequence with any of them, not the grooms nor Thomas, the handsome underbutler with green eyes, nor the brewer nor any one of them. And I wondered often enough if my father had ever had a civil word for my mother. I recalled to myself though I hated to do it, how Ned Loft broke my poor Ellen's heart after she was already so harmed and after he'd promised to love her forever. All my life I'd seen lovers fighting with words and fists and still I wanted some for myself. I wanted to tell someone about my rise in station and have them give me a squeeze and say, "That's the way, Susan. We'll save together and soon enough, we'll have a nest egg. Now, give us a kiss," but no one did.

Master Freddie, of course, wasn't someone for me to love. He was born too high, of course, and also, though he and I met in the pantry once a week or so, I didn't think of him as a man. No, I don't mean that as harsh as it sounds. He was kind enough, and to be as truthful as I can be, I even derived some shameful pleasure from our act, but what I mean is that I thought of him as my master and needful. And that was like no man I wanted. I craved a man bigger than me, someone like Miles the smithy, whose arms were as big around as posts.

When I met Master Freddie in the pantry, it was because he'd come downstairs to ask the cook for a bit of cheese or a piece of pie or some such, and I learned that that meant he wanted more than just a morsel of something to eat and that if I should choose to find myself in the pantry later, I wouldn't be alone. It pleased me to think that he wanted me. That's what kept me awake when I should've been asleep. And that's what kept me going back when I was quite sure that if I didn't, no harm would ever have come to me from any unwillingness. I wasn't unwilling. I was sinful and lustful and also, though it makes me blush to say it for it's so pathetic, I felt pleased by his attentions.

Attentions, really, is a big word. We had little talk to our adventures, to be sure. We'd meet, we'd kiss but just a bit, and soon I'd be on my back. He was kind, as I've said, but we both knew our places in our arrangement, and for that, words weren't necessary, not really. I could sense that it saddened the young master a bit, that we hadn't more than we did, but there was naught I could do for him. I'm not learned enough to make a pleasant conversation, and besides, what could I have told him that would have been of interest to him? The art of black-leading a grate?

I don't mean to say, not for an instant, that he could have loved me. I mean only that I believed he missed the sort of tenderness that I did not feel for him and that I did not care to receive from him. I did not miss it. I knew it would never grow between us and so I did not yearn for it. I did not grow to love him, ever, though it seems clear that many maids in my particular position, and by that I mean on their back in the pantry, would have grown to love their masters. I knew better. As I've said, I have the gift of foresight, but even without it, I'd have known that Freddie wasn't the one for me. Once only, did Master Freddie talk to me in the way that lovers talk. The moment felt horrible to me, but I shall repeat it here.

After we had done, on that particular night, he lay on his back for a moment longer than was usual while I was pinning my bodice back together. It's worth a note, I suppose, to say that I met him in my maid's frock, while he came to me in his nightgown. A servant cannot be casual the way a master can, not even in that circumstance.

At any rate, he spoke suddenly. "It seems I'm to be married," he said.

I looked at him in surprise, at his saying such a thing to me, but it seems that he thought that I reacted to the words he spoke rather than that he did at all.

"Yes," he said, "my mother's great friend has a daughter. Maude is her name, and she and I have been slated for each other since we were tiny. It is both our mothers' fondest wish."

I did not know what to say. I did not know what he might have wished me to say. He was looking into my face and so I smiled a bit and continued to tie my strings.

"She's . . . that is, Miss Maude is . . ." Master Freddie seemed to stammer, "Pretty."

I felt embarrassed for him, that he would tell me such a thing. It was no business of mine. Miss Maude's station was high and mine low, especially now that I'd fallen, and he should have known better than to speak her name to a maid in his house. It was wrong of him and it made me angry with him that he knew no better. And I felt angry for another reason. It put the image of the two of us, Miss Maude and Susan Rose, standing next to each other, into my head. It made an awful picture and I wished it away as soon as it came to me.

"I do hope she's a person of some sensibility," said Master Freddie almost to himself. "I do hope we can talk to each other."

It did not seem to occur to him that I stood there, still smelling of his seed, still tying my strings. But I realized again then, as now, that he'd have just as soon had a friend to have tea with as have had a lass like me to lie with. I'm not saying that Master Freddie cared more for boys than girls the way some of the high folk did; what I'm pointing to instead is the fact that he just wanted a bit of human companionship, and if it had to come from a housemaid, well then, I say he was lucky to have me to give it.

I sometimes wondered about Miss Maude, how pretty she was and how much she'd be able to care for Master Freddie, but as it wasn't my concern, I didn't dwell on it. I turned to my new work with a great deal of vigor and won the approval of Mrs. Hart more than once or twice. The young master and I still met on occasion, and thus it was that as the summer waned and the family began to talk about their sojourn to London, I found that the smell of coffee made my stomach turn and that I no longer needed the rags that I'd used every month since I was thirteen. You will not be surprised, dear Reader, to learn that I found myself with child.

LADY PRUTHY'S REASON

My Dearest Sophie,

I write to you with good news. James has finally been offered a position at the House of Lords. He shall visit there tomorrow in order to fully understand his duties, but I daresay they shall never be as arduous as those he has fulfilled these past years as undersecretary to . . . well you know about whom I speak and I dare not write it. It has been a trying time for him but he has kept his dignity about him at all times and I have been extremely proud of him.

Pray forgive me . . . I have launched into our own news without wishing you the very best of our prayers and thoughts. I miss you every day and wish that we lived but closer, so that our children, cousins after all, might grow to the same closeness we enjoyed as girls. Ah well, with husbands as busy as your Charles and my James, it seems that we shall have to do with summer parties and weddings. It is the way of progress, I daresay, but it does seem cruel, does it not.

If we were together, I would whisper all the latest gossip into your ear, for life in London does afford some of the most delicious tidbits. Imagine, if you can, what we all thought when Lady Bradshaw attended a ball in a gown that did nothing to hide her delicate condition. But be satisfied, dearest Sophie—the bump on her belly, though evident enough, did nothing whatever to detract from that famous bump on her nose about which we have tittered so often. Oh, I do long to laugh with you as we did when we were young!

The children are very well. Colin is quite the little man now that he is out of his skirts and I do truly think that Netta believes that she is his mother. It is vastly amusing to watch them as they play. I can only hope, dear Sophie, that your sweet Anna and Margaret are as pleased to play with each other as Netta and Colin seem to be.

As for the baby, well, he will have to go out to nurse. I had a nurse in the house for the older two, but the other servants were quite jealous and there was a deal of strife. Twas almost a full-time occupation to keep them in line. It seems that they felt that she ate better than did they, which is of course ridiculous, but you know how servants will take a thing and worry it to death. This time, as James will have me travel with him, I must leave the house alone at times, and thus will not be able to control the servants as much. The nurse I have found lives in Leighton and the baby will go there presently.

I must close and post this letter. I expect Lady Lily Bateson and Mrs. Albert Graves for tea. All my love, darling.

Your Cousin,
Elizabeth Pruthy

Three

These Chandler twins had a trying night, bless their heads. I blame it on the cabbage soup I ate, but perhaps it's the colic. One twin awakens the other, over and over, til you'd think they'd be too exhausted to even squall but squall they ever do. Only the breast will help, and so I've learned to suckle both at once. It made me giggle to think that I could, but that's what comes from having tits as big as I have. I sit on the bed, with my back against the wall, and put each baby on a pillow beside me to raise it up enough so that its mouth will reach me. Even with the pillows I have to lean forward, which burns my back, but they'll sleep sooner if they suckle than if they don't, so I suppose it's worth the ache.

I must hope the soup passes soon, or else they'll be up all of today as well, and none of the three of us will sleep at all. I'll tell Cook that it's just bread and cheese and tea for me today and I'll pour the milk out of the window. I'm given plenty of fresh milk, which even my mother would tell me to drink to help my own, but it makes my stomach roil and my farts stink, and I've never learned to like it. I pour it out the window when I can, or invite the cat upstairs to drink it from a dish I took from the kitchen. I take care to shoo the cat out as soon as he licks the plate clean lest he sneak into the cradle and steal the babies' breath.

I'll tell you how I got here, Reader, though it's a long story. A long story is a good story though, for a one such as I who must sit and be patient through the days and nights, watching and caring for those who can't keep themselves.

❧

The Bonney family left for their London season in October. It had rained all the week and the wind whipped the Great House as if sorry to see them go, though Lord knows, the rest of us were not. We lined up to see them off which wasn't much done, according to Letty, who'd had it from a cousin of hers in another house, but the master demanded it. We waited in the rain while the family picked their ways to the carriages. The young master, who was to ride with his mother, gave me a nod which his mother, who had his arm, marked, I was quite sure. It gave me a start though in truth, I told myself later, what does it matter now? I thought I must quit or be sacked soon enough, after all.

Though I was well on, no one knew. I am that large anyhow, you see. By my luck, I wasn't bothered much by sickness in the morning which always troubled my mother so. My apron and my bulk hid what needed to be hid. I still did my work well and had Mrs. Hart's approval, and to be truthful about it all, I hated to disappoint her as much as I feared my father's wrath. It was right amazing to me that she'd never caught on to my condition, seeing as she'd see a pin out of place in a curtain, but I suppose she never thought of me as that sort of girl. Letty was that sort, and I know that Mrs. Hart often scolded her to be careful of herself. I, on the other hand, didn't seem to need the same advice.

First, I kept myself to myself as far as boys went. Second, they didn't cast me a glance, anyhow. I knew how she'd feel when she found out: as if I'd cheated her because she hadn't caught on to me herself. That doesn't make sense, does it, but Mrs. Hart would hold a grudge against a person for a thing that didn't.

I hid myself from Mary easily enough. I waited til she changed into her own nightclothes and had her shift over her head and then quick as a blink I'd change mine. I've always been quick and anyone's quicker than she is so it was easy as cake.

Even Master Freddie hadn't caught on, though our meetings had continued just up til he left for town. It makes me blush to say it, but as my front grew, I just turned so that I wasn't on my back, you see, and that seemed to both please and distract him. I knew that he'd wonder where I'd learned such a thing, but I didn't want his weight on me in the front, and that's what made me remember how animals couple in the fields and wonder if it would work for us too.

Only once did someone cast me a look and that was Mrs. Bonney herself. Just two days before they left for London, I had climbed up on the library ladder to dust a shelf of books when she walked into the room. I curtsied from up there, and she waved me back to my work and walked over to the window to stare out of it for a moment. When I glanced at her again, she was staring hard at my stomach. I realized I had my arms up over my head, one hand steadying myself against a shelf above my shoulder while I dusted the books with a cloth, and that in this posture, I stuck out a great deal. I quickly lowered my arms and turned my face back to my work, but I could feel her eyes on me til she walked out of the room. For a few days after that, every time Mrs. Hart spoke to me, I'd hold my breath, but nothing ever came of it and so I calmed myself.

When I finally resigned my position to Mrs. Hart, it plainly shocked her and made her angry. I wouldn't tell her my real reason. Instead I told her that it had to do with my mother's health. It seemed to me that it was all my business and that I was less likely to poison Mrs. Hart against the young ones in our family if she didn't know the truth. In a village like ours, and unless you have a trade which none of us Roses did but for my brother John, the Great House is the best hope for employment that we have.

I told Mary because, after all, she's family isn't she, and then I had to threaten her to keep her peace about it.

"But, Susan," said Mary, "who can have done it to you? I never saw you with a man, not once."

"Aye, well, that's my secret and I'll keep it, if you please. Only don't tell anyone here about why I've gone and if they think they've guessed, you deny it for me, Mary."

"Susan," she said, suddenly all over horrified, "it cannot be that it was the master, can it? Not like Ellen?"

"As if I would have let that bastard near enough me to . . ." said I. "No, twas someone else, someone you do not know of."

"Oh," said she, sobbing, like she always does at the slightest little grief, "they'll all find out anyhow and we'll be disgraced. You know it's true."

"Mary," said I, "just you make sure it's not you who's told them. For if you do," I said and clenched my teeth so she'd know I meant it, "I'll tell Father about what you do with Timothy out behind the kitchen garden, and then he'll flay you for sure."

Well, Mary's afraid of me and so I knew she wouldn't tell. But I spent yet another sleepless night thinking about my father and what he would do to me when he saw the truth.

❧

I let my mother and father wonder why I'd come home for a day before I told them. But then I had to do it. My father called me a slut, a slattern, a whore, and all that. He slapped me so hard I had the handprint a hour later and then he went to find as much ale as he could swallow.

"It's simply another excuse for him," I said to my mother as she bathed my cheek where he'd smacked it. "He'll blame me for his headache tomorrow but he'd have had it anyhow and you know it."

"Yes, I know it," my mother said. Then a doubt crossed her face. "Susan, the same as happened to Ellen didn't happen to you, did it? Surely not?"

"No," I told her as I'd told Mary, but gentler, for she was my mother and still grieving from poor Ellen's fate. "No, Mother, it came about in the regular way." I tried to speak nicely, for to be sure, I felt the shame of it, though the shame was mostly for getting myself in trouble than for the deed itself.

"But who was it, Susan? Your father'll smack you til you tell him and I want to know too."

"Mother, listen," said I. "Father'll never get anything out of the man who did this, believe you me. It's impossible. We might as well pretend it's a virgin birth for all the good it'll do him to try."

It upset my mother and my father too that I acted so calm about it all. But I did not know how else to be. It might have made my father soften if I'd cried more but I didn't so he didn't. In truth, I had drawn so much from my pot of tears for Ellen that I could hardly pull up more for this. It caused me a great, hard pang to think that I had ruined myself to be married, that's true. But my mind excused it thus: no man whom I'd accept had ever looked at me twice and it might never have happened even if I'd kept my virtue. And if it came to pass that I wanted to marry, say, if my father continued to abuse me forever and I had to leave his house, there'd be some ugly widower in need of a mother to his brats who'd take me. There was always such a one.

The fact is that I did not hate the creature inside me; not at all. I recall one day, as I walked through the snow to milk our cow, I felt a kick so hard it took my breath away. I found a stump to sit on and watched my stomach, even through my heavy skirt and apron, as it moved like a basin of water carried too fast. It was astounding, it was.

I remembered watching my mother, time after time, as she stood in the garden or at the table, with her stomach jutting so that she could hardly do her work. She was a woman who looked rosy when she was with child and prettier then, than when she wasn't. Carrying a babe would put some flesh on her and she wouldn't look as gaunt as she often did between times. My father seemed to see it too; he'd sometimes give her a kiss or a squeeze in front of all of us, just to see her blush and smile.

My brothers and sisters, the older ones still in the house, seemed ashamed at first of my condition, but as time waned it became a matter of course, the way things do when you're living with them day to day. Indeed, round as I became, I was still stronger than most of them and worked harder than any of them. In my time away in service, they'd forgotten that I could hold my own quite well, but they learned it again soon enough.

When Bill, who was seventeen and between Alice and me, called me "saucebox" under his breath when I wouldn't fetch something for him that he wanted, I caught his hair in my hand and pulled it so hard he cried like a baby. "If ever you say such again," I said to him, in a calm, scary way I have made my own, "I will crush your parts with a brick while you sleep. Do you understand that I mean what I say?" He whimpered and refused to answer so I twisted tighter. "Say, 'Yes, sister,'" said I, til he did. He walked away glowering, but I could see him recall to himself the way I had been and realize that I had not changed, babe or no babe. Later, I made him a special tart from cherries my mother had dried from the springtime and smiled when I handed it to him. I was pleased to see that respect for me had crept back into his gaze as well it should for I am his older sister. Anyhow, I see no call to shrink and mewl when I'm as big as any boy and fiercer than most.

⚜

Reader: we are told it was payment for Eve's sin to suffer so when babies come, and so may it be. Twas torture for me, that's sure. But when the midwife handed me my Joey, I thought no more of the pain and the muck of it, for I was all over with love for the little mite that I had pushed into her arms. Twas then and will always be a miracle, whether it's them high ladies or us low girls that do it.

Perhaps overhearing my shrieks had lessened my father's anger to me. Maybe I yelled a tiny bit louder than what I needed to do, just so the screams would reach him in the cowshed where I hoped he sat. In the end, though, it must have been the baby's aspect that took the murder out of him. He would not even cast a glance toward the mite for the first week but then, once he laid eyes upon his sweet face, he softened some. "My first grandchild and a bastard," he said aloud to me as if he hated me, but I didn't care what he said when I saw him like the look of my Joey.

There hadn't been a baby in the house for a year. When we were all growing up, there was always one in the cradle, and sometimes two, if my mother had one of her own. She'd nurse hers until they were old enough to eat a little solid food, and at the same time she'd nurse the paying babies til they were old enough to be replaced. There was always a paying baby so she never dried up. It's just like a cow works, if you want to know. If there's suckling, there's milk.

I'd remembered her words when we went home to bury Ellen. "Well, Susan, this one's a foundling, and they don't pay much," she'd said when I asked her about the one in the cradle. "I'm past forty years now and the wrinkles in my face frighten away the clients. I know it: I look as if my milk is sour and perhaps it is. They want someone younger and plumper anyhow."

She'd looked sad when she said it but then we were all sad.

***

When my baby, who I'd named Joey, was about four weeks old, we had a visitor.

"How de do," called a voice from over the door. We had the upper part open and Mother told Ada to see who called, as her hands were all amuck from the kneading and I was just dozing for a minute after having been up at night with the baby. I waked right up when the lady came in though, for the novelty of the new face. Even my father, who was at home, stood and bowed his head when Ada showed the guest in.

"Oh, sorry to bother," said the lady to my mother. "Are you Mrs. Rose, then? I am Mrs. Potts, niece to Sarah Carter that lives over near church. Can you spare a moment?"

After she was all welcomed in and sat down, we all agreed that old Sarah was a good soul and that the day was cold but fine and that we'd none of us never seen such a winter for turnips. And then she told us why she'd come.

"I work up in Aubrey," said Mrs. Potts, "as cook for a very nice young family, the Holcombs is what they're called. Mr. Holcomb works at his father-in-law's business, which is dye making, and they do a very good deal of trade. Why, half the time, Mr. Holcomb is late for supper but when he's not, they eat very fancy and often with guests. I'm up at dawn with them, is what I can tell you."

We all listened politely.

She continued. "Now, Mrs. Holcomb, the dear, just had her first baby, a wee little thing. And that's why I'm here. He needs a nursey, for she," and here she lowered her voice, "she can't provide for him from herself. I heard that a nurse for hire lived here and that's why I've come."

"Oh, Mrs. Potts," said my mother, "I'm afraid you're too late, by a year or more. I've all dried up."

"But what about she?" said Mrs. Potts, pointing straight at me. "She could."

It so happens that Joey had been sleeping for some time, and I had leaked along my front, as will happen when the vessels are all full and in need of emptying. And it happens also that I'd been thinking just that: that as I seemed to have more than enough for my own baby, it would hurt no one were I to share it with another baby who might need it. I had even said as much to my mother after a week or two of feeding Joey. "Mother," I'd said, "now that I've caught on to it, I could do as you did." My father had heard me say it and since then his mean words had tamed some, imagining the extra shillings I could draw, I suppose.

"Yes," he jumped in quick, "couldn't you, Susan m'dear."

I threw him a look for the sweet words where there hadn't been any in so long and came forward. "Yes, ma'am," said I. "I'm sure I'd have enough."

"Well," said Mrs. Potts, "and what would your husband say, though? Would he mind?"

"He died," I said as quick as I could. I said it too quick, and it made her look at me quite sharp, but she hadn't said that she wanted a saint for her mistress's baby, had she.

"Ah," said she. "A shame. Well, as the baby needs a nurse, and as you seem quite clean and very healthy, well, I think you'll do. They'll pay nicely, a pound a month, minus tea and sugar."

"A pound!" said my father, though I winced at him saying it. "The rates has risen!"

Mrs. Potts nodded at him. "And I'll see to it myself that she's fed well."

My mother and I looked at each other, confused.

My father replied in his gruff manner, "She'll eat what we eat. I've provided well enough for my family these long years: Susan needs nothing more than my wife had and she was nurse for a faggot a years."

"Yes," said my mother smiling, "ever so many."

Now Mrs. Potts looked confused and then suddenly, she understood something that we had not. "Oh, Mrs. Rose," said she to my mother. "Now I see what's befuddling us. The girl is to come with me. I'm to take her to Aubrey. The Holcombs wish for a nurse to live in their home. It's the style now, you know, and there's no worry for them, as to the cost of the thing."

"But," I said right off, "what about Joey? He'll need me for ever so long, still."

"You're going, girl," said my father. "Don't try to wriggle out of it."

Mrs. Potts looked back at me. "How old's the mite?" she asked, and when I told her she wrinkled her brow. "Well, yes," she said, "that's young but he can be hand-fed, can he not?"

"Mother," I said, turning, "Mother, you know it's too soon to leave him. You know that."

"Yes, dear," she said, "but a whole pound . . . and now that you're not at the Great House . . ."

"Mother," I said. "But how will he live?"

And then it was I made my mistake. "Father," I said, though I oughtn't to have done it, "you're soft for Joey. You don't want to see him without his mother, surely? How will he live?"

At that, his eyes hardened. "He'll live," he said. I could tell it: if Mrs. Potts weren't in the room, I'd already have a black'd eye. "Didn't you hear your mother? She said she'd feed him by hand."

"Well," said Mrs. Potts, standing from her chair, "I'll be at my aunt's house for two days more. I leave on the Thursday coach. You can make up your own minds, but, girl," and here she looked me in the eye, "it's not often you'll have the opportunity to help your family as much as this." Then she added, "Especially . . ." but did not finish her sentence. I wished her dead at that moment, because her words, as she'd meant them to, made my father's hand tighten on my arm.

❧

Of course I ended up going. My father made my decision for me. He beat me til I shrieked and then, out of his mind, he made for the cradle. When my mother stood in front of it, he smacked her til she bled from her nose. My father had a vicious streak in him, and though I couldn't believe he'd hurt a baby, twas hard to know what his anger would let him do that a milder man wouldn't have. In the end, I could do nothing else. I packed my two frocks and my aprons and my caps and then I nursed my baby one last time. He suckled something fierce, staring at me til his eyes drooped and he slumbered. I wept and wept and wiped the tears off his sweet face before I put him in his cradle.

"I'll see to him, Susan," said my mother, kissing me gently, as her lips were still puffed from my father's fists. "Don't worry your head. He'll be right as rain, never you mind."

And so with a last sob into his cradle, I took up my bundle and went to meet Mrs. Potts and go to Aubrey.

MRS. MOORE'S REASON

I am Mrs. Moore, first name of Prudence. My husband is half-owner of Cranford & Moore, which I am sure you have heard of. He owns exactly half of the company, not a bit less, though our name is second, but do not let that fool you. Someday, and I think it will not be very long, my husband's name may be the only one on the sign.

The shop you see on the street is only a small part of the business. There is a warehouse of some size here in Seagrove which, as you must know, is a town that is growing like a foot grows out of a shoe. Seagrove is not simply a holiday seaside spot, not anymore. It's shipping that's made it grow so. That's how my husband, who started in the navy I am proud to tell you, made his mark. He learned the ins and outs of the shipping business from Mr. Cranford—there's no denying that the old man knows that part of the trade.

Mr. Moore, my husband, says he cannot do without me. I do not need to boast, I only repeat what he says. He consults with me quite constantly. Just the other day at dinner with Mr. and Mrs. Steele I heard him say this, "I know shipping, but it's Mrs. Moore, here, who knows the shop. I've never seen a head for business like she has. Knows just what to stock, she does, and . . ." then he whispered, "If the baronet's man has special-ordered a fancy silk, well then, he might have to pay a bit extra for it, not that he'd know it." And he cast me a naughty look and then didn't we all laugh.

It was no trouble to me to take care of Charles and Henry when the shop was smaller. I had only to bring them with me and the ladies of Seagrove thought nothing amiss about it. But now that the town is growing and we are serving the likes of baronets, well, it's different. Mr. Moore and I were both surprised when I realized, though it was late in our marriage, that I was with child; after all, the boys are both big enough to be away at school, which gives us our days to attend to the business. We talked together about it as we do with all our business deals and thought to put this one out to nurse.

Before the child was born, I had made my inquiries and had found a fine spot with a lady named Mrs. Rose down in Leighton, not five hours away by coach. I reserved the spot and pre-paid an extra half-shilling in advance, in order to hold it. I knew better than to depend on the shopgirls to keep the business going while I hunted for a wet nurse. Sometimes, I told my husband, money spent is money earned.

"That's the way to do it, Mrs. Moore," said my husband to me when he'd heard what I'd done. I also told him that I'd made the nurse sign her X to a paper that said if the baby died before the first three months, I would deduct that same extra half-shilling from her year's wage. She agreed to do it and we had a contract.

Four

When I walked into Mrs. Holcomb's bedchamber, I think she would have liked to hug me around my neck, though she'd never set eyes on me before. She was that glad to see me. She was sweet enough, as was her baby, though my Joey was ever so much handsomer.

"Oh, Susan," she said, friendly right off, "this is the baby! His name is William," she said as she handed him over. He was tiny and grayish, though his eyes, I noted, seemed to fix quite well on my face for a mite so young. I told her so and she smiled at me from her bed where she'd been holding him.

"Oh, Susan, do you see that too? And you will take good care of him?"

"Of course I will, ma'am," said I with a curtsy. We were alone in the room, she and I, or else I might have been too shy to say what was next. "Ma'am, do you think he might be hungry now? I have been traveling a long way and . . ." And then I spoke no more because my blouse spoke for me. I felt in somewhat of pain and I needed to be milked, to say it blunt.

"Oh, do try and see," she said, sitting up in her bed. "May I watch?"

I felt shy at a lady's eye on me like that, but I needed that baby to suck or else I'd be drenched in no time. So I sat in a chair and undid my blouse and my shift and gave the baby to suck and suck away he did, the dear. I looked down upon him in his bliss and it made me smile and weep, together. Then I heard a sniff from the bed.

"What can be the matter, ma'am?" said I alarmed. I made to give the baby back at which he started to squall, having his meal interrupted.

"No, Susan, let him drink," sobbed the lady. "I am only jealous. I meant to nurse him myself, but the pain in my tit was more than I could bear. He's been living all this time off the nurse next door who our neighbors said we could share til we found someone of our own. I meant to nurse him myself, I'm sure I did. I'm sure there is something wrong with me. I think it may be the tightness of my corsets. . . . I have always liked them quite tightly laced. Perhaps they shaped me in some way that did harm." Her tears flowed.

I thought to tell her that it always hurt at first but then the pain subsides. I had had it from my mother, who had told me so, and I found it to be true. I thought to say that a compress of cold tea leaves would ease the pain and toughen the teats, but then again I thought not to. My employment depended on her needing me, after all. Now that I had been parted from my own darling and landed here in this lady's house, I might as well perform my duties. After all, if I went home, my father, now that he had the idea that city people paid as well as they did for a nurse, would find me another spot in a breath's time. At least here, the mistress seemed kind.

Later that night, as I sat in my room—my own, though tiny!—the master of the house came to meet me. He was a nice-looking man with handsome ginger whiskers but he said this, "Susan, is it? Yes, well, we are very glad you've come and that Baby William has taken to you as well as he has." I nodded and waited. "Lucinda . . . Mrs. Holcomb . . . feels greatly her inability. I don't wish it to depress her. I ask you only, Susan, to use discretion in the performance of your duties." He said it kindly but he looked straight at me as he did and I understood. "Yes, sir," I said. "Of course." And that was that.

Mrs. Holcomb would have liked to have kept the cradle in her bed-chamber, but Mr. Holcomb could not sleep through the night because of the baby's crying. She wept more tears when the cradle was moved to the lovely nursery all set up.

"Oh, but Mrs. Holcomb," said I as I set the nappies out and the lard, "this is quite a good thing, it is. It means he's growing so fast, you see, that he cries during the night. He does it because he's hungry!"

And then there were tears afresh because, "Oh, Susan, I hate to think of him growing! I know you'll think I'm silly" (which I did, rather), "but he's so perfect as he is, isn't he."

I looked at her sitting in a chair, all a'ruffled and a'laced, holding that baby like he was a precious jewel and I had to smile. "Yes, ma'am," said I. "He's that."

It surprised me, it did. I figured society ladies like herself cared not a whit about their babes; after all, I'd seen enough rich people's babies in my own house for months or even more than a year whilst I grew up. One lady, very high born, sent her baby through her footman, who told us that his mistress traveled abroad and thus could not care for him herself. Indeed the little boy stayed with us for upwards of eighteen months without that we heard a word from the lady, but only received her payment. But Mrs. Holcomb was different than that. She liked nothing more than to be in the nursery, watching while he slept or changing his nappies or singing and rocking.

Wait til I tell Mother about this, I said to myself, because she will not believe it. "That's how it goes with those who farm their babies," she had said to me once. "They aren't near 'em, are they, so if the baby was to die, well, the pain of it's slighter than with us who lives with our own."

I thought how amazed she'd be to hear how much Mrs. Holcomb dotes, though she's rich. And then I thought about myself, who don't live with my baby but loves it like my own life. For, Reader: how could I be happy? All the time my thoughts were with my own child. I prayed for his health and wept for a sight of his little face. I recalled to myself the portrait of Master Freddie and his mother which I had seen when still a scullery in the Great House, and I cried to think that when next I saw my child, he would look so different from the last time. I asked Mrs. Potts when next she would visit her aunt so that I could send a message and hear a word, but it was not to be for a long while, and so all I could do was to wait and hope that all was well at home.

One day, after about three weeks of my time at the Holcombs', the mistress came into the room whilst the babe nursed.

"You needn't turn away, Susan," she said, sitting across from me. "I am resigned to it now."

"It's just that the master . . ." said I, but she interrupted me.

"Yes, James thinks that I am more fragile than I am, in fact," said she. "I am just glad that we found you and so quickly. Really, you are just the thing for the baby."

I thanked her.

"But really, Susan," said she, her eyes wide, "I have heard such stories about nurses! A friend of mine . . . do you remember her, Mrs. Hughes who came in a pink gown . . . had a nurse that dosed her baby with laudanum to keep it quiet! Mrs. Hughes caught the woman one day as the horror tippled it into the baby's mouth! The nurse said it was all the done thing in London. Mrs. Hughes had begun to suspect something was amiss when her baby's eyes did not focus as they should have. Laudanum for a baby that small! Dreadful."

"Gracious," said I, "what a thing to think of!" And then I thought, oh, is that why she spends the time she does in the nursery? To catch me at something? I looked at her and it must've been reproachful-like, because she started and then she said, "Oh, Susan, do not think that I ever suspected you of any misdeed. Never have I. I have only been glad that you were here, that my darling child had your gentle care and your . . . softness."

I laughed because I was relieved. "Ah, miss," said I, "soft is certainly what you might call it. I'm like a pillow for the baby, amn't I." And then my own tears started up and fell.

"Susan," said Mrs Holcomb, "is it your own baby you're thinking of? Poor dear, to have lost a baby. I am indeed a lucky woman."

"Why," said I, staring, "my baby is as alive as yours! He is at home with my mother, who is feeding him by hand whilst I am here for yours." Then, as I saw her face change, I realized that I spoke too brashly. I said quickly, "I do miss him but your William is sweet and you are so kind."

"But, Susan," said she, still horrified, "what of him? How could you leave him?"

I shook my head and thought how stupid rich people can be. She would not like it, I knew, if I told her I was there because she paid me. She wanted to think that I suckled her baby because I loved him and that I accepted the money like it was an afterthought. "There was nothing for it, ma'am," I said, "it was how it had to be."

"I cannot understand it," said she, "but I tell you again: I am glad for it."

"He's asleep now," said I, looking down. "Shall you hold him or shall I put him down?"

"I'll hold him for a moment," said she, and she grasped him like she hadn't seen him in weeks.

I closed the door soft when I left the room. I saw that Mrs. Holcomb could not understand how things were at my house; how my father would drive me and Joey both out if I were to leave this position. A pound a month wasn't nothing to turn a back on in my family. I doubted that even Mrs. Hart back at the Great House earned as much. But that was life in town, and whether it was to my misfortune or not to have the slot, Reader, I leave it to you to say.

❧

One day, after I had been with the Holcombs for over two months, Mrs. Potts told me that she planned to visit her aunt in a fortnight and that if I could work it with the household, I might accompany her. I was right wild with joy. It was the evening and I was having my dinner while Mrs. Holcomb sang the baby to sleep which she liked to do now and again, before he slept. He was a dear little thing and had grown fat and rosy and slept as well now as anyone could ever wish. I could not wait to ask her permission for my visit home.

The Holcombs finally finished their dinner, and since they had dined without guests, I thought to ask the butler to beg for a moment of their time for me. I was shown in and I curtsied deep and then looked up at Mrs. Holcomb's worried face.

"Susan," said she, "surely there is nothing wrong?"

"Oh no, ma'am, the baby is sleeping like a little angel."

"What is it then?"

I tried to be dignified but my happiness made my words tumble. I described the opportunity. "And, ma'am," said I, "William will be well cared for. I have seen to it. I asked Mrs. Kildare's nurse Ratliff whether she could take him on, just for a very few days, and she said she thought she could and she would ask her mistress. And you could cut my pay for that piece of time . . ."

Mrs. Holcomb interrupted me. "Susan, you are ahead of yourself.

How can you wish to leave William in the hands of someone he does not know? He knows you, Susan, and would perhaps be too shy to sup from anyone else and might take ill!"

"Oh but," said I.

"Really, Susan, I am shocked that you . . . that is, I know that you want to see your own child, I'm sure you do, but you know that William is delicate . . ."

"But, ma'am, he's plump as a peach, he is. And twould be three days only, and . . ."

"That will do, Susan," said Mr. Holcomb in a sharp voice. Mrs. Holcomb had jumped up from the sofa where she'd been drinking coffee and had turned away. I could see her slender back shaking. My shock had made me numb and I could not yet believe that she would not grant me leave to see my child.

"Susan," said Mr. Holcomb, "please leave us. Mrs. Holcomb and I will discuss the matter and be sure to give you a final answer very soon. I know that you are distressed but please compose yourself. I have heard that the baby's milk may be affected by the nurse's moods. Please try to collect yourself as best you can."

I opened my mouth and closed it and curtsied and left the room. My despair was very great. The "baby's milk," he'd called it, as if I had been born for them, as if my own sweet Joey had given me my milk for my masters and their brats.

❧

The next morning the door to the nursery opened quietly, and I rose from my chair and bobbed my curtsy for Mr. Holcomb. My face had swelled, I felt sure, from having cried all night but there was naught I could do for it. I put the baby in the crib and he was good and did not cry.

"Susan," said he, "Mrs. Holcomb feels she has been too hard. She wishes you to know that you may have the three days you wish for."

I gasped for I had not thought it would turn thus. "Oh, sir," said I, my voice hiccoughing with new tears. "I am so grateful to you."

Mr. Holcomb cleared his throat. "She worries, Susan," said he, "that you will decide to remain in Leighton. She feels that it would be difficult to immediately find a replacement nurse for William and that his health would suffer for it."

"I promise to return with haste," said I. "I promise . . . on Jesus' own name, sir."

He smiled. Then he said quickly, as if he were explaining, "Mrs. Holcomb is herself so innocent, you see. She feels . . . she believes . . . that you care as much for William as . . ." and then he bit his tongue. "Well," he said, "I have said too much and perhaps made the both of us uncomfortable. Susan, you have been careful of Mrs. Holcomb's feelings these months; please do not let your sensibilities diminish in this regard." And then he bid me good morning.

I hardly knew what he meant with that last, but I was so happy I hardly cared. My milk let down just to think of my own baby's face, and I thought to pick up little William and offer him to suck which he did do. I smiled down at him in my joy. I thought about what Mr. Holcomb had said about Mrs. Holcomb and how she wished for me to love the baby, not just nurse it. She has learnt a hard lesson, I thought, and perhaps a bad one for me. It's like King Solomon did with the two mothers who wanted the same baby. When he threatened to halve the baby and give each woman one piece, one of them agreed and the other refused, and that's how he knew which was the real mother and which the false. Perhaps that's what my mistress is thinking to herself even now: that I would let her baby be cut in twain if twere to serve my purposes. "Ah," I whispered as I looked down at the sucking baby, "your mother's near a fool, isn't she, my dear."

I waited anxiously for the days to pass. While I watched the babe in the night, I burned a tallow candle that I might sew my Joey a bonnet from a scrap of muslin I had bought in the shops. I have never cared for needlework much, but I wanted to bring a gifty with me. I had some ribbons for Ada and some loose sugar for my mother and I meant to buy an orange for the children, once the time for leaving came close.

Once Mrs. Holcomb came in and saw me sewing at the bonnet in candlelight and gave me a smile before she looked at her baby in his cradle. I saw how it was: she did not offer me the use of one of the house lamps, which she would have done before I had asked for the leave.

Three days before our journey, Mrs. Potts and Mrs. Holcomb both wished me to make an errand to the baker's shop while the baby had his nap. Mrs. Holcomb had neglected to advise Mrs. Potts that there'd be company for tea, and Mrs. Potts had naught but brown bread in the cupboard as the next day was her baking day. I welcomed the errand. Partly, it felt lovely to be out of doors as I had been in the nursery for many hours that day; William was hurting with a tooth coming in and squally. And partly I wanted to make up to the mistress, as I knew it would go better for me once I was back in her good graces, so I thought to do the job fast and well.

I was diligent in my errand and bought a lovely plum cake which I got for less as it was crookedly rised but, I thought to myself, Mrs. Potts will serve slices after all. I took up the cake and walked quickly back to the house and meant to give it over to Mrs. Potts as quick as could be but she was not in the kitchen. I put it in the pantry and when I came out, there was Mrs. Potts and Mrs. Holcomb both, having come down the stairs together. Behind them was someone I could not see as both those ladies tended toward tallness.

"Oh, Susan dear," said Mrs. Holcomb and I curtsied and wondered at her face, teary, but that was almost usual, and then I saw Mrs. Potts look at me with great concern and out from behind them stepped my own sister Ada. Her face was struck with sadness and I did not know why.

"Mother?" I said, clutching her. "It's not Mother?"

"No," said she, shaking her head. "Mother is well. It's . . ." And then she stopped and gave a sob.

"Ada," said I, "tell me quick," and then she said, "It's the babe, Susan," and then I sat down hard on the floor like my legs had broke and I could not move.

❧

When I remember next, I think I was sick. The doctor had come and given me a dose which had put me to sleep, and when I opened my eyes Ada sat by me holding my hand. "Susan," she said. "You've woke."

"Tell me, Ada. Tell it to me."

So she told me that our mother had tried her best to feed the baby by spoon and by sucking rag and that it had seemed to work at first. "She did it for the little babe with red hair, do you recall, Susan?" said Ada. "Perhaps when we were nine or ten years? His mouth was misshaped, remember, and he couldn't suckle at first? She fed him by hand for ever so long and remember we all took turns? And he lived so nicely!"

Joey had seemed fine at first, though he wished for the breast, you could see it, she said, but then, two or three weeks ago, he began to turn away his little mouth at the spoon and then, when a fever came, it took the little mite, and so very fast.

"We buried him on Tuesday," said Ada, "and oh, Susan, you would have liked to see it, the little coffin, so clean and white."

"Oh, Ada," I sobbed, "my baby, my sweet darling, and I never got to see his face again, not once. He needed his mother and his mother had to work and that's what killed him. I shall burn for it, I hope I burn for it. Poor little thing. His little hands was so soft. Do you know: I would go to him as he slept and feel the smoothness of his little hand. I thought I was touching a cloud." And I wept.

Ada stayed with me and soothed me and petted me. Later that night there was a soft knock on the door and Mrs. Holcomb came in carrying a tray with her own hands and with tears on her face. I thanked her, but I could not speak well for crying, and so she spoke to Ada in a quiet voice. Ada said that she had said that I should not worry about little William for he was being looked after by Ratliff, the same as who would have suckled him when I was with my very own child. But I did not care who nursed him. It did not matter to me.

I wondered if I could bear to suckle little William ever again. But as it turned I woke in the morning with one breast red and hard as a rock and so painful that I had to bite on a rag to keep from shrieking even simply to change my shift.

"Susan, it is milk fever," said Ada, "like Mother had once and she said that the only thing for it was to suckle. It is because your milk curdled with all your tears!"

"Ah," I said, "I am so weary. It's not the tears, it's the milk lying fallow because there was no baby at the tit. Go get him then, for this pain in my heart and on top of it both will make me mad."

And Ada said, "What shall I tell them?"

"I care not; just get the baby." And then as she made to leave the room I said, "Wait, Ada. Tell them that I miss little William so and please may I have leave to hold him. Tell them like that."

Ada brought him to me, and he suckled though it made me groan and groan, but whether it was because of the pain in my breast or because of the loss of my precious Joey, no one knew, nor I.

ঙ্গ

I remained with the Holcombs for I had no desire to return to my home with that Joey was not there. When their baby was ten months old, Mrs. Holcomb thought it best that he be weaned but she found me another spot with a friend who needed a nurse. The Holcombs made me a present when I left, of two pounds over my salary, because, as Mr. Holcomb said, "It is a melancholy reflection that our William was sustained at the expense of your child." I thanked them kindly for the gift but thought it not enough, considering.

My new station was at the home of Mr. and Mrs. Cooper, also in Aubrey. I stayed only a short time in this position as I could not make myself understood because of the broadness of my accent. Mrs. Cooper was from London and had brought her servants with her from there, else she'd never have eaten any dinner or had a carriage brought, for not being able to speak with her men and her maids. I lasted only six weeks there until she brought in another nurse all the way from Parkingham, where I reckon the accent was more to her ear. By my luck, Mrs. Holcomb from before had called by to see how Mrs. Cooper's baby fared. When she heard that I was to be turned out, she took it upon herself to ask around, and that's how I come to be in this position I have here with the Chandlers. And so I sit and nurse the babes and dream of what's behind me and too, of what's to come. I recall that I asked Mrs. Cooper to thank Mrs. Holcomb for me when next she saw her, but I do not think she understood the words I said.

MRS. DUNAWAY'S REASON

By God's grace and love, I was delivered forth of two healthy babies yesterday evening. Ever have I had an easy time of it in childbirth for which I can only thank the good Lord in Heaven. I was calm though my labors were fierce, for I thought only of His trials and tortures on the cross, and in this way my own, in my bed, seemed insignificant.

My own sister Hannah attended me. When she discovered after birthing the first that there was a second at his heels, she wept that my labors would be protracted. I recall that I rejoiced through the pangs, to know that another Christian soul lay in my vessel and that he should come forth to be raised in a household that holds the commandments so dear. "Pray for me, sister," said I, over and over, through my pains, and she did as did I.

The babies are healthy and please God may they remain so. My husband named the first to be Luke and the second to be John and this pleased me. I meant to leave the bed and kneel in a prayer of thanks but he begged me to stay where I was.

"My dearest wife," said he, "our Lord in Heaven will hear your prayers from your childbed as well as if you were on your knees." As he is my husband, I conceded to his wishes.

Though I was full set to nurse a single babe, two were more than I could manage and still yet assist my husband in his parish duties. "We are fortunate," said I when I spoke of it to him, "and I cannot abide it if I am unable to help you as much as you help those who have not what we have." He kissed my brow when I finished my speech and thus I knew that he approved my plan. I inquired after a wet nurse and was directed to a Mrs. Rose in Leighton. I was assured that she was as good a Christian woman as could be had and that she would watch over little John with love and care. My intention was to nurse Luke myself for a half-year and then to trade him with his brother's place, so that each might benefit from my own breast as is God's plan for us mothers, and that is what I did.

Five

The Chandler babies are learning to keep a schedule, bless them. Their eyes follow me now and they smile when I come to lift them from their crib. The boy smiled first and will show his little gums at whatever's in his view: a pigeon at the window, a candle, a bonnet string. The girl's more serious-minded and only smiles at me if I smile first. The boy is very dear but it's the girl I prefer. I cannot care much for smiles yet, even from babes, and she does not demand them of me as he does. Their names are Richard and Anne, after their parents.

Yesterday, Richard had a small fever, which worried his mother, though it did not stop her from going to dinner with her husband. In truth, it was I who persuaded her that all would be well and that she ought to go so I cannot blame her. I would not have let her persuade me to leave my child if our roles were reversed, but that's the way of those with money. And even as I muse, I bite my tongue. Susan, says myself to myself, were you there when your Joey was sick enough to die? No, you were not.

On Friday last, I was given an afternoon to see the dentist, for I had a great pain in my tooth, and the cook said it looked black and ought to be pulled. I squeezed some milk into a basin before I left and covered it with a cloth and Barbara, the downstairs maid, said she'd see to the babies and feed them with a spoon if I was long. I walked down toward the part of town I knew, the part where the Hebrews live, as I had seen a dentist's sign hanging there next to their worship house. I did not much like to have my tooth pulled next to a heathen temple, but as I was in somewhat of distress, I could not choose too nicely.

As I made my way toward the dentist's house, it quite amazed me to see the bustle in the streets; so many people with such bundles! Indeed, the people were in a queue outside the baker's shop, and when I looked in the window to see what could be the cause of it all, I could see nothing but backs. Soon I came upon the dentist's door and knocked. He answered quickly but looked at me with surprise.

"What business has brought you here at this hour?" said he quite sharply.

I looked around me, astonished. "Why," said I, "my tooth aches so and you are a dentist, are you not?"

He cast me a look even sharper and then he said, "Has your pain caused you to forget the Sabbath? Come in; if I work quickly, I may be able to help you before I must close up."

I sat and he looked in my mouth and drew down his brow. His face was very close to mine. His eyes were brown and his reddish hair curled, like the fleece of a lamb. He saw me looking and he smiled at me. I know I blushed.

"Open your mouth as wide as you can. It will hurt, do you know that?"

I nodded.

"But I will try to be quick."

He reached in with his metal tool, and gripped my tooth and pulled hard. The tooth was more rotten than he had expected and at the strength of his pull, it fairly slipped out. I yelped and he flew back across the room and landed on his bum, his legs straight out in front of him, holding his dentist's tool aloft with my black tooth in its jaws. I gaped at him and then I realized: the worst of the pain was gone.

"Lovely!" cried I, holding my hand to my cheek, and at that he grinned very wide, still there on his floor. And then we both laughed and I helped him up from the floor and paid him plus a small extra for that it had hurt me so little when he pulled the tooth out.

"Thank you, Mrs. . . ." said he and he waited and I said, "Rose." I did not tell him that I was not missus for there seemed no need for him to know it.

But he did not let go. "I see you wear weeds," he said. "Are you widowed?"

I must have blanched because his brow lifted.

"I have said too much. I am a dunce and you will forgive me. I lost my own wife, you see, and since then, I seem to see more like me than I understood there were before."

I saw what he meant and I nodded. "Yes," I said, "and my baby . . ." but then I could not continue. We stood still for one moment and gazed at the floor.

"We were not blessed with children, my wife and I," he said.

I said nothing.

"Well," he said, "if ever you need a dentist again, remember the name Abrams, Harry Abrams." And he smiled.

"I shall," said I. "And I'll tell those I know that you've the grip of a Goliath."

I smiled to myself as I walked back to the Chandlers', at his pleasantries though he was a Jew, as well as because I was afflicted no longer. But his name, Abrams, reminded me of Isaac in the Bible, and the story of how his father would have sacrificed him. I never could bear that story. And now I thought to myself, that is how it was with me. I sacrificed my own child for a pound a month.

❧

I am sitting in the nursery with the Chandler twins. One's suckling; the other's already asleep in his cradle. I can hardly believe who came into this house just now.

Earlier this morning, I had visited the kitchen for a cup of tea and a bit of a chat with the cook while the babies slept. In came Mrs. Chandler, her nose tilted up as is her habit.

"Cook," says she, "there's guests for tea and we need, I think, something quite good. What can you do?"

"Better than scones and sandwiches, ma'am? Well, let me see: it's early enough that I could get a cream cake together, will that do?"

"And chicken mayonnaise, I think," said Mrs. Chandler. To me she said, "I will perhaps ring for you to bring in Richard and Anne. Make sure their smocks are not stained and put them in the lace bonnets."

When she left we looked at her maid, Alice, who had come to bring her mistress some tea. "Oh," said Alice, "it's just a friend of hers and her mother. They're richer and Mrs. C. feels it."

All day long, Mrs. Chandler was on the knife's edge and wouldn't be content til the rest of the household was as well. She ignored the babies and me, and I felt the luck of it, for when I peeped out of the door, I heard her shout at the scullery for some spot that had been there since that girl was in swaddling and then I saw her hand snake out and slap her as well.

Finally, the doorbell rang. I changed the babies into their prettiest little frocks as I'd been told. I waited for the bonnets because of them being scratchy, but when we was rung for, after the ladies ate their cream cake and mayo, I popped on the bonnets and carried both babies out, cooing so as they wouldn't cry. I am big enough, see, in my arms and elsewhere, that I could easily carry two babes. And they are little mites, having been two instead of one.

When I walked into the room with the ladies, I kept my eyes down as is proper. I know'd they wasn't looking at me, those ladies; they wanted a peep at the mites and then Mrs. C. would say, "Thank you, Susan," and I'd bob and leave. That's how it'd all happened before, and I'd say, if you asked me, that a big part of my job here at the Chandlers' house is to look like a perfect servant, whether I am one or not. So I was as surprised as I could have been when I heard a voice I knew say my name.

"Why, it is Susan, is it not?"

When I looked up I stared right at Miss Eliza Bonney and who was sitting on her left but her mother. I might've dropped the babies if I'd been a smaller lass, but as it was, they was in no danger.

I smiled at Miss Eliza because what else was I to do and mumbled my "yes'm."

"Oh, yes. Susan," said Mrs. Bonney in that way she had that I remember quite well, like she's about to fall asleep over her milk, or some such.

I bobbed again, but could not look at her full-ways.

"Oh, was Susan yours?" said Mrs. Chandler, all surprised and thrilled, quite, by the discovery that what she had now had been good enough for them. "But surely not as a nurse, I don't expect."

There was a little pause, just tiny, not hardly so you'd notice. And then Mrs. Bonney said, "No, not as nurse. She was a maid in our house, I believe."

"And how do you do, Susan," asked Miss Eliza all cheerful.

"Well, miss, and I hope you are."

"Oh, yes," she went on, "we are in town for Freddie's wedding. But, oh, look how sweet—two babies, Anne, how smart of you to do it at once!"

And then they all remembered what I was in the room for, so they coo'd and smiled til little Anne got squally and then Mrs. Chandler told me I could go. I'm sure I felt Mrs. Bonney's eyes on me til I was out of the room.

I considered all that could be known about me if someone were to ask Mrs. Chandler a question. That I'd had a baby that died. That I'd been a nurse here in this house and somewhere before and also before that. Mrs. Bonney could do the adding up if she liked. And she might, at that. She might not have much in the way of spirit but there was cunning there. She'd realize, I thought, she'd realize about Master Freddie and me, and then I thought: what of it? What if she knows? It means little to me. Most likely, if Mrs. Bonney thought about me at all, she thought, well, if Susan Rose wanted to ask for money she would have done it by now. But I made up my mind to not be much disturbed by it. And the reason is that I feel quite sure that ladies do not converse about the lives of their servants much when there's frocks and balls to be spoke of.

The summer was so hot. Twas all I could do to keep the babies' bottoms from chafing with their sweat, and I came up with a rash under my left tit that itched til I thought I'd go mad. The Chandlers took two days at Seagrove—my mother'd been hired by a lady there once—and left the babies and me in Aubrey. I was sorry because I have never glimpsed the sea and would like to do so. But Mrs. Chandler felt that it would be difficult to carry all the things the babies needed and I suppose it is so. Oh, but for a chance to see the sea, I would have washed a barrelful of nappies.

At her return, Mrs. Chandler's evil mood turned the house topsy-turvy. Her maid reported that the lady had found an old school acquaintance at the seaside who was to holiday in Switzerland up in the mountains where the weather was cool. She'd invited Mrs. Chandler to accompany her but Mr. Chandler wasn't willing to give her the money. Alice said she was pouting something terrible. She made our lives a misery for about a week but I daresay Mr. Chandler felt the worst of it. It wasn't long before he told her she could go after all and weren't we all pleased then. Her being gone was like our holiday, after all.

And that was indeed how it came to be. Mr. Chandler ate at his club and came in very late. The cook asked for a few days to visit her brother in Manchester. Barbara, the downstairs maid, went across town for a day or two to see her sister's new baby. Mrs. Chandler had taken Alice, her maid, with her to Switzerland. That left only Lottie the scullery, and Lucy, who was the upstairs maid, and George the butler, and me.

I felt sorry for myself. Of us all, only my duties had not changed; the others were either gone or lazy, not that I could blame them. I was glad for them but I wanted a holiday too. That's the way of a nurse though; no one can stand in for me. What I do's not the same as scrubbing or baking. It's not as if I can stay abed late because the mistress is gone. When the babes are hungry, I'm on my duty. And they're hungry right often. No one had told them that their mother was gone on holiday and you can't blame them if they didn't notice, can you? What I do is God's miracle, I know it, but it seems sometimes like a burden nonetheless.

I asked Lottie, one day, if she'd trade with me—to a point—I said, pointing at my chest, and after we both laughed, she said yes. She agreed that if I'd make a bit of milk for the babes, she'd look after them and give me an hour or two of my own and then I'd do some grates for her on the very next day. (In truth, I'd had my eye on the hob in the parlor, which hadn't never been properly cleaned, at least not while I'd been at the house. I might have taken it on before but that I didn't want to do work for free, did I?)

I thought to take my outing in a new part of Aubrey, where I hadn't been before, but almost like I didn't have naught to do with it, my feet led me once again to the Hebrew part of town. It was so strange, see, and that's where I found the attraction.

All my life I've liked a bit of what's not the usual. Me and my brother John were alike in that way: we chafed at never getting to see anything new. When I was little, I used to beg to go to church on Sunday just for the stories you might hear if the curate were in a telling mood. I liked to dream of the ancient places and how they looked, so different from my workaday world.

I felt the same when it was time for the Great House. Knowing I was to go into service there had been exciting for me as a lass; to know that I'd see things what I'd never seen before. I wasn't like Mary or even Ellen, dreaming of the day when I'd wear lace or take tea—I knew those days wouldn't never come. I just wanted to see the stuffs they wore and the food they ate. I'd never even dreamed of the pictures on the wall: they came simply as a wonderful surprise.

Once, Gypsies came to Leighton. Father hated them for tales he'd heard of them and told us to stay put around the house, but John and me were crazy with wanting to see them and so, though we knew it would go poor for us in the end, we ran off. We hid in the bushes around their camp and though their dogs knew we were there, the Gypsies themselves did not seem to.

There were perhaps twenty-five of them, men with soft hats and women with hair black as mine and children in bedgowns, mainly, and a smattering of babies. One of the children finally saw us and pointed, so we came out of the trees, but the adults ignored us and we would not play with the children as we were too shy; we just stood there and looked at them. I remember that I looked upon one of the smaller girls, who had dark skin and gold earrings, and felt that I wished to be her and wear her earbobs and her skirt and eat from the stewpot that a woman stirred over one of the fires.

While we were there, several riders rode up and dismounted. They were young gentlemen and ladies from a manor house in the next village from us, come to have their fortunes told. A crone came forth from a tent and motioned one of the young ladies inside, but she was afraid and none of her lady friends would go with her, and the young lady would not accept any of the young men as an escort. They laughed very much but the young lady much desired to go inside the tent, you could see it, and the Gypsy woman wanted her to, as well. Finally, one of the gentlemen pointed to me and said, "Faith, take her with you, she'll be your chaperone," and though the young lady laughed, she did take me.

Inside, it smelled strange, and I saw the lady wrinkle her nose. I did not mind it at all. It smelled spicy and I thought, in my fascination, that it was perhaps the way tents in the Bible smelled. The Gypsy gave the lady a seat and then grabbed her hand and peered at it for a long time til the lady chirped with a giggle, but I think it was just nerves. She kept looking at me as if I, a child, would protect her if something ran amiss. Then the Gypsy murmured something about a man with a red waistcoat which made the lady put her glove to her mouth and blush. But I did not think that it had been difficult for the Gypsy to tell that the lady loved that gentleman, because she had looked at him more than at the other men when we were all outside together.

But then the Gypsy gave me a sharp look and she asked the lady, "Tuppence for the little one's told," and the lady shrugged and gave her some coins and then left the tent, giggling about her own business. The Gypsy came toward me and took my hand up in hers, and I did not look at my hand but only at her face which was dark and hard, I thought. And then she looked from my hand to my eyes and said, "You'll see to yourself, girl," and that's all she said. And she threw my hand down and left the tent to bargain with the other young ladies on their horses. I have always remembered that time though I did not understand what it meant.

Our father never found out where we'd gone, even though John scrapped with one of the Gypsy boys and got his nose bloodied for his trouble. Later that week we heard that one of the women in the camp died from having a baby and that the sexton wouldn't allow her to be buried in the churchyard, though her family had plenty of money to give him. They buried her outside the gates and after a time, the Gypsies left in their wagons, with their dogs following behind.

I thought of the Gypsies for the first time in many years as I entered the Hebrew district. I passed the dentist's house, Mr. Abrams is his name, I thought. The streets bustled. The air smelled of spices; perhaps it was this that recalled the Gypsies to me especially. There was much to look upon and to hear: great vats of pickled cucumbers and what looked to be bits of fish in brine. To be sure, this last smelled disgusting to me, but truly I have never cared much for fish—it floats in the belly as much as in a pond. The old-clothes sellers wore their wares on their backs if they did not have a stall; one man had hats to sell all piled up on his head.

I looked down at my weeds, that I'd been wearing since Joey died. Mrs. Holcomb had bought me this dress as a kindness. I thought perhaps it was time to change it. Mrs. Chandler gave her old frocks to her servants but of course there was none my size, ever. I found myself in front of a stall as had ladies' used dresses on the wall; the keeper kept a stick with a hook to get them down.

"Anything in my size, then?" said I, and he looked and indeed, there was a sprigged muslin, worn a bit, but large enough to fit. And the buttons were at the front, what's more, which is where you need 'em in my profession. So I told him to take it down and he did, and I told him I must try it, and he showed me a curtain to get behind, and it fit. Mrs. Chandler would approve of it, I knew, as it was quite plain and well-made. We wet nurses have no need of a uniform; I can wear what I like, and that's a blessing. It did right up, so I kept it on and paid the man near what he asked for but not all because I showed him there was a rip in the hem and a button almost loose at the waist, but it'd stay, I thought, while I took more of my walk.

"Miss," said the seller as I looked in my purse for a coin. "Look at this lovely ribbon, here. It matches just right, do it not? Why, this is ribbon as only a grand lady might wear."

I have always liked a ribbon. For those as us who cannot afford to put ourselves in smooth stuffs, like silks and satins, a little piece of ribbon is a luxury. I was feeling so gay that day! I looked at his ribbon—a lovely brown, just like the chocolate Mrs. Chandler drank for breakfast. I nodded.

"Just a small piece," said I. "Just a bit."

The seller cut a piece for me and wrapped it round and round. When he turned round for a moment, he dropped a little loose end of it onto the ground. No longer than my thumb it was, but waste not want not, I always say, so I knelt and took it up as fast as ever I could and he did not even see me. So I got my ribbon plus a extra bit and that was a piece of good luck for me.

When I came out of the rag seller's I found myself very near a main thoroughfare, where two streets crossed. There, just across the road from where I stood, I spied their temple. The building was large, with two stone columns. Many people were going in, and before I could stop myself, I had crossed the street and as if I knew what I was doing, I climbed the steps and entered the building.

Reader, it was like I had been pulled there! What would my father say to such news as his own daughter inside the worship-house of the heathens. He had not himself an overabundance of religion, indeed he hadn't, but he would beat me til I died if he could see what I was about. I stared amazed at my own Christian feet, that they would not stop me from entering the place, but as they did not, I decided to look around.

To my surprise, it was quite like the church I had visited on a Sunday when I went with Mrs. Holcomb, though of course I had sat in the balcony. Indeed, the temple was quite clean and decent. Previously, I had not wasted one thought on what their temples would look like on the inside in the whole of my life, but if I had done, I would have told you that there would be no clean seat to sit on nor any clean person sitting on them. That race is not known for cleanness, somewhat like the Gypsies. But in fact it was quite respectable and on the whole the people did not smell worse than a usual crush would.

I saw that men and women did not sit together, for once inside the men went one way and the women the other. Indeed, a wall stood between them so they could not see each other at all. I followed a group of women and noted that they pulled their shawls up over their heads if they had no bonnets; my black bonnet did fine. I felt like giggling to think what I was doing. It was like spying a bit, wasn't it, and I knew the sin of it, but it was exciting and made me feel very brave. It would not hurt me really. I knew that, because I am firm in my faith in the Lord.

The service was not like a decent Christian service where the people sat quietly. The whole while the Hebrew women chattered and laughed with each other in their strange language. Children ran up and down the aisles and hid under their mothers' seats. Sometimes, it is true, everyone would stop their talking and say a prayer together or sing one of their mournful hymns. At one point, some men opened a box on the platform and lifted out a scroll with a very ancient look to it, and then everyone quieted down and bowed. There was very much to look at all the time.

I sat on a bench in the midst of four or five young mothers. Two of them had babes in arms and others had small children in their laps. There were no boys over ten or so; I supposed that they'd been sent to the other side of the wall to sit with the men. At one point during the service, a quarrel broke out between two of the children who were playing together at the back of the room, behind the women's benches. At the sound, the woman beside me, who had a baby in her arms, turned and spoke something to the children. The noise did not abate though, so she sighed very loud and shook her head and stood to go break up the spat. I looked up at her as she stood and our eyes met, and she smiled and thrust her little baby at me for me to hold while she went to make the older children be good.

I have held other women's babies all my life, since I was a wee little lass, and I've always liked them. I like the tiny ones the best, when they're breathing so fast it's like they've run a race and must gasp for air. And they're so dear when they're older and smile and reach to touch your face. But there's something about knowing you're being paid to care for 'em that holds your heart a little away, don't it, and it's like that with everything in the world. What's your own is dearer to you, and that's all there is to it.

I recall watching my mother see her sister's baby for the first time. My mother's sister was very dear to her, and so when she first put my little cousin into my mother's arms, my mother cried. I remember because it seemed that strange to me: all the day my mother held babies, her own, the paying babies, and she had done so for years, every day, babies. And here my aunt puts yet another little child into my mother's arms and she weeps.

And here I was looking into this little baby's face, like I'd never seen a baby before, my heart full. It was just this: I wasn't being paid to hold it. I guarded that baby for a favor for a woman who'd never yet seen me before but who looked at me and thought me safe enough. To her, I simply looked like another woman from the district, in my neat sprigged frock and my covered head and my smile. I seemed to her to be a woman as would know how to hold a baby and keep it quiet. Which I was.

The service went on a bit, but not as long as some I've been to. I remarked to myself that as people left the building, they seemed as busy as ever. They did not have the peaceful expression on their faces that Christians have when they leave church. I thought this to be odd. But when I thought more, it seemed to me that often I have seen a peaceful expression turn to anger as fast as a whip cracks, and so the look on the face might mean less than what it seems to be.

"Mrs. Rose," was what I heard as I made my way down the steps of the temple.

I felt startled near out of my skin. I felt like I'd been caught robbing. I'm sure I blushed scarlet. "Mr. Abrams," said I so I almost couldn't hear myself, I said it so low. I was that ashamed.

"And how do you do? How is your tooth?"

"How can it be, when it's not any longer in my mouth?" said I, trying to banter. "You took it, so you ought to know."

He laughed, bless him, and then he introduced me to the lady on his arm. "This is my sister, Henrietta. Hen, this is Mrs. Rose." We bobbed at each other but I was still too embarrassed to look up much. I thought that I was lying not to tell that I wasn't a missus, but I also couldn't imagine the purpose it'd serve to set him right. So I didn't.

"Mrs. Rose," said he, "how've you come to our service here? I have not seen you here before, I think?"

"No, sir," I said, low again. "You have not. I was in your part of town here, where I come sometimes to do some trade." And then, as if I was a puppet in a Punch and Judy show and someone's hand was in my back to move me, I said, "I felt drawn to come here, for I though I was raised in a Christian home, I am of your blood."

They gaped and I am afraid I did as well. I cannot say what made me do it. Twas such a lie! But I was afraid of being caught in a place where I did not belong, you see, and thus the fib came forth. And as well, as I had sat with the women of the district, and watched them talk and pray and scold their children, I had noted something else: a resemblance between them and me. Often, in a place—in church or the market or the street—I thought that I seemed darker of hair and complexion than other women. But there, sitting in the Hebrew temple, I thought I looked quite at home, though I might not have felt it.

"I confess," said Mr. Abrams, "I am amazed. I have never heard such a story. How did this happen to you? Where did you . . ."

But his sister stopped him with a hand on his arm. "Harry, leave off your inquiry!" she said. "You will frighten Mrs. Rose away!" Then to me, "I'm sure you didn't understand much this evening. Did you not find it tiresome?"

"Oh no," said I. "I quite enjoyed myself. It was strange to me, it's true, but it was different."

Mr. Abrams laughed. "Some would call 'strange' and 'different' both to be bad things. I see that you do not."

This confused me so I said nothing. But I did look up and smile and they smiled back.

"Mrs. Rose," said Miss Abrams, "must you return to . . . well, where is it that you go to?"

"I'm a nurse for a family in Compton," said I, "but I'm having my half-day."

"Well then," said she, "come with us to have some supper. Our mother will have cooked a lovely Sabbath supper and she always prefers to feed more than just us. Do come."

"We will not bite, if that's your fear," said Mr. Abrams. "Neither will you eat anything you'd rather not." He smiled when he said it, and I knew he referred to the fairy tales we hear where the Jews are cannibals, like.

His sister laughed and pushed him a bit, so that he stumbled. "You're an imp, Harry Abrams. Whatever will Mrs. Rose think?"

"Please," said I, "call me Susan, do."

"So you'll come?" said Mr. Abrams. "Good."

Their rooms, which were behind Mr. Abrams's dentist's parlor, were clean and proper though not so much as to size. Their mother welcomed me very nice and we sat to a dinner of beef and potatoes with white bread in a braid. We drank a glass of wine and after dinner, there was stewed apples. It was very pleasant and I told her so. I learned that Miss Abrams did fancy sewing, and that her work and her brother's kept the family since their father, who had been a spice seller, had died with an abscess not two years before.

They asked questions of me and I answered as I could. I told them the story of Ellen at the Great House and part of how I had become a nurse. I left out the part that Freddie played in the story and let them think that I'd had a husband and lost him. I felt my nose swell like I would cry when I told them about my Joey.

"Look, my weeds are in this parcel," I said, pointing. "It's just today I've bought this frock at the old clothes seller near your temple."

"Just today," said Henrietta in a pitying way.

"I lost two," said her mother, and we sat quietly for a moment til Harry told us a joke to shake us from our sighs.

Supper had been lovely but it soon came time for me to go along home. When I said so, Harry said he'd walk me which I accepted his favor, though it wasn't at all far. It was dark though, so I was glad for the company. We chatted a bit but were mostly silent as we walked the short mile.

"Thank you for walking me," I said. "And thank your mother again for me, because I had such a nice time. It's not usual for me to sup away."

"Well then, you shall come again," said Harry. "Next time you have a half-day." And he shook my hand and I went inside to the twins, who were more than very glad to see me.

I wondered if I would have been invited to dinner if my hosts knew that indeed, not a drop of heathen blood flowed in me. I thought not. And so I was glad for my lie, for I had a very nice time that evening.

❧

Soon enough Mrs. Chandler returned to her husband and babies and for two days she was glad to be there. Quicker than ice melts, though, she turned snappish and it was all the maids could do to please her. I kept myself out of her way and hardly left the nursery if she was at home. The babies were growing up lovely and strong and they were beginning to eat a little oatmeal from a spoon now. I thought to when they should no longer need me and what I should do. Twas a complication: I did not want to put the idea in Mrs. Chandler's head as to when I wasn't needed no more, but neither did I want a surprise about it one day. If I could've asked her, please, ma'am, might you know how long I should expect this employment, just like that, straight out without being scared that it would give her the idea, I would have rested easier. I knew her well enough, though, to know that I couldn't ask lest she stamp her foot and say, "Well, just go now, if you need to know so much."

When it came time for my next half-day, Cook begged me to stay and help her rather than take my time off. Mrs. Chandler had invited twelve for a fine dinner party for that very night and Cook was up to her ears in eels and asparagus.

"I'll cover for you some other day, Susan dear, if only you'll stay and help us this afternoon," she begged. "Twelve's so many, and if you bring the babies down to the kitchen while she's out, you can surely lend your hands, can you not?"

I agreed to help her though it meant I'd miss the Hebrew Sabbath. I'd been gleeful thinking of it since the last time; how I'd sit in the strange temple again, how I'd perhaps take dinner with the Abramses again; how, to tell it truthfully and since, Reader, you've guessed it anyway, I'd see Mr. Harry Abrams again. When I did walk down to their district the next time I had some chance, I did not see anyone I knew and I felt too shy to call at his door.

RACHEL CHANCER'S REASON

I cannot read nor write but have never been the less for it. If ever I had got a letter, which I never did, I might have gone to the Reverend Battle with it for he can read, and write too. But it were never necessary.

I married when I was but sixteen, and it's just as well to do it young, for most girls do it sooner or later, and there's no need in waiting if you're ready. My Dick and I were set to make a home together for we'd been courting since I was fourteen and he but a year older. My sister had already married her man and had a happy life and I was set to have my own home just as she had hers.

Dick farms his bit of land with straw for the hats they wear down in London. I can weave a hat as pretty as you would like. The weaving brings in good money, but the straw brings in better, so as the children came, we would all work the fields with Dick, and I would weave at night or during the cold months or when the weather was too poor to be outside or when I was too big. That last was often for I had my share of brats and several of them lived.

I suckled all of them that would suck and that was six. I birthed ten in all, but four of them died as they was born, two with the cord wrapped around, one from breech, and one lived for a day but could not learn to swallow. Every one that died I cried more than with the last. Losing a baby is not a thing that you could ever get used to, I don't believe.

My youngest child who lived—twas Ann—was born in June just as the straw was a'coming in. The crop was very big, as Dick had applied with the manor house to plant a extra parcel of land and had been granted it. Twas a fine crop, for the spring had been wet and then dry, just as the straw likes it. Our family had worked very hard in the fields all the spring and was hoping for enough to buy a horse with the money that the extra crop would bring. If we had a third horse, we could keep Peg and Nag as plough-horses, and use the third as a dray which would set Bill, my oldest, up just fine.

When Dick asked me nicely if I would be able to bring in the crop I kissed him and said yes I would. I walked over to my sister's house—her name is Rebecca Rose—and gave Ann right into her arms and asked her to keep her for a week. Rebecca had a babe-in-arms and was not nursing anyone else's babe at the time, which I knew, for we are devoted sisters and take a meal together twice a month if we can. She said, "Well, I'll do it but I'll take a bonnet for my trouble."

By all of us working from the dawn til the dusk, we was able to bring in the crop in just a week. Dick and Bill went and bought the horse and it was a good horse, but it died by being struck by lightning, which was a freak accident and no one could have expected it. Bill is a hard worker though and has since bought another. Ann grew up very lovely, and I kept her away from the manor house, for I had a niece that came to a bad end there and it broke her mother's heart.

Six

Every now and again on a Sunday morning, when the Chandlers were gone to church, I would bring the babies to the kitchen so as to take a cup and a chat with the servants downstairs. This day, being a fine spring one, we were enjoying a lovely gossip when there came a knock at the back door.

"I'll get it then," said Barbara. She came back from the vestibule with a odd look on her face. "It is a man for you, Susan," said she.

I could not fathom who in the world it could be and I felt afraid, for always did I fear bad tidings about my mother who, now that Joey was gone, was the person I loved best in the wide world.

I quick gave the baby I was a'holding to the cook, and went up the stairs and looked out. Was I not surprised! For there was Mr. Abrams. He stood very proper on the back stoop and smiled when I looked at him.

"Why," said I, "Mr. Abrams! What is it you do here?"

"Hello," said he, and then he opened his mouth to say more but no more came out.

"Are you quite well?" I asked him, for I noticed that he pulled at his collar with his forefinger.

ERICA EISDORFER

"Yes, yes," he said, and then he laughed, which seemed to make him more easy in himself. "I have come to return something to you, which I think you dropped when you supped with us. I had hoped to see you on our streets, but as I did not, I thought to come and return it myself."

"I cannot think of what I dropped," said I, "for I take care of my things." After all, those of us as has few things to begin with must take care, lest we have fewer.

He held it up and, Reader! It was nothing more than the thumb's length of ribbon I had filched from the old-clothes seller in the Hebrew district. And though I had not much experience with a man's feelings, neither was I stupid, and I knew that a person did not walk a minute, much less a mile, to return something so small, without that that person wanted something else.

I thought that what Mr. Abrams might want was somewhat like Freddie had wanted. Freddie had wanted a bit of company but took what I gave him in its stead. Not that he snubbed what I gave him, no indeed. But as I have told you before, if I could have talked to him about books and such, well, he might have forgone the other.

I did not think that about Mr. Abrams. I thought that what Mr. Abrams wanted was . . . well . . . everything. He wanted to talk to a woman about his day and hers. Plus he wanted a lass to drink a glass of gin with and if that drink should lead to a squeeze and that squeeze to a kiss and that kiss to somewhat else, well then, that would be fine with Mr. Abrams. He did not tell me any of this, of course. This is just what I guessed from that bit of ribbon in the palm of his hand.

And, Reader, I felt the same. I liked him very much, and if I could have told him so, I would have. But of course I could not, for it would appear very forward in his eyes, and I wished to seem like a good girl, for in my way, I was. So I made my face look innocent and I said, "Ah, I wondered where that had got to. Thank you very much for your effort in returning it to me."

He smiled a nice smile and I smiled at him. We stood for just a moment and then I said, "I hope your mother and sister are well?"

"Very well," he said.

I wished I could invite him inside but of course, him being a Jew, I could not. So I said nothing and he was about to say his good-bye, I believe, when there came the sound of a baby's wail, very loud.

"Oh," he said, smiling, "your master calls you, I hear."

"Thank you again," said I and he tipped his hat and went away.

I went back to the kitchen and took the baby from the cook. I noticed very quick that the room had come over quiet and I thought I knew why. Now, I have often thought that if you have a blister come upon your heel that is paining you very much, the best thing to do is to burst it yourself rather than wait for your rubbing shoe to do it for you. It will heal ever so much more quickly that way. I put a look on my face like I was much surprised and I said very clear, "Did you see that Jew on the stoop?"

There was a pause, and then they all sighed like as if they was relieved—the cook and Barbara and Lottie did.

"Only I saw him," said Barbara, "but I told the others quick!"

"Barbara was funny, she was," said Lottie, "in what she said to us. Do listen: she said, 'Why, fancy, there's a regular Mr. Disraeli on the back stoop!' and then didn't we all laugh!"

"What could such as he have wanted at a respectable house like we are?" said Cook to me, with cold eyes.

As ever, I thanked the Lord that He had made me a fast thinker. "Oh," said I, "you will not be surprised. Do you recall that I had a tooth pulled some weeks ago? Yes, back here, see the hole? Well, he was the dentist and I owed him a shilling which I forgot to pay to him. Imagine, walking all this way for a shilling!"

"And on a Sunday!" said Barbara.

"But how did he know which house to come to?" said the cook, still wondering.

"Oh," said I, "he made me tell him, when I was short the shilling, so he could come and get it, if he had to."

"And so he did," said the cook, finally satisfied, that bitch.

You will think it strange that I could like a man and speak so of him. But I thought it best that the other servants mind their own businesses and not my own. If they did not like a Jew or a monkey or a loaf of brown bread, I did not care a whit. I recalled to myself what Mr. Abrams had said to me the night I had supped with his family—that I was a person who liked a thing that was different, just for its being different. I liked very much that he noticed that about me.

And there was something more. All my life I have been a watcher. I watch, is what I do, and this is how I know how to act. And it seems to me that most others do not. They act first, and then they watch what happens to them with their mouths agape. But this watching habit of mine has set me apart from others: from my friends, from my family, from the other servants in whatever place I was in. And it seemed to me that this is the same thing that Mr. Abrams felt all the time. That feeling of being set apart. And that feeling is sometimes bad, but at other times, well, it may be very good indeed.

So you see, Reader, I thought I knew how Mr. Abrams felt about the world because I had oft felt the same. What I did not feel for him was pity. I only admired him. I did not like to hear the other servants speak badly about Mr. Abrams, who seemed to me a fine man and whose hair curled very nice. But it could do him little harm after all, and thus I thought it best to keep my own counsel.

❧

I saw Mr. Abrams again only once before I left the Chandlers' house. Mrs. Chandler wanted some fancy whale candles for her sitting room like they use in London, not tallow. I'd told Barbara that I'd seen some of the very same for sale at a good price, just in our talking together, and she told Mrs. Chandler and she said I should go and get them. As the babies had just gone down for their nap, I thought to go out quick and come back quick.

I walked to the candle stall and you have already guessed which neighborhood it was in, I daresay. In truth, servants like me who are hired for one particular thing and that thing only, did not see much of the town or country around the house we worked in. I did not often go on errands. It quite annoyed me, in fact, that I knew so little of Aubrey after having lived there for nigh on two years and more. But I did not. I knew but a few of the streets around the Holcombs' house and a few more around the Chandlers', and I had made myself familiar with the place the Jews lived, but that made the whole of my world in town. Twas all I knew.

So it was there I made my way. I went right to the candle stall and made my purchase and then, as I turned back for the Chandlers' home, I saw Harry Abrams's face in my view and he smiled at me.

"Good afternoon! I had begun to despair of seeing you ever again," said he. "I said to my mother and my sister, just this morning at breakfast—say a prayer today, I told them, that Susan Rose's tooth might hurt her and perhaps she'll come for a visit."

"How unkind," said I with a smile, "for I am sure that without my teeth, I should very soon wither away." Then I laughed at my joke for withering is not what you'd think I'd do soon, if you saw me. But he did not laugh and looked at me like I'd said a riddle that he could not solve.

"And what is it that brings you here to our neighborhood?"

I showed him the candles I had bought.

"But you may not tarry, then?" said he. "I had hoped that you might."

"I may not, sir," said I. "And you yourself; surely there are plenty of maws for you before supper?"

He sighed and ran his hand across his cheek. "Yes, there may yet be. But it is such a lovely day, is it not? It is a lovely day, Susan Rose, and you look very lovely in it," said he which made me laugh and blush.

"Sir, I know how I look. You ought not tease."

He looked at me a bit strange. "I believe you never saw a mirror, from your speeches. Why, you look no worse than any one of the ladies on this street and better than many."

"What you say is the truth," I laughed, looking around me at the people on the street. "It is truly as if I was a lone Gypsy who stumbled into a camp of them! Is that not funny? It is how that would look!"

Mr. Abrams stared at me. He could not understand me, I knew it, and I could barely understand myself.

"Forgive me," said I. "My head is turned. I feel gay for the first time since my little child died." And I smiled at him.

He smiled back and then his face changed. "Will you come with me, Susan Rose?" he asked with quite a sober look, and I knew that my strong feeling had charged him with his own, and I knew what he wanted and I wanted the same. And so I nodded. We walked a short distance to his house and went into the shed behind it which had a door that could be closed. Our embrace was tight enough that neither of us had breath to speak again for a good long while.

~❧~

Twas soon after that that Mrs. Chandler spoke to me and said I might seek employment at the end of the same month we were in, that being October. I was surprised, just as I wished I would not be, because I thought I should stay with the Chandlers til the springtime.

"And the babies . . ." I began to ask.

"They shall be weaned," she said.

"They're young, though," said I, quietly, "still not a year yet," and she told me that she thought ten months to be quite enough at the breast and that now they could eat, it was time for them to drink from a cup. I waited to hear if she would ask me to stay on as a nurse—a dry nurse, my mother would have said—but she did not. Later, I heard from Alice that Mrs. Chandler's sister would send her own children's nurse from Durham, since she was done with her. I recalled to myself how Mrs. Chandler much better liked what she had when she knew that others had had it before, as when she found that I'd been a maid for the Bonneys.

I asked Mrs. Chandler if she knew of anyone who needed a wet nurse and she said she would inquire. When I asked again, she said that she had not heard of anyone who needed me, but I believe she never could recall to ask. I walked to the hospital one afternoon when Mrs. Chandler was out and paid a penny to have my name placed on a large board, near the front of the building with those of other wet nurses who sought employment. Indeed, someone sent a boy to ask, but when I went to call on the lady, she had already found another. Only one other sent for me, but that was the wife of a minister, who wanted to give her baby to nurse so that she could accompany her husband on his town missions better. She inquired quite close as to whether I had been married and told me that she could check if she was of a mind to, so I said I had not, and she said she would find a better girl. The skinny chit. I was surprised she could have ever had a baby herself, seeing as how it is you get one and I told her that, as I left the house.

I began to fret about not finding a place and so I went to the newspaper which was the *Aubrey Illustrated*, as it was called, and asked to place an advertisement. The man there told me I had to have an endorsement, and I asked him what that was, and he said I should get one from Dr. Sims at Highbridge. After spending a shilling, I was finally able to take a spot in the newspaper which said that if anyone needed a good and careful wet nurse with references, they should inquire of Dr. Sims and he would know how to find me.

I did finally find a place with a family that lived near Hittyfield, on the other side of Aubrey. This was a relief because twas nearly All Souls' Day, and I had begun to think that I would have to go home to my parents if I could not find employment soon.

When I kissed the twins good-bye, I shed tears for them, for they were dear to me, though not mine. I have told you how it is with us who is paid nursing: our feelings go only so far and then no farther. But I am not a stone girl and those babes had carried me through a terrible sad time in my own life, to be sure, and that was Joey's death. As I nursed baby Richard one last time, I thought that nursing the Chandler twins had dried me of my tears somewhat, for having a baby's sweet face so close to your own, for so long a time as it takes to nurse 'em, is a great tonic for a sad soul. Indeed, I thought to myself looking down at the little boy, they nursed me from my distress as I nursed them for their health, and I will always love them for it.

The other servants could not spare time for much of an adieu; Mrs. Chandler had invited guests for another fancy supper for that evening. Indeed, the mistress had forgotten that I was to leave on that very day, and as the dry nurse had not yet arrived and the twins were fretful, all on top of the fancy supper, Mrs. Chandler became quite frantic and begged me to stay an extra day. I could not though, because I had promised the Clarkes, which was the name of the new family and I thought better to make the old angry than the new. Mrs. Chandler was quite furious at her plight and shouted at me but I simply bobbed and left, though I must say I smiled as I turned my back. She was not a good mistress nor either a good mother and I wish those mites the best with what they've got.

I made my way to Hittyfield to find the Clarke home, which I did, but only after being much turned about and lost. When I found it at last, I waited on the back stoop for ever so long before the door was opened by the cook, who looked frowsy with some worry of her own. She took me upstairs herself which I thought odd and I was shown to the master of the house. He had been drinking, I saw, but he said a few words and told me where to put my bundle. He took me then to a door and knocked and we went in.

It was very dark and close and smelt of sickness.

"The nurse is here," said Mr. Clarke to his wife. He went into the room and motioned me to follow and he showed me to his wife, who looked at me from her bed, but did not speak. I bobbed at her but she did not see much, I could tell. I heard the baby in its cradle make a mewl and as no one said any word, I walked over to it and picked it up. It was very tiny, born too soon, I thought, and it did not look as if it would last.

"Shall I try here?" said I, and Mr. Clarke just nodded. He gazed at his wife but did not look at the baby. I sat in a chair and turned away from what he could see, though he did not look, and undid my buttons and my shift and gave the baby to suck. It hardly could. It was too small to know how, I thought. I squeezed a drop of milk into its little mouth and it tasted it and then tried again, very weakly, to suckle. Of a sudden, my milk let down and spilled into the tiny mite's throat and it coughed.

At that, the mother raised her head and murmured something to her husband, who said something back but I could not hear what it was. I saw he did not touch her but stood at her bedside for some time before he left the room.

I tried for a long while to nurse the babe. It would suckle, just a drop, and then cease its pulling too soon. It fretted but did not seem to learn how to swallow without that it coughed. Finally, it dropped to sleep and I put it in its cradle and went to seek some supper.

"How's the mistress?" said the cook when she gave me my stew. "Does she stir?"

"She sleeps, though not well," said I. "Is she a good mistress?"

"They're quite kind, the both of them," said the cook. "This'll kill her, I think. Her others are at her brother's house."

"And how many?" said I.

"There's five others, though there'd've been more, had she borne 'em. But she's lost as many as she's had. Tis a pity he can't leave her alone."

I nodded. After my supper, I went to see about the child again. It waked up and suckled a bit more, but not enough to last, I thought. The mother moaned and I went to her with the babe at my breast, thinking it would do her good to see that it was suckling at all. But she was very feverish and could see nothing. Her shift draped open and I saw from her tits that she'd nursed her babies, the ones that had lived, by herself. I thought that from the looks of things here, she'd never nurse this one.

It came to pass as I had thought. The baby lived for five days and suckled each day; not enough to keep itself alive, but enough to use my milk but very gradual, so that when it died, I was very reduced. Its mother died two days before it did. Twas a sad thing, to be sure. I was hard put to find someone to pay me for the little I had done; the mistress's sister finally saw what I was about, and paid me a pound which was more than I deserved for the time I was there, but she did not know that.

I took it from her though. Having sent my wages home except for what I secretly kept back, I wondered how I should live. I stopped by the hospital to inquire if they knew of someone who might need my services but the doctors had no good news for me. "The foundling hospital could use you," one of them told me, but I did not want to go there as they do not pay enough to keep a mouse in crumbs. I thought I would go home. I knew from my mother that my milk would freshen if I could find a baby quick, and that was what I hoped to do when I got there. I thought that my father would send me to the city again and soon, but I wanted to see my mother's face so I waited for two days at a public house til the coach came for Leighton to take me home.

MRS. GAINSBOROUGH'S REASON

I am Henry Gainsborough which name you might know as my great uncle daubed and made his way with it. My uncle is the Earl of Q**** and sets the finest table you can imagine: we dine with him often. We are intimate friends with Lord and Lady S**** and are often invited to their country manor to shoot. Lord S**** is most considerate to his guests and Lady S**** the very picture of elegance.

My wife, Mrs. Gainsborough, and I have been married for ten years. I rescued her, not to put too fine a point on it, from her eccentric family. Her father and mother both hail from ancient British lines, and yet they seem to deem themselves irresponsible as to their duties: they cannot conceive of how they should and must set themselves as examples for their lessers. They do as they wish. They have no house in town, they do not visit, they set but the meanest table I believe I have ever seen and explain that they are vegetarians and therefore may serve no meat: no mutton, no beef, not even pork!

I am amazed that my poor Aerial survived her childhood intact. I chanced to meet her at the opera—twas *Il Capelli de la Luna,* which I recall because that very evening I bowed to the viceroy and he caught my eye and bowed back! It was indeed a high point. At any rate, at intermission, I immediately noticed that old Mrs. Beaumont was attended by a lovely young girl who shone as brightly as the many diamonds she wore in her hair. I made my way to Mrs. Beaumont at the conclusion of the opera and was introduced to Miss Westin, as she was then. She was staying with Mrs. Beaumont, her aunt, because her parents did not care for London. I must have looked surprised, for the poor girl blushed and turned aside. Mrs. Beaumont explained that Miss Westin's parents were not much in society, but by choice not necessity. "No indeed," she told me. "If they wished, they could afford a palace here but they do not." The next day I called by to speak with Miss Westin and then again the next and the next until I had sealed the fate I so desired.

When I asked Mr. Westin for Aerial's hand, the conversation passed strangely but I shall relate it here for your amusement.

I had ridden out to visit the Westins at their home in Oxfordshire where the family had lived for centuries. The manor is enormous, but much of the surrounding land is quite wild, with deep forests very near to the house rather than the tidy green lawns that we think of as the proper setting for a place of such size. The family was friendly but very sparsely waited upon: indeed, I watched with my own eyes as Aerial and her two younger sisters cleared away the dishes after we had breakfasted. Supper was more decent, with several servants to do the setting and the clearing, but they spoke to both Mr. and Mrs. Westin whenever they liked and even laughed at the jokes and parries that the family passed at the meal.

After supper, when the ladies had retired to the parlor (and I must confess, I do not think that this was their habit, in general), I asked Mr. Westin if I might have his daughter's hand in marriage.

Rather than the smile I had anticipated—for my name, I assure you, is at least as good as his own—he asked me if I loved her.

"Ardently," said I, "and with all my heart."

"And she feels the same?" he asked in what seemed to be some astonishment.

"She tells me that she does," I said humbly.

"Aah," he said, and then was quiet for a moment. "But, sir," he continued, "what is it that you do?"

I was quite amazed and somewhat insulted. What was he about?

"Do?" I said. "Sir, my family is . . ."

He interrupted me. "Ah yes, your family," he said, waving at me as if shooing a fly from his face. I felt most abashed.

As you have surmised, we overcame his objections and were married in the springtime of the next year. Aerial found herself to be with child soon thereafter, and our baby, Elizabeth, was born at the Westin manor, so that Mrs. Westin could attend at the birth as is, of course, proper.

After the baby was born, Aerial and I found ourselves at a small crossroads of opinion. Aerial was quite ready to nurse the child herself, as it seemed to be—and I must say it did not surprise me to hear this—a tradition among the women of her family. But I stood against it. I explained that it was simply not done, that it would misshape her, that it was not good for the infant's health and that, of course, it would limit our ability to go into society for yet another five or six months, when we had already lost almost the same amount of time due to her pregnancy. She wept and carried on, but I remained fixed to my opinion. It is simply no longer done in our set.

In the end, she capitulated to my wishes, and a wet nurse was found, a Mrs. . . . , well, it does not matter. Suffice it that the nurse lived in Leighton which was a good distance from London. It is too bad that little Elizabeth perished under her care from a fever. Two other children born to Aerial fared well enough at their wet nurses, including my son Henry, who will inherit.

Seven

My mother laughed and cried to see me and I did the same for her. The family seemed well. There was news to hear. Mary had married and moved to Seagrove; her husband had got a job on the docks there. Father boasted that he would take Mother there for a holiday one day, but I saw my younger brothers roll their eyes to each other at that. Our cousin Ann had just posted her banns. John, my eldest brother, was groom at the Great House and had men under him and told them what to do. He had taken Bill to teach him but Bill would not attend, so John had thrown him off, for which my father complained bitterly, but I said I thought it was the right thing, for if you cannot do the work, you ought not to be allowed to stay. The little ones still ran amuck, as my mother would say, in and out of the house. The littlest one looked so much like Ellen that I caught my breath when I saw her.

"I thought I saw a ghost, when I saw Janey," I said to my mother, and she nodded and caught the little girl to her and kissed her. "And my Joey," said I, looking at my mother's face and she nodded and said, "And Ellen and Ada," and then we wept together, wiping our tears away with our aprons.

After supper, with my father off at the tavern, I told my mother about the two years since I'd seen her and the adventures I had had. Then I asked her if she knew of an infant. "It would have to be an older one," said I, "for my milk is drying up fast, so what needs to suck, must suck hard." But my mother did not know of any baby. I thought I would ask at the doctor's on the morrow.

"If you do not find a babe," said my mother, "you can return to the Great House, can you not?"

And I thought I would try. I thought to ask at the laundry house, for then I'd avoid both the housekeeper, who was still Mrs. Hart, and also Mrs. Bonney, the mistress. I did not know for certain whether Mrs. Hart knew that I'd left the house for being with child, but if I hid myself in the laundry where she needn't see me, then it might not matter. And the same with Mrs. Bonney. I decided to go there and ask for a position for what else was there to do but that?

It turned out easy enough. The laundry mistress was Mrs. Hubbard and you could tell she tippled, but she seemed kind enough and let me in right away. "You've great arms; you can stir," said she and there I had my job. It was a deal of toil and I hated it soon. The sheets were heavy to stir and the room, hot, but as I had not found a nursing baby in time, I had dried up and had no choice but to take what work I could find. Twas not all gloom, though. The other maid, called Martha Campbell, was a girl I'd known when we were small and as I'd always liked her, we had plenty to talk of and no one to tell us not to.

The laundry building stood some steps away from the house and the treat was to deliver the fresh linens to the kitchen entrance. I always gave my turn up to Martha which made me seem queer, for the break from stirring or ironing or wringing was our great delight. But I did not want to take the chance to see Mrs. Hart or any of the family. And so I always made an excuse about my foot hurting, or that I was doing some delicate stuffs and had to take care, or that I needed to piss, could Martha please go. Soon enough, Mrs. Hubbard no longer asked me if I'd like a turn and that was that.

A big difference between us laundry girls and those who worked in the Great House was that we did not board. Martha and me and Mrs. Hubbard might live in town if we wished and we all did. It meant a deal of walking, but I've never been afraid of that. I walked with Martha, and either we went through the fields if it was fine or if we was tired, we used the road. Most times, a carter would stop and give us a ride. So I could go home at night and see my mother which was a great comfort to me.

At this time, Reader, it seemed to me that I'd lost my way. Joey was dead, my earnings diminished, my life seemed to have got a deal smaller in a short while. I had agreed to work on Sundays in exchange for my own evenings and thus was never in the church which was a sadness to me. In Aubrey, at least, there was new things to look at on my half-days but while I lived here at home, the faces of those lost loved ones rose up at every turn. Twas the doldrums, for sure, though to say the honest truth, if I had known what I would yet gain and lose, I might have been content to stay and stir the laundry til my arms stretched to twice their length, and never once look up from the kettle.

One day not long after I'd started at the laundry, Mrs. Hubbard asked if I could stay on a little to help with the great pile of ironing we had to do. The Bonneys had many guests that week and it seemed they'd all soiled their shirts. Martha was all crampy with her bleeding and lay asleep on a pile of sheets; when she woke, Mrs. Hubbard said she might leave a bit early. I stayed extra and ironed perhaps twenty gentlemen's shirts: in between the buttons, starched cuffs folded just so. Mrs. Hubbard thanked me for staying and then she told me I might go on home. The road was quite empty as the carters mostly had gone home for their suppers. I sang as I walked to pass the time.

After a little while, I heard a horse's hooves come behind me and pass me. I looked up to see who it might be and though it was a'gloaming by then and the light quite dim, I made out the face of Master Freddie and I gasped. He seemed as surprised as I and stopped his horse and jumped down.

"Susan," said he, "you've come back!"

"Yes, sir," I said, keeping my tone level. I had much I wished him not to know. "I have and I am walking along home."

"It surprised me to find that you'd left your position," he went on. "No one could tell me why."

I wondered at that. Who had he asked? I wondered. Had he really asked Mrs. Hart and if he had, what had she thought of that? I could not conceive that he had actually asked his mother. I imagined it thus, in an instant:

Freddie: Mother, where is that scullery maid, the one named Susan Rose?

Mrs. Bonney: Who?

Freddie: You know, Mother. The scullery, the fat one? Susan is her name. I no longer see her in the house.

Mrs. Bonney: Freddie, darling, why on earth would you want to know?

Freddie: Oh. Well, it's just, I , well you see . . .

It made me right sick to think of it, really. "My mother fell ill, sir," said I. "And so I had to go home."

He looked at me with concern. I noticed that his waistcoat bulged at the buttons rather more than when I'd seen him last and that the skin on his forehead looked quite white with flakes, and very raw.

"Is she . . ." he said and waited.

I thought to myself to remember the lie I'd told him. "Oh," said I, "thank you, sir. She is in excellent health, that she is. A proper recovery."

His features came all over with relief. I felt touched in my heart to think that he might feel so much about the mother of one of his maids. I thanked him again and smiled.

He smiled back. "I am glad, then. And, Susan, how do you fare?"

I thought of what he did not know and felt the lie I'd tell by saying naught, as well as what a baby he was himself, to be protected from such a thing as I would not tell. That's the difference between us and them, I thought. We know all of what's bad because we can't keep from it. They live in their big houses and the walls are thick enough around them to keep the bad out.

"Me, sir? I'm fine," said I. And then, "What's that?"

As we stood, a horseman came up the road very quick. The rider was hunched over, like he was racing, and he whipped the horse very much.

"My God," said Freddie as the rider came toward us, "that man will kill that horse. He must be bent for the doctor for what else could need speed such as that?"

We stepped off the road to watch the rider pass, which he did, but not before his horse's hoof threw a small, sharp stone at me which hit me on my leg, above the knee. I yelped and almost fell, but Freddie caught onto me and helped me across the ditch, where there was a bank to sit on.

"Shall we look at it, then?" said he, his voice all worry.

"I shall look at it while you may not, sir," said I, for I could feel that it was just a prick. I felt myself flirting, but I was relieved to be safe and not have suffered a worse wound.

He smiled at me and turned his head away to protect my modesty, but pretended to snatch a glance at my leg as I picked up my skirt. He acted all rolling eyes and snickers, which made me laugh.

"Tis nothing," I said and put my skirt back down. "There'll be a blue mark and nothing more."

"I'm delighted to hear it," said Freddie and then, with no warning except what you've picked up already, Reader, he kissed me very deep and squeezed my bosom with both his hands.

"Sir," said I, "you are married now, are you not?"

He drew himself a little away and looked ashamed. "I am," he said. "Yes, I am. But she does not like . . ."

I giggled, though it was wrong of me to do it. "What is it that she does not like?" I asked, pretending to be innocent about it.

"Me," he said. "She does not like me."

Which was not the answer I'd thought it would be. I looked at him in pity and when he looked back it was with such hope, Reader. I remembered him, you see, how sweet he'd been, and I remembered my Joey, and though it shames me to say it now, well, it's likely I don't need to say it at all. I gave myself to him right there on the bank of the road though we pushed into the wood a bit so that if a traveler happened by, we would not be seen.

From then on, for several months, we would meet just thus. Twice a week, on Tuesdays and then again on Fridays, I would tell Martha that I had an extra job at the Great House after the laundry was done and that she should go along home without me. She had no reason to disbelieve me. When she had gone a distance down the road, I would walk on my way and very soon Master Freddie would find me and we, along with his horse, would walk up into the forest. It was his wood, you see.

We flirted a little but did not talk much otherwise. The same melancholy came upon me as had when we met in the pantry; the sense that he'd just as soon have talked as screwed. But the screwing seemed to give him some comfort as, in truth, it did for me.

Once he said thus to me:

"My wife befuddles me, to be sure."

"Why, how can she," said I, "for you are surely more learned than is she."

"It hasn't to do with education," he said. "It has to do with what she likes and what she doesn't."

I did not speak.

"She does not like a kiss," he said, giving me one.

"I like a kiss," I said.

"She does not like a squeeze," he said with his hand on my ass.

"I do not mind a squeeze," said I.

"She does not care for a suck," he said, putting his mouth on my nipple and suckling.

"Aah," said I.

"My God, Susan, your breasts give nectar."

I did not answer.

"She does not like a finger just there," said he.

"I like a finger just there," said I.

Etc.

Another time he said to me:

"My wife is in love with another."

I did not answer.

"His name is Stephen Whitt and he is handsome."

I said nothing.

"She told me so last night. She said she wished that my horse would throw me and that I would break my neck."

I took his pecker in my mouth.

We met thus for two and one-half months.

❧

This second time, my father was not so angry. He knew what I could do for him if I went out to nurse. So he called me a slut and slapped me for a week or two, but then he left me alone. He did not even seem interested in who the father was. He was dreaming of the gin he could buy with what my milk would bring.

I schemed too, of course. I had hidden some money from my father out of each month's pay, as who would not? I told him what was not true: that the town ladies took money from my wages for beer, when they did no such thing. I told neither him nor my mother any word about the extra money I had as a bonus from the Holcombs nor about the pound I got at the house of the baby and mother who died. I kept it secret. I made a plan for myself and my babe; when it was born, we would flee my father's house and we would go to the city where I could wet nurse to keep us. I had heard of women who would be taken on with their own little babies, if they agreed to nurse the paying babies first. If I could not find work like that, I would go to the foundling hospital though they would pay but little. They might not pay a shilling, I thought, and it would matter not at all. This time, I would keep my baby. This time, my baby would have its mother near it to keep it quite safe.

Freddie, bless his soul, never gave me a problem, when I told him we must stop our nonsense. (I called it nonsense to ease it a bit; he must not think he was being thrown off. Sweet he might be, but master he still was. It had to be managed, see. But he gulped at the bait.) The last time we met, I simply told him that I had another young man in the village, and though he sighed, he nodded. "But I wish I had thought to bring you a present, one of these times," he said. "I have enjoyed our meetings."

I almost laughed. He spoke as if we'd been sitting thigh to thigh in church, listening to the sermon together. I wondered what he'd say if he thought for one instant that he'd been father to my Joey. I could not imagine what he would do. He was so like a child himself; I thought that if he found out, he might cry and run to his mother. He did not seem to like his wife much, but that she scared him was for certain. A bastard, even with someone as low as I, would be the makings of a ripe scandal, especially if it came uncovered that it was the second brat with the same servant woman. Now that's a story as could make even the cold Maude burn. In families such as the Bonneys is, scandal's what they're most afraid of, you see. Well, the why of it is clear. When such as us have to do with who we oughtn't or drink more than we should or have a brat without a husband, there's no story in the newspapers. Them who writes newspapers and them who reads 'em, don't much care about us. "We're the humbler contingent," is what my father used to say.

"What's a contingent, Father?" John would ask, because that was the way of the joke; it never seemed as funny if one of us asked as it was when John did.

"If you must ask, lad, you mayn't know," my father would say, and then we'd laugh.

It seems quite small to me now, that jest. But I do like to think of it sometimes, especially when my father's eyes turn hard. Yesterday, when my mother put her hand on his shoulder as she gave him his stew, he growled at her. She quick snatched it back but I saw how she remembered that he'd used to let her put it there if she liked. She looked quite downcast and I hated him, as I often do. And then the baby roiled in me and, for no reason that I could think on, I recalled the joke. And so I said it. I said, "What's a contingent, Father?" though it belonged to John but John was grooming so he wasn't at table. The little ones didn't remember it but Mother did and Bill did and so did Father. He looked at me like I'd asked him for a shilling but when he saw our faces, like we were expecting something, he said, "If you must ask, you mayn't know," and though he didn't smile, we did.

As for Master Freddie, well, I was glad of my quick mind, that I'd thought of the phantom young man in the village. Twas the perfect fool. I saw him smiling sadly to think that I, of whom he was doubt-less fond, had found my own true love. That was Freddie all over. He preferred something to turn out happily. Myself, I prefer what's real to elves and fairies, all the time.

I continued my work in the laundry til almost the day I dropped my baby. Twasn't easy. When I stirred the sheets, the baby stirred me. Sometimes it would kick me so hard I'd lose my breath, and then I'd have to sit and catch it. "Why, Susan," said Mrs. Hubbard, "why do you pant so? Are there too many sheets in the kettle?"

"Tis nothing," said I. "Tis a heavy load, is all."

Gossip made the time pass. I am afraid that Mrs. Hubbard and I corrupted Martha that way. She was a quiet girl who minded her own, but Mrs. Hubbard and I enjoyed to tell what we could by the linens. And oh, there's clues.

We could tell when a lady had her monthly of course, from the stains. We knew when Mrs. Bonney had one of her bad colds; her bed-sheets had a special trim and she had the habit of blowing out her nose into them. Freddie's wife, Maude, had very fine things and very many of them. The three of us laundry women would examine them close to see the stitches and the fabric: the finest silk, the finest muslin. That Freddie wore his underdrawers longer than he should surprised me not at all; Martha laughed and laughed at them and would hold them on the end of a stick like a flag, to tease.

We could tell when there were visitors by the extra laundry we had to do. The gentlemen's blouses resembled each other's very close; we had to take care to know whose was whose so as to return the right shirts to the right man.

One of the gentlemen's shirts was finer than any of the others, finer than Freddie's, and his were always very good. That was Stephen Whitt, the very one who Maude loved. His shirts were of the finest cotton I've seen; Mrs. Hubbard, who knew about such things, said the cotton was from Egypt where the pharaohs lived. He'd had small letters embroidered in the ends of the shirttails, and Martha, who could read a bit, said they spelled out "Whitt." "That way," said Mrs. Hubbard, "he won't take a chance to lose a blouse, I suppose, and get it traded for something less."

"Fancy," said Martha as she admired the stitchery. She had an interest in sewing and loved a perfect seam.

One sort of stain made Martha blush. They appeared most often on the backs of ladies' nightclothes and sometimes on the sheets. When Mrs. Hubbard spotted such a stain she'd most likely sigh and say such as, "Well, we all do it, whether we be rich or we be poor, but it's the poor as has to clean it," and then I'd giggle and Martha would turn her head away or put her hands on her ears. What I noticed, though I think the others did not, was that when Stephen Whitt visited, Miss Maude often had stains of that sort on the back of her petticoats. Twas easy to remove those stains as there was no color to 'em, but they told a lot of story, for being as small as they were.

❧

Twas the middle of the night when my time came. I thought perhaps I would die like Ada did. We were right surprised, Mother and I, for with my size we thought I'd never have a problem slipping out a baby. He was breech, and she had to reach her hand in me and turn him. Twas like hell. I vomited in a basin she had for me, over and over. She'd reach up and turn him a bit, then I'd vomit and then she'd give me a rest for a minute and then turn him a bit again. I screamed til my voice hurt me and when I could see at all, I saw the tears rolling down her cheeks.

"Mother," I shrieked, "Mother!"

"Don't die, my love," she sobbed. "Don't die, Susan, my own," and with that, she reached up inside me one last time and grabbed the baby's arm and pulled it down so he pointed right. And so, she saved our lives.

The slightest little mite, just lovely he was, with hair black as black silk.

"Such a little thing, to make such a fuss of it," whispered my mother as she stroked his little cheek to make him suck. I was so worn with my labors that she had to hold him up to my breast and watch that he knew what he should do. But he did, the pet. After he had dined, she swaddled him and put him in the crook of my arm and we, all the three of us, slept like kings.

I named him David. It seemed fitting, exactly. David was small when he fought Goliath; my baby was small, but when I looked into his serious eyes, it seemed to me that he would someday do something great, though I might never know what it would be. David was a great warrior; when I looked at my baby's form, I thought he would be a sturdy man, able to defend them who needed it. I knew that David from the Bible wrote the Psalms; I made up my mind that my David would learn his letters. The name David was a fine old name—from the Jewish Bible to be sure, but fine nonetheless. And I thought that if it ever came to pass that his father was to see him, he would be pleased to think that his son's name came from that testament. It would signify to him that I had chosen that name out of that book. He would take it as an honor, for him and for his race. For you see, Reader, Harry Abrams was my baby's father.

❧

You will think that I am a Jezebel. You will wonder how I could bed Freddie, when I knew I had another's child growing in me. You will wonder what sort of slut I might be. Indeed, it's not easy for me to explain what I might've been thinking as I accepted Freddie's attentions. Of defenses, well, I have none. More, it's explaining that I can do if I must.

It was Tamar from the Bible that I was thinking of when I did it. It was the Hebrews that made me remember her story, and then her story that made me lie with Freddie. Here's my meaning.

When I lost my Joey, I might have died from the sadness of it. Women have lost their babies before me, I know it, but that does not mean we who next lose ours don't feel it just as hard. And when I lost Joey, I wanted to die but I did not die. And instead, I found myself in the Hebrew section and then in the arms of a Hebrew himself.

I learned that in the Hebrew temple, the people read the Bible, just as we do in church. And the very day I went into their temple, their man of God read to us from the story of Tamar. I did not know it then because he spoke in their tongue which is rough enough to give you an earful of splinters. I recall that, before I thought if it was polite, I said such to Harry and his sister when I ate supper at their house, but they laughed and so I knew I hadn't vexed them much. It was they who told me that the man had been telling of Tamar, and I recalled the story and wished I could have understood the words it had been told in, as I always did like that one in particular.

"And what is it that you like about it?" said Harry to me as we were eating.

I remember that I paused because I had not before thought about it overmuch. "Well," I said to him, "I like it because she does for herself."

"But think," said Harry's sister, "what she does! She's a disgrace, if you ask me."

I nodded. She acted the whore, did Tamar, and with her father-in-law. Twas a disgrace, Harry's sister was right.

"Still," said I.

"Still?" said Harry. "You're not ready to throw Mistress Tamar to the likes of my sister just yet, or so I see?"

"No I amn't," said I. "Not quite yet. What I like about her is that she didn't just sit back and let herself be tilled under. She could have just pined away and never had not one thing for herself. But she'd been promised a husband, and a husband she meant to get. I suppose it's that she didn't give up, that I admire."

"Oh well," laughed Henrietta, "I'll have to take care never to try to cheat you at a game of cards, if I know what's best for me, now won't I?"

"What's it to do with cards?" said I, not understanding her city talk.

"Nothing," said Harry. "My sister just means that you like what's just, is all. And of course you're right to do so."

So, as it was Tamar who'd been talked about at dinner that night, and since Mr. Abrams and I didn't speak much more than that, that's the talking I remember. And I did remember it. I went over and over it in my mind because I had enjoyed it, that talking. I liked that we all three knew the story, and I liked that he asked me my opinion of it, and I liked also how though my opinion wasn't usual, still I kept firm to it, and that made me proud.

And so that's how the Jews put Tamar in my mind. And how they caused me to lie with Freddie is this: when I had lost my profession and I was with child and I lived once again under my father's thumb and I could not ever hope to be with Mr. Abrams again, it was a dire thing to me. I had feelings for Mr. Abrams even though he practiced his heathen faith, but because I am a Christian, it meant that I had sinned double in lying with him. I could not see how anything could go right for me anymore. And then I remembered Tamar and how she was not afraid to get what she wanted. I thought to myself that I did not know how to get what it is that I wanted and so I thought, Well then, Susan

Rose, you may just as well do as you like. And that was how I came to lie with Freddie. It may not follow to you, Reader, but I have found that things of this nature rarely do if they ever do at all.

But a baby's a whole new thing, as my mother would say whenever she held a little one, and there's nothing truer. How they come hardly matters once you've got one in your arms. I gazed at my Davey and wept: for joy and for Joey, too, and I suppose, for the things I'd like to have had but never would. And then I opened my shift and gave him the breast and nursed him til he was satisfied.

MRS. BOATWRIGHT'S REASON

I am Mrs. Hiram Boatwright as was Miss Lucinda Tanner. My husband and I are married seven years. I have borne five healthy children and every one of them has lived, for which I thank the Almighty every day, for I know that not all women are as blessed as am I in that way. My father farms his land just outside Aubrey and saw to it that I had the pleasantest childhood you can think on. He made a good living and we were very happy and had all the fresh milk in the world to drink. My brothers had very good white teeth. As do I, I am proud to say.

When I was seventeen, I married Mr. Boatwright as was a widowed man from Aubrey. He was still young and had no children as his wife had died in the childbed with their first. We met in church, and as a suitable time had passed and as he no longer wore his mourning suit, my parents agreed that he should court me and so he did. He had to ride a good five miles just to have dinner with us, but he paid me that compliment several times before he asked for my hand.

After we married, I moved to his house in town. I had not much lived in town, but I found it very congenial with many entertainments and people to see. Soon enough I found myself with child and we was very happy waiting for the baby. As my time came near, I began to fret. Though I did enjoy my town life very much, I worried that my dear little baby would suffer from it. When I took a turn out of doors, it seemed to me that the air was thick with dust and that the streets were not clean. I recalled to myself my own wholesome childhood on the farm: the clean air, the green fields, the blue sky, and the good, fresh milk. It came to me very strong that my own dear babe should have those things that I had! I felt a relief like the hand of God on my brow to have thought of it.

I told Mr. Boatwright that I wanted to put the baby out to nurse in the country where it could breathe the fresh air. He agreed. We got the name of Mrs. Rose from a doctor who once lanced a boil on Mr. Boatwright's foot. When I heard that she lived in Leighton, I knew that she was just the one. I have been to Leighton and it is a green little village, in the old English style. That was just what I wanted for my babe.

That first baby, our son Hugh, became quite huge with Mrs. Rose, and when we took him back into our home, it was time to give her our second, little Alice. Each of my babies has gone to nurse (though only those two went to Mrs. Rose) and that is the reason, I am sure, that they thrived as they have done. Country air is the thing for babies as it reduces colic and helps a baby's lungs to work properly.

Eight

For a fortnight after Davey was born, all fared well. I stayed abed a deal and my mother brought me soup and porridge, and I nursed my child til he began to unbend a bit and his lashes unpeeled and shewed themselves. I loved little ones like this, with their head a'bobbing. And this one was mine! I thanked God for him.

He was strong for being so little, able to hold his head up very early. If I didn't take care to swaddle him tight, he'd kick off the cloth with his scrabbling. At night, I placed him on a pillow so that he was like a gem in a ring and then took him to bed with me. When he woke in the night and began to bawl, I needed only to bring him to my breast and he'd suckle away very serious. Ofttimes, when he had just waked and was ravenous, his little chin would judder with the wanting. Every baby does this same; this one was mine and thus it seemed charming to me.

At first, my father had little to say about the baby. For a man as full of anger and ale as he, it seemed strange that he was quiet. I watched him, as he pretended not to watch me, and never left the baby alone for long. I did not know what he might do, and I trusted him not at all.

One day he spoke.

"You'll go to nurse, missy?" said he.

I had been waiting for it. "No, sir, not just yet," I answered. "I will not lose another. I'll wait til this one is set before I go."

He growled. "And how long might you be planning to loll around, eating and drinking what all's in the house?" he said, his lip curled like a nasty dog.

"Six months, perhaps."

"Six months! And who's to pay for you and your bastard?"

I looked at him straight. "Why, Father," said I, "did you drink it all away, the money I sent while Joey was here dying?"

He slapped me but I'd thought he would, so I'd turned my face away in time to miss the worst of it.

Once, when I was a little girl, my father saved a man's life. Twas a mild spring afternoon and my father and my brother John were mending a stone wall that stood between our house and the road. The snow of the winter past had tumbled the wall so that it took a good day's work to fix it. The stones were large and old and they needed scraping of the old muck, which I was doing along with Emily. John and my father together would fit them back to their holes in the wall. Twas like a puzzle and they were amused by it, though it sweated their shirts right through.

"Look, Father," said John, "this big one goes right here, can you see? Here at the bottom, where this point is, is how it fits in."

"Yes, I see and why don't you go ahead and put it there if you're so smart then?" my father said and then stood back and laughed while John tried to manhandle the giant stone by himself. Twas funny indeed to see the scrawny little boy try and we all laughed together at the fix John found himself in.

"He looks like him who takes the world on his back," said I. "John, you told us about him who did that, that Mr. Guzzardi told you in school. What was his name?"

"Ninny," panted John. "I cannot talk to you now, I have this thing up and I can neither put it down or pick it further up. Father, help!"

I remember that afternoon, for what occurred later that night was so serious that the whole of the day stood out to me. It acted like it was in a frame in my mind, that day, like it was one of those pictures on Freddie's wall that I'd gaze at.

That night after dinner, my father had begun to snore in his chair and we girls were helping my mother with the dishes when there came a soft knock on the door. I opened it and there stood Mr. Guzzardi, the schoolteacher.

"Come in, Mr. Guzzardi," said my mother. I heard the surprise in her voice. "Tom, look who's come to visit," she said loudly so my father would waken. He did.

Mr. Guzzardi stepped in and when the fire lit his face, we saw that he was much frightened.

"What's happened then?" said my father to him as my mother led him to a chair and poured him a mug of ale.

We children had gathered all around, and of course Mr. Guzzardi was used to a crowd of young ones, but now he looked at us tongue-tied. My father saw this and yelled at us. "Get to bed, all you brats, and now." We scurried but John and I, being more curiouser and braver than the others, opened the bedchamber door as soon as we dared and listened through the crack.

"I swear it, sir. I swear it to God," Mr. Guzzardi was saying.

"Why do they accuse you, then?" said my father back, very gruff.

"Tis my faith," said Mr. Guzzardi. "You know it is. They call me Papist and spit at me, though they send their children to me nonetheless. Now they look for me to hang me!"

I heard John gasp from just behind my head. I pushed the door open a bit more, just enough so I could see some small piece of anything. I saw my father's back which made me brave as his face would have not. Mr. Guzzardi had not kept to his chair but instead paced, back and forth in front of my father, with his head in his hands. My mother must have been in the room but I did not see her.

"I did not touch her," Mr. Guzzardi said. "You know I did not, Mr. Rose. I did not care to touch her! That she is with child is not my doing. They accuse me wrongly!"

"She is but a child herself!" My mother said that from a corner.

"She is!" said Mr. Guzzardi. "She is! She's but twelve years. It's a blasphemy. It makes my stomach turn."

"Why did she say it was you?" said my father in a stern, loud voice. "Why, man?"

Mr. Guzzardi burst into tears. I had never seen a man cry before. John grunted; when my father turned his face toward us for a sip from his mug, I saw his curled lip.

"I know why! Her father had her and she's afraid to say it!" said Mr. Guzzardi. I couldn't imagine what he meant but I heard my father say, "The bloody bastard."

Suddenly, a banging came at the door. "They'll take my life from me," sobbed Mr. Guzzardi. "I did nothing."

"Tom," I heard my mother whisper. "What shall you do?"

John and I watched as my father leapt toward Mr. Guzzardi, grabbed him and twirling, shoved him toward our very door. We stepped away just in time, for the door flew open and my father thrust Mr. Guzzardi in and closed it shut again.

John and I stared at Mr. Guzzardi and he at us and then, quick and without a word, the three of us pressed our ears against the door.

We heard my father open the door.

"Who's there?" he said.

Mr. Galbraith spoke in his high voice. Father had laughed at it be-fore. "He flutes like a little girl in a frock," he'd said, just the last week.

"Are you hiding that bastard Guzzardi? Mike said he ran here, didn't you, Mike? He said, 'He ran on to Rose's house,' didn't you, Mike?"

"I did," we heard Mike say.

"I may be," said our father. "He may be just inside my house. He may be just on the other side of the door."

I saw Mr. Guzzardi's eyes widen.

"But you'll never know," said my father. "For you're not invited in."

"If you know what's good for you, Tom, you'll send him out."

"They're all drunk, Tom," said my mother.

We heard a low rumbling from outside. "Sounds like a pack of dogs," John whispered. Mr. Guzzardi's breath came quick.

"Galbraith," said my father low and mean. "Get your filth away from my door. It makes me sick."

"If you don't send him out," said another, "we know how to come in."

"Galbraith," said my father, very loud this time, "shall I tell them what I know?"

There was a silence.

"What do you know?" called a voice.

"I know," said my father clearly, "that Pat Galbraith should be God-damned for a hypocrite as well as for much else."

"What's he mean? Galbraith, what's he saying?" yelled the voices.

We heard the crowd quiet themselves a bit. Then Galbraith spoke. He sounded like he'd been punched in his guts.

"I believe he's bluffing, lads. The bastard's not here. He's probably run off by now. Aah, my poor lass." He began to sob like drunks do. The men outside began to disperse; we could hear them walking away from where we were. One of them even said, "Sorry, Tom," to which my father answered, "Fuck off, then."

Then he slammed the door. John and I ran to hide behind the chair in our darkened room so Father didn't see us when he yanked the door open and pulled Guzzardi, who seemed about to faint, out of it.

"That's enough of my trouble for you," said my father. "Tomorrow night they'll just drink more and be after you again. Here. Take this and get ye gone. God only knows why you came to me anyhow."

"Thank you, sir. Thank you," groveled Mr. Guzzardi. "You saved my life, sir. Thank you for the coins. I shall pay you back, I swear."

My father grunted.

"Good-bye, Mr. Rose. Thank you. Thank you, Mrs. Rose. I am in debt to you."

Then he left and we heard the door close behind him.

Twas suddenly silent, except for the sound of my father pouring himself more ale.

My mother spoke very softly. "It's because you can read, I expect," she said. He did not answer her.

John and I looked at each other, amazed. We had never before known that our father could read. He had never tried to teach us, nor even told us that he could.

For a long time, twas a mystery to us—why he'd kept it secret—and we would together try to work out why it is that he'd kept it from us, when other men might be proud. But as time passed and our father succumbed more and more to the drink, we did not speak of it to each other anymore.

I think now that my father did all he could to forget what he might have done, but did not do, with his life. That he came to naught, he blamed on us: on our mouths, always open and crying, like a nestful of baby birds. And of course he blamed my mother. And the blame made him so mean.

I try to see it different from how he did. If only, I think to myself, if only he could have seen that to be a good father and a good husband is the most Christian of all the world's duties, well then, he might not have champed so at the bit in his mouth. He might have kept himself some dignity and some pride. But then I think: well, Susan, that's what you did too, is champ, and hard. I champed hard enough to forget the good teaching I'd had as a lass. I'd champed hard enough to lie down with whomever I wanted, commandment or no. And so this way, I understand my father better, though I hate him still. After all, my sin never blacked an eye nor yet chipped a tooth.

❧

When Davey was but two months old, my mother came to me with a message. My mother's cousin, Patsy Garnett, had a daughter who had a baby just born. The daughter's husband made hay for the manor house in Butterfield, just a little way down the road, and he wanted his wife's help in gathering it in. She must be in the fields all the day next provided the weather held, and she worried about her child as there was no nursing woman in all the town. Patsy wished I would come up, just for the morning. "It would ease her mind so, my dear," said my mother to me, "because hers is such a tiny mite, it cannot go for longer than an hour and she'll be away from it all the day. My cousin Patsy said she'd feed it by hand for the afternoon, but if they had you for the morning, it would help a great deal."

"And Davey?" said I, a little short, for I still smarted from my Joey's fate.

"He's a fat little man, isn't he now," said my mother, smiling and rubbing Davey's tummy as I held him in my lap. "What a milk belly you've given him!" We both smiled at the tyke and were rewarded with a burp and a smile.

"Well, I'll do it," said I, "to help her out. But, Mother," and I lowered my voice to say this, "watch Father around my baby."

My mother looked at me with something of reproach but then her face changed. "Aah," said she, shaking her head, the tears starting from her eyes, "I can never forgive myself for letting your Joey go. I have kept so many babies, and hardly ever lost a one. Just that little lass with the fever like your Joey and then the tiny boy who died in the cradle. Woe is me, it'll be a sorrow and a cross to bear, all my life, to think what I lost for you, my dear." And she wept.

"Now, Mother," I said, drying my own tears and then hers, "I could never blame you for it and I never have. I know you did what you could for him. It's Father I blame more, for it was he forced me to go before Joey was able to lose me. And listen: I do not mean for the same thing to happen again. I don't, Mother, no matter what occurs." I looked at her in her face to see if she understood.

"Yes, my dear," said she, "you must do as you see fit. But he may yet come around, Susan, you shall see. He was such a good man when I married him." 'Twas hard for me to believe it at all.

Patsy's daughter sent a horse for me and off I went early the next morning. I'd had it in my mind to wonder how a woman, so recently on the childbed, could stand a day of baling, but as soon as I saw her, I understood. She was as tall as a man, and as broad, with arms veiny and thick. 'Tis not often I feel dainty; in her presence, I rather did. Vincy, as was her name, acted right glad to see me.

"I am so obliged to you," she said, "you see how small he is yet, having been born a week or two early. He's my first and came so quick, though the pains was fierce. He sucks like a monster though." She looked at him fondly.

"He'll have a deal of growing to do to reach your chin," I said, taking him from her.

She laughed a great laugh. "Ha, you should see his da," said she. "He's right like a tree! Yes, if he takes after us, he'll be a giant, true enough. Thank you once more for helping me this way. Bob said I might work but half the day." She laughed again. "I told him that in that half-day, I'll do as much as most men will in a whole." And off she went.

So I took her little mite to the breast, and just as she'd said, he sucked like a fury. When he was sated, and his little head nodded, I put him in his cradle and he slept. I looked under the cloth she'd showed me, and there was a lovely pasty and some cheese as well as a nice mug of ale, and so I had a little rest. Twasn't usual for me to just sit. In my mother's house, when I wasn't nursing, I was hard at work in the kitchen, or churning, or mending, or twisting wicks, or anything else I could do to make it so I wasn't just a leech on my father's arm. But here, where it wasn't my house, I could just sit and wasn't it heavenly.

The baby suckled three times before his mother returned, all brown and blown, from the fields. She came into the door laughing and grabbed him from the cradle to kiss his head. He cried some, as babies will do when they sense their own mothers are there, and this just made her laugh the more. Twas sweet, though sweet's not a word you'd think of first when you saw that giantess. Still, that's what it was.

I had to wait a bit for the carter she'd hired to come along, but then he did. The journey wasn't a long one, but by the time he got me home, I was half asleep from the rocking, as well as from the second glass of ale Vincy had pressed upon me as we waited.

I thanked the carter, and jumped down to go inside. Little Janey, sitting in the doorway, blocked my way in.

"What's amiss, Janey?" said I, squatting to look in her little face. She was only seven years old, and for most of her life, I'd been off to nurse so she was shy with me yet.

"Are your brothers horrors?" I asked, putting my hand on her head. "You must learn to fight 'em back, you know," but she looked up at me and wiped her nose with the back of her hand.

"It's Father," she said. "He oughtn't to hit Ma."

"True enough," said I, but then a dread came over me. I stepped by her into the house and there I saw my mother, sitting in her rocker, holding a rag to her lip and weeping. "Mother," said I, rushing up to her. "What'd the bastard do this time? You're all right, aren't you? Let me see." But she would not.

"He took him," is what she said, "and I could not prevent it."

My eyes nearly sprang from their sockets; I could feel them pop. I ran to the cradle but it was empty. Empty! Davey was gone! I looked at the shelf where his things were and it too was bare. No nappies, no lard. I know I screamed loud enough to raise a soul from the deepest part of hell.

I felt as if my very skin could not contain the horror. I thought I was stuck inside a hideous fancy. The pasty and the ale came up and I ran to the sink to vomit. Suddenly, but I could not tell you why, my hair seemed ridiculous; why my hair? I cannot say. But it seemed to me that I must rip it from my scalp so as to be able to again take a breath.

"Mother!" I screamed. "Where's Davey? Where has he taken him? What has he done with him? Mother! What shall I do? Mother, tell me what he said. Make haste! As you love me, tell me now!"

And this is what she told me.

Even as I carried Davey inside me, my father must have determined to find the baby's father and make him pay. And "pay" he meant; he did not care that I become an honest woman; he cared more for the shillings that could be got out of me and my situation. He may have sus-picioned on several young men of the town, but if he did, I'm sure they laughed in his face. I imagine those meetings: Gar, I'd rather fuck a cow than your daughter, Old Tom. But then, said my mother, one evening as my father sat in the tavern, a man he didn't know told him a story.

The man said he'd been walking in the wood—and by that I expect he meant poaching—near the Great House and he'd come upon a couple going at it in the dirt. He told my father that he had sneaked to watch—the nasty thing—and had heard the gen'lman—he could tell he was a gentleman by his boots, my mother told me and then she colored in her cheeks—say how he's used to having roses under him. I knew then that the story was true because I remember Freddie saying just that to me and how we had laughed at it.

I suppose the man hoped to get a shilling for his trouble in telling the story; it's more likely that my father broke his nose for him. But however it ended in the tavern, I do not know nor care. My father did not tell my mother a word of it until that very morning or she would have warned me. When she tried to stay him from snatching the baby right out of her arms, he yelled the story at her, broke her lip, took my Davey and ran.

"My God," I said to my mother. "He's not taken the baby to the Great House?"

And my mother, holding the side of her face, simply wept.

"But he doesn't understand," I screamed. "Davey's father hasn't anything to do with the Great House and them. He's a man I met in Aubrey!"

"What can you mean, Susan?" said my mother. "Is the story your father heard a lie, then? Oh, I knew there was no truth to it. I knew it."

When I saw what my deception and slatternliness had done to them I loved, I felt a wish to die. If I had known what there was yet to know, my heart might have refused to beat further. My mother beaten and confused, my baby kidnapped, and all because I had some evil in me that was bent on coming out. But there was no time to muse on my badness just now.

"When did he take him, then?" I cried, dashing away my tears. "Will I catch him?"

"I don't know, my dear," said my mother. "He has been biding his time. He told me that he found out about you and the young master," and then again, she looked muddled, "but that's not the truth, I now know . . ."

"But when did he talk to that man?" I asked.

"Ah, it seemed to me that it was ever so long ago, before even Davey was born. And now, to think it's not true!" And again she wept.

"Mother, you must dry your tears and talk to me! When did he take Davey? How long ago?"

"Twas not long after they came to get you this morning, my dear," said my mother. "I stood in front of the cradle, but he split my lip and threw me hard against the wall. He had a horse from someone, and he took the baby up like a sack of apples under his arm, the little thing just crying . . ."

I screamed as loud as ever I could. "But I must go!" I said. "I must go and get back my baby!"

I ran to my trunk and pulled out my bag and threw into it my other dress and an apron. Then I made haste into the barn and there I grabbed our shovel. I dug in the southwest corner and found my money, and I wrapped it tight in a kerchief so it would not clink and give itself away, and I put that in my bag. And then I went back to the house to hug my mother and we were both crying. She handed me some coins, and I did not thank her with words but instead just kissed her again on her mouth and her hand.

"Take care of yourself, Mother," said I. "I will always think of you, every day of my life. I will see you again before the end." And she clutched me and cried and then I found myself on the road walking as quickly as ever my legs would carry me. I did not look back for I could think only of what lay in front of me, though I might not know what it was.

❧

I could not get a ride. There was no one on the road and those few who did ride by were but single horsemen who, when they saw my size, ignored my pleas and rode past me at a gallop. It took me a good forty minutes to get to the Great House, and the whole time I was thinking thoughts that made the walk seem like the path to hell.

I supposed my father would go to the Great House to tell them what he had heard about the baby's father and try to get some money out of them. I supposed Mrs. Bonney would intercept the problem so she might protect Freddie from his father if she could.

But what if I could not get to Mrs. Bonney? What if she refused to take the baby, what would he do with it? What if she did take the baby, what then? What if the family was not at home: what would I do? Where would next I go to find my child? What if one of the few riders coming down the road was my father? Would he hurt me bad enough so that I could no longer search for Davey? Who would feed Davey? I tried to banish thoughts of feeding from my mind immediately, lest they bring my milk down, but it was too late: that familiar tightening arose, and my breasts filled and leaked onto my shift. I could not run; my bosoms was too big and it hurt to bounce them. I made do with a trot, more like, and finally, there in front of me was the Great House.

I made my way as quick as I could to the downstairs entrance and slipped in. Twas late by then, but the house was lit and I could tell by the kitchen that there was a fancy supper upstairs. The soup had been served; I could see the big silver tureen on the kitchen table ready for washing, and for an instant, it recalled to me my hours of polishing when still I was a maid and a maiden, too. The Bonneys and their guests upstairs were on to the meat course, which I knew because the cook and the kitchen girls were sitting at their own table, eating their own suppers, which they might do before the salads were served.

I knew the place like I knew my Davey's hand. I snuck by the servants as they ate and turned left down the hall toward the pressing room, where we laundry girls would stack the sheets and shirts after they was all cleaned and ironed. I went in and closed the door. I did not know what to do next and felt quite wild at being so very close to them as perhaps had my child. I wondered if he was in that very house, hungry, while they ate their quail and drank their wine.

Then the door opened and in came Mrs. Hart. She opened the door very sudden, just as she used to do when I lived at the Great House. The other girls thought it was so she could catch them at some sloth, which often she did, but I knew better. She was just a fierce one, was Mrs. Hart, and she opened doors the way she did because it was in her nature to be rough. I knew this about her because I am the same. Strong and rough. We looked at each other in our eyes. She was surprised to see me.

"Susan Rose," she said sharply. "What do you here?"

"Mrs. Hart," I said. I could hear that my voice was harsh and hoarse with the passion of my situation. "I believe my baby is here in this house."

I could not tell what was in her look: was it fury or was it pity? I could not say. Footsteps rang in the hall. Mrs. Hart turned so that she blocked the door and said to the person outside, "Maggie, come back later." Then she turned back toward me, closed the door behind her, and locked it.

"How do you dare to come here?" She did not sound angry now, but more curious.

"I believe my baby is here," I repeated. "I mean to get him back. Is he here?"

"Why should he be?" she said.

"You know," I said. "For the love of Jesus, tell me."

She said nothing and looked me up and down.

"I have money," I started, but she shook her head.

"They say," said she, "that it's Master Freddie's baby you carried."

"No, mum," said I, quite fierce, "it's mine."

Mrs. Hart pursed her lips and raised her eyebrows and suddenly I knowed exactly what she wanted. She wanted to know. She was over-come by curiousness and that was all it was. I saw it clear: to such as her, the knowing what others don't is what keeps her above them. She was a breed apart, was Mrs. Hart: not part of us servants nor yet part of the masters of the house, and that in-between place was where she'd found her betterment in the world. If she'd been a man, she'd have gone to sea or she'd have been a general in the army. Instead she was a housekeeper of someone else's house and she might hate it, but the power of it was what kept her alive.

So I fed her. I told her about meeting Freddie by the side of the road, which made her nostrils flare in anger, but whether she was angry at me for reaching so far above my station or because she did not like Master Freddie or because she did not like what we did, I cannot know. I told her what I knew about my father's meeting with the stranger in the tav-ern, and she listened closely, but no expression showed on her face.

I did not tell her that Freddie was not Davey's father. I thought to do it and then bit back the words. Mrs. Hart had no care for me after all. Her cares were only for the Great House and them what was in it. If she knew that Davey was not Freddie's, why, there'd be nothing left in my story to interest her. And I needed her to want to know more, and yet more.

I debated in my mind about whether to tell her about Joey and I decided that I would. She may have heard that I had had a baby before, and leaving it out might set her against me. She might ask me how I'd made my way in Aubrey and I thought the fewer lies I told her, the bet-ter it would go for me, as she was shrewd enough to catch me in them. And I thought that if she had a spark of pity in her breast, which I did not know if she did, but if she did, it would soften her up to think that I had already lost a child before this one. I did not know: perhaps she had had a child herself, though she never spoke of one nor had a like-ness that she shewed around.

I did not tell her who Joey's father had been. I knew that of all the things in the world, it would make her angriest to think that one of her maids had been lying in the larder with the master under her watch. So I did not tell her about that. The truth, I thought to myself as my brain worked at what to leave out, is a very good thing, but only if it steers you in the right direction.

When I finished she nodded. Then she looked down at her hands that were folded in her lap.

"There was a baby here this morning," said she.

My eyes popped. "Is he still?"

"No," she said. "He is not."

I panted. She continued.

"Several months ago, a rough man with blue eyes . . ."

"My father!"

She nodded once. "He came here one morning and asked to see Mrs. Bonney. I quizzed him as to what he wanted but he would not tell me. I almost turned him away, but he told me that his message concerned Master Freddie so I thought it wise to tell the mistress. I made him wait outside til Mrs. Bonney had dressed, which was a good hour and a half, but he waited. When I told Mrs. Bonney that a Mr. Rose wanted to see her, she seemed quite curious about what he might want. She called in Miss Anne as a chaperone. Their meeting lasted for a good while.

"I did not see Mr. Rose leave. But for a week following, Mrs. Bonney took to her bed and refused even to move to the sofa in the morning room. No one could attend her but Miss Anne . . . not even Master Freddie. This was perhaps four and a half months ago."

I could not keep my moan to myself. It was horrible to me that my father had laid his terrible plan, the particulars of which I did not know, while I was still big; that he'd kept it close to his chest while I labored; that he harbored it as I nursed his grandson.

Mrs. Hart continued. "This morning, quite early, he came back. Rawlings showed him right in to Miss Anne, who seemed to have been expecting him. They did not sit, but left the house immediately and made for the stables. Later, Miss Anne ordered that a bowl of milk and a spoon be sent out. I never saw her again inside the house til after the cart came."

"The cart?" I croaked.

She quit her speech. I stared at her but her mouth was pursed as tight as a mail slot, as if sudden-like, she realized how much she was giving away for free.

"Please," I said.

"Before noon, a carter drove up with a woman riding along. He hopped down and went inside the stable and was out in a trice. He handed a bundle to the woman, who took it in her arms and then they drove off."

"But how could you be sure it was a baby?" said I, weeping. "The stables are a good bit from here, too far to see clearly."

"It was indeed a baby," she said.

I stuffed my apron into my mouth lest my howl overcome the household. "You must help me," I said when I was able to speak. "I beg you to help me. I must speak to the mistress as soon as she can be got. Please help me."

She looked at me. She might almost have been made of stone, for as much as her expression gave away. I had nothing to give her, nothing she might want as a bribe for her to let me see the mistress. But it might be . . .

I calmed myself, but not so much that she would think me a conniver. "Perhaps," I said, "perhaps you are right. Perhaps it would do better to talk to Freddie himself."

She looked at me, suspicious.

"He will know what to do, I'm sure he will," and then I stopped speaking.

She looked at me and I at her. She knew that Master Freddie would never know how to do anything at all. She knew that I knew it too. She did not know what I was up to exactly.

I cast my eyes down as if I was humble. And I prayed.

She thought a minute. I hoped that Mrs. Hart was thinking that her mistress would better like it if I stayed away from Freddie once and for all. I hoped that Mrs. Hart was thinking that if she told her mistress on me, right then and there, that she would get the credit for saving the poor boy from the unpleasantness of my tears. I hoped that Mrs. Hart was thinking that this was my punishment for reaching so far above my station and that if the mistress cast me out, then all I got was what I deserved.

"Master Frederick is not at home," said Mrs. Hart. "But if you like, I will see if the mistress can be disturbed from her guests for a moment."

"Not at home?" said I like I was distressed. "The mistress?" I said like I was afeared. "Well, I suppose that will have to do," said I, thanking God under my breath. Mrs. Hart left the room and I waited.

MRS. PADGETT'S REASON

Mrs. Padgett—my own Elizabeth—and I had loved each other as tiny children. I distinctly recall holding her little hand in my own as we tripped across the lawns of her home at Mansfield in pursuit of a jackrabbit. Our mothers were cousins and admitted to us, after we professed our fondness for one another, that they had both long harbored the hope that we each would find our hearts in the other. When I asked her father, Lord Elliott, for her hand, I believe that I saw him dash a tear of joy from his eye as he agreed.

Our engagement was lengthy; Elizabeth had come into society but recently, and her mother wished her to have a season in London before we married. We were eager to wed, but she, always the best of daughters, would bow to all her parents' words with perfect obedience. This innocence was in part why I had remained so attached to her. I hoped to feel that same perfect trust one day from her as my wife as they did as her mother and father.

Our marriage trip was among the happiest in the world, I am certain. We visited Florence and Venice, and when her brown eyes widened with the splendors of those ancient cities, I realized once again that in her I had picked a rare and perfect blossom.

Elizabeth found herself with child after a half-year of our marriage. As is the custom for the eldest son and his family, we lived in my father's manor as it will one day be mine to inherit. I had previously taken on much of the responsibility of the estate, and when we returned from our wedding trip, my father was very glad to shift the remaining work to me. He is older now and more and more interested in his botanicals and I was glad to take the burden from him.

Elizabeth and I were very happy. But then a shadow entered our lives. As her slender frame grew round, she found less rest in her sleep and began to be troubled by dark and terrible dreams. Often she would waken in tears and would sob words of nonsense, about black horses and horns. Her morning illness, so common in the bearing of a child, did not lessen but only grew as time passed, and her eyes, once so bright, seemed to dull. She sometimes mumbled and when asked to repeat herself would quake and quiver as if threatened with some physical violence. The doctor prescribed a healing purge and then cupping, but these did no good.

One terrible morning, she came to breakfast in her shift, upon which she had vomited. The look in her eye was frightful, and when I took her poor arm to assist her up the stairs I heard her mumble that I was a demon and that this was hell.

By the end of her time, her plight was very dire. No one could help her, she knew no one, not even her dear mother who came to be with her. Dr. Frame refused her the laudanum that might have soothed her, and I think he was right to do so: he feared that it would hurt the child she carried and that no good could come from that. When her pains began, he had to tie her down so that she would do no harm to the baby as it was expelled from her body. He did not tell me so, but I saw her binds when I looked in from the next room where I waited.

Her labors were fierce and lasted for twenty hours. I prayed constantly for God's mercy, that He would find it in Himself to free her of the shadows that had taken her, so that she would be able to love her child. And, I wish to say, so that she would come back to me the Elizabeth I have loved for so long.

It was not to be. When shown the babe, she shrieked and would have scratched it with her fingernails had not the nurse quickly removed it. I must confess that I was in despair at this time. Dr. Frame, who is a good and wise man, knew of a wet nurse in Leighton, a Mrs. Rose, whom he had trusted for some years. He told me candidly but with great gentleness, that he had recently ascertained that she did indeed have a place for an infant. I understood that he had assumed that my Elizabeth would prove inadequate to the baby's needs, and I thanked him for his foresight. My brother Harold took my mother and the baby to the lady's house on that very day since she lived but one hour hence by chaise.

Mrs. Rose kept the baby, a girl called Elizabeth after her mother, and nursed her for sixteen months at which time she was weaned and came home to us. She brings light to our lives. My wife lives in an asylum some leagues hence where she is dosed by laudanum daily, lest she do damage to herself or others.

Nine

Mrs. Hart told me to stay where I was and locked the door when she left. I had nothing to do but pace like a prisoner before the gallows while I waited. I wished I could break down the door and kill Mrs. Bonney. My baby! I blamed her as much as I blamed my father. I did not know exactly what he'd said to her to convince her to take Davey off his hands, but I did know that she was a mother too. She was not so old and her children were not so old as to keep her from remembering the smell of her own baby's head. And she took mine away. I prayed to God that after He gave me my baby back, He would cause a canker to grow inside her so that she might know the pain that I suffered now. As for my father's fate: I only hoped that he drank himself to death and drowned in a ditch.

My pacing did not hide the rustle of her silks. When she opened the door and came in, I curtsied. I thought it best to keep whatever manners I could lest right away she have enough of me. Oh, what I needed from her! Twas a horror to me that she had so much power to refuse.

For an instant I recalled young Mrs. Holcomb in Aubrey and how she wished to deny me my visit home to Joey. The rich—they have more than what they need and yet they take so much from us. Tis like the story of David and Bathsheba: David had plenty of wives while Uriah had but one and that's the one David wanted so he took her. Twas the same then as it is now.

"I should like to sit down," was the first words out of her mouth. There was a chair not three steps from where she stood, but I quickly fetched it and put it behind her knees. She smoothed her dress before she spoke again.

"You needn't worry. I have made the best possible arrangements for Freddie's son. He'll be raised as a gentleman. If you are a good girl, you will thank me and leave it be."

I stood in front of her, my mouth agape. Her words surprised me more than I can say. I had thought that she would scold me, that she would call me a repulsive ugly thing, so far above my station as to be unnatural. Twas the farthest thing from my mind that she might be calm and in fact not cruel.

"I did not see him myself, but Anne told me that he resembled Freddie very much around the eyes and the forehead," she said. I started. I had thought to tell her right away that the baby was not Freddie's. But when she told me that she had taken care that the baby would be cared for well, I was not so sure. Whatever might she do when she found out it was not her son's? Would her wrath thrust Davey into some danger that I could not conceive of? I could not take the chance.

"Ma'am," I said hoarsely, "he needs me. He is my baby. You have a mother's heart, I know it. Please, I shall die without him."

"Susan, is it?" she said quietly. "Please think of what is best for the child. Does it not occur to you that he will be given a good education, a fine upbringing? It is best this way. After all, girl, it is not as if Freddie is the first young man to be tempted by a servant, nor you the first servant to birth her master's bastard. I might've simply dismissed your father when he came to see me, but I wished to do something for the child. Be grateful, girl," she repeated, "and leave it be."

"Mrs. Bonney," I said, standing as still as I was able, "I did not ask you for anything. I want nothing from you nor from . . . the young master. I ask only that you return my child to me."

"You believe that now, Susan," said she. "But I expect that soon enough you would come to want something from us and then something more. You might not mean to do it, but you would begin to expect what you may not expect from us. It would never do."

I could see that my father had put that idea into her head. He had explained it to her thus: give me money now, he'd said, and take this brat, or I will haunt you for the rest of your days.

She began to look distracted. I talked fast. "You said yourself, ma'am," said I, "that this is not such a uncommon thing—for a gentleman and one such as me to have . . . done what . . . to have it happen as it did. It's true, just as you said. It does happen, indeed it does! Why then did you not turn your back on my father when he came to bother you?" I was panting as I spoke, for I spoke quick so she would not quit me before I had done with her. "Listen, please, my lady," I said. "I am sure you gave him money, my father. And that is all he wanted and I am very sorry for it. But if you will give me my son back, I will never bother you again . . . indeed, I will take the child and go away and never bother you anymore, I swear it to God, if you will only do that."

"No, Susan, I cannot," was all she said.

"But why," I wailed. "Why do you spend a care on what happens to him, as he is but a bastard and means nothing to you?"

"Because it is my Freddie's!" she said very suddenly and loudly.

I was astonished. Twas not the blackmail, then. Twas the tenderness for her own son.

"Surely Master Freddie does not know of the child? I know that I never told him!"

"Certainly not," said Mrs. Bonney coldly.

"And what if I were to tell him then," I said wildly. "I shall tell him!"

"You shall never find him," she said. "He is in Italy and you, I think, will not go there. Now, my guests await me."

"Please, ma'am," I said, "please. I cannot just forget my child. I must know where he has been taken. Please," I began to panic as she moved toward the door, "please! Please! You owe it to me! You owe it to me!"

"And what do you mean by owe," said she, whirling, her mouth tight. "What could we possibly owe you?"

"My Ellen," I sobbed to her. "You already took Ellen from me. You may not have Davey too."

She looked down on me to where I knelt, on my knees, on the floor of her folding room. Her mouth softened just a bit. "Ah," said she, "that was a loss, was it not. But you know," and she became stern and cold in her look, "I could not chance that you'd lose this child too."

"What do you mean?" I whispered.

"Your father told me about your first child. I assume he was my son's as well. Do you not see, you stupid girl, that the baby is far safer where he is now? Let it go. I am afraid that if you do not, your father may beat you. He seemed a violent man."

"He was not Freddie's," I shrieked. "Freddie is not this baby's father."

She stopped in the doorway and turned. "Is that true?" she said, very low.

"Yes," I cried. "Yes! My father's wrong in his story. He believes it but it's false."

She looked at me, abashed. Then she shrugged. The gesture was familiar to me. I had seen the same, more times than I could count, when she had done with what she was at and wanted to be on to the next thing.

"Ah well," she said, "it's done, anyhow, and so best to leave it."

And with that she turned and walked out the door.

I had not the luxury to bask in my horror. I ran from the folding room to the stairway, praying that I should meet no one. As I had expected, the maids were busy with the dishes and the men were clearing the table or serving coffee in the drawing room. With any luck, I could slip upstairs unnoticed. The back stairs, while creaky, were blessedly deserted.

I climbed two flights, taking two stairs at once, and opened the stairway door slowly. Just across the hall, I found the room I wanted. It was the least desirable room on the hall, for how near it was to where us servants came and went like ants, all the livelong day. Twas the perfect room for a poor relation. I tried the door. It opened right away and I went in and sat in the chair next to Miss Anne's bed to wait for her return.

Twas but a quarter of an hour. She had entered her room and closed her door before she saw me. She started and almost screamed but did not. I sat very still. I felt quite desperate.

"I cannot help you," she hissed at me. "You would do well to get out before I call someone and the constable is summoned. They would put you in the stocks, you know, or worse."

"Where did they take him?" I said calmly.

"I will not tell you anything," said she. And then she said, "Slut."

"Thief," I parried.

Her eyes flashed in anger but then I saw what I wanted. I saw fear.

"If you do not tell me this instant," I said, rising and walking toward her, "I will tell them about the things you took." I knew only about the necklace I saw her take that one day she had helped Mrs. Bonney with her letter whilst I cleaned the grate. But I gambled on more and I saw that I was right for she had paled.

"I do not know what you may be speaking of," she said, but her hand trembled where she rested it on her bedpost. She spoke very soft. I could see that I had hit a nerve.

"Tell me where they took him and I shall keep what I know about you to myself."

"I do not know," she said, but her eyelids fluttered very fast.

"Shall I tell them now?" I said so loudly I almost frightened myself, but it worked: she shushed me with her finger to her mouth.

"I shall tell, only please, I beg you to speak but softly," she said in a panic.

I did not allow any hope to come into my eyes, lest she feel she might disarm me. I cared only to look dangerous, as if I would do anything at all, which was only the truth.

She told me that she and Mrs. Bonney had a cousin who was an officer in the Royal Indian forces. He had married a young woman some years ago and taken her to India with him, but she had become ill there and so he had brought her home and then returned to fulfill his commission. Mrs. Norval lived in London. Not three months earlier, Mrs. Bonney had received a letter from Captain Norval, stating his concerns about his wife: that she seemed quite turned with loneliness. He begged Mrs. Bonney to do something for the lady. He thought it would do her good to have a companion, or perhaps a child, as she had always loved children and yet had none of her own. Mrs. Bonney received his letter the exact day before my father had come to her first. It seemed a natural fit, then, and so it had become a plan.

Norval—I cached it tight in my mind.

"Have you an address?" I hissed at her as I made myself up to leave.

I saw her: she almost spoke and then thought not to and instead, shook her head as if she'd changed her mind about it. "No," said she with a shrug, the same shrug as Mrs. Bonney had shown, the same as if she'd learned it like a lesson at her knee. Twas not that she didn't know, no, not at all. Twas rather that she didn't care to say. What care had she if someone else was in pain or worse? I could hear their thoughts, hers and the lady's: how could it possibly matter to me, they would say through those pinched, false red lips.

I am not a violent girl, though I'm big. I can fight if I need to fight, mind you, but mostly I don't need to, excepting when my brothers used to need stopping. But that shrug made me see blood behind my eyes, and I tell you, Reader, twas a good thing for that heartless bitch of a Miss Anne that I was in a hurry to get out of that house and find my baby. Even so, my hand darted out and I struck her, hard enough to knock her to the floor. She lay and looked up at me in fear and I felt how good it feels to cause it when it's wanted. My pleasure must have showed in my eyes, for when I looked at her again she whimpered, with her hand to her face, and said, "Hampstead Street," in a small, scared voice.

Then shame rose up inside me like a curtain. Twas not that I felt guilty for striking her, not at all. Twas more that I had not hit Mrs. Bonney, though she'd shown me the very same shrug. I had turned on Miss Anne instead, whose life was not so sunny as to afford it. No, Susan Rose, I told myself, you suffer the rich to do as they wish and hold the less fortunate to a higher standard. Tis unfair and tis the dirty part of the world that we all live in, but there it is just the same.

She yet lay on the floor when I slipped out of her room. I ran across the hall in two steps, down the back stairs and the downstairs hall and out the rear door. I cannot say if anyone saw me or not and nor did I care. I had the information I required and it was needful for me to say good-bye to the Great House for then and forever.

❧

I stepped into a dark night. I knew that at that time of night there would be no transport to take me to London, which was a very long way. I crept to the laundry, snuck in, and lay on a pile of dirty sheets. My tears would not stop and no longer did I try to make them. I cried til my heart ached inside my chest.

After a while, I opened my shift and let it hang down around my waist. Then I stood over a sink and like as if I was a cow, I milked my own full dugs and watched the wasted milk as it dripped down into the drain. Each breast was very full. I squeezed and squeezed and rung myself out like I was a rag. I mirrored each drop from my bosom with the tears from my eyes. Twas a long and tedious business, but it was important that I do a job of it. Only Davey himself kept me in milk, only his suckling filled me again. I knew that unless I emptied myself completely, my supply would dwindle and when I did finally find him, I might have nothing for him, and a trouble as bad, no way to earn our keep. I meant to find my child. If you have ever fed a child, with breast or by hand, you will know how long it took me.

In the morning, I rose before the sun and went out onto the road. I had taken a bit of bread and cheese from the small larder that Mrs. Hubbard kept in the laundry for her midday meal, but, as I did not have my letters, I could not write her a message to tell her who her mouse had been. I walked out onto the road and started south toward London. Soon, it began to show some life with horsemen and farmers with carts. Twas not long at all before a carter picked me up. I asked him what he hauled; he said parsnips. He asked where I was off to; I told him London. At that, he looked me up and down and said, "Blimey. And what'll you do there, love?"

"I'll find work as a nurse, is what I sincerely hope," said I.

He nodded as if he approved of my plan and then he filled his pipe and smoked as his horse trotted down the lane. My heart lay very heavy and I was glad to be quiet with my thoughts. The day before, on my way to the Great House, I had felt that I could not move fast enough, that my skin was tight around me, as if I should have to shed it to breathe. I could not sense where my hands should go or what expression my face should wear. All the little things that my body knew how to do, like blinking my eyes or swallowing, all seemed too silly to go on with. I felt like I was breaking into parts and I feared madness, I truly did.

Today, I felt better. I was no less anxious but I felt a bit calmer, more as if I had a plan. For that I did. I had the name of a lady and I had the name of a street. And each turn of the carter's wheels brought me closer to that lady and that street and to my Davey.

During my night in the laundry, I had prayed, like Hannah prayed for Samuel til God heard her cries. And I believe God heard me. For when I awoke, I felt as if He had poured strength into me that I might not use up were I to walk for one thousand miles. It was not that far to London, but far enough. I had no time to walk. I must ride or perhaps be too late.

The carter, who seemed a good enough fellow, said that he would let me ride with him almost to the gates of London itself, but he went too slow and I could not abide it. I bade him let me off in Christchurch, and there I paid a fortune to take a night coach so I would not lose time. The coach was full of travelers but we did not speak to each other overmuch. It is as true as my nose: decent folks don't travel at night unless they must. There were four in the coach with me: an old man with but one leg who hawked through the night and spat into a crock, also a younger man who kept his eyes tight shut til he resigned his seat, though I think he did not sleep, and also a woman in weeds and her daughter, about my age, also in black. The daughter wept for hours, til her eyes were swole up as tight as nuts. Her mother sat still and stared out into the dark.

We departed from the coach in Mansfield. I had heard of the town, for my mother'd had a baby from there. I stepped over to the inn and asked if I might use the outhouse and there I milked myself as dry as I could, though again, it took some while. When I had finished, I went into the inn and ordered a bit of bread and a glass of ale and inquired of the keep as to when the next coach to London would come.

"Not for some hours, miss," said he, "for the regular coach has gone and broke a axle, and they're hard put to find another."

"But is there naught else than that coach?" I asked, very upset, and he shook his head with a no.

As I sat and fretted, a man stepped over, very polite-like, and told me that if I should give him a shilling, he would give me a ride to Longbourne Village where I could pick up a coach that very afternoon. I thanked him and asked when he would start off, and he said that he would wait for me to finish my ale and then we could leave. I drank it in a gulp and jumped up from my bench, which caused him to smile. He was a nice-enough-looking man, though his teeth were rotted.

His cart, I was glad to see, was sturdy and not too full so as to weigh it down. I told him as much, so as to be a hint that I would like a fast ride, though in truth I was at his mercy and must accept whatever speed he saw fit. But he laughed again and said, "You are in a hurry, are you, miss?"

"Yes, sir, I am," said I. "My young man in London and I have posted the banns and are to marry before the week is out. He has found good work there as a smith."

"Your young man?" said he and he looked at me and smiled again.

"Yes," said I. "He is a smith," I repeated. "He has a house set up for us."

"Doesn't that sound comfy, then," said he.

Then he said, "He must be a big man, I suppose?"

"Yes," said I. "He is like a Goliath in his way."

He laughed. Then he said, "Miss, I must beg your pardon. We must make one stop, just up the road a bit. I'm hauling a batch of brooms to town for my neighbor, and we must stop by his warehouse and collect them. It will not take a moment."

I nodded though I felt that I did not want to stop at all.

We traveled in silence for a few minutes and then he said, "Aah, do you see it ahead, his storehouse?"

I nodded again.

"Like Goliath, is he?" said the man.

"Yes," I said, willing him to speed the horses just a bit.

"Well," said he, smiling, "a man like Goliath will do well with a big girl like you, then."

I looked at him to see if he was up to something, but he was giving his thought to driving the horses up to the storehouse door and I could not well see his face. When the horses had stopped, he jumped down from the cart and unlocked the door with a key from his pocket.

"There are but a dozen bundles," said he, "and if you will not mind waiting, I shall have them loaded in a moment."

I waited while he brought the bundles out, one by one, where I could have carried two at one time. But he was such a jolly fellow, he did not think to do it. After the third load, I thought that I would have to help him or else we should be parked outside that storehouse forever. I jumped down and walked into the door of the storehouse, and he came at me and knocked me down.

I am not easy to knock down. But he was a big man himself, and I was not prepared for him wanting what he wanted which was what was between my legs. I fought him, but he had got on top of me and was holding me down with his knees on my stomach. I could not breathe nor roll over nor move much at all.

I hollered in his ear and I spat and I tried to kick him but he would not let me go. I tried to reach up with my mouth and bite him but I could not. He had me firm but yet he could not do what he wanted, though he had his thing out of his pants. He kept trying to move my skirts with his one knee and push the other up between my legs to part them, but he could not both hold me down and do all he wanted to do. We both cursed and fought at each other but he would not get off and I would not give in.

"Damn you, girl," he said finally, "give it to me or forget about your ride."

I stopped my struggling. "Be quick about it then," I said to him, "and forget about the shilling."

Very quick he was. When he finished, he did not help me up but instead smiled, did up his breeches and took up the next bundle of brooms. I cleaned myself a little and then got up to help him.

He did it to me once more before he left me in Longbourne Village but it was worth it to me because between times, I made him whip the horses so they would go as fast as they could and he did so. He wanted to do it to me more than that, but I did not want him to stop the cart, so I gave him what he wanted but in another way. Freddie had taught me how to do it when it was my monthly so that we should be tidy together and thus I knew the trick of it. After he saw that he could get what he wanted from me, he was as pleasant as a spring day. He chatted away and sang songs and laughed very much. He told me his name was Jim and asked me mine, but I would not give it to him. When I refused him my name, which was all I had refused him after all, he looked at me like a dog who had its feelings hurt. He was ridiculous.

I know it is not a pretty thing to hear—that I gave in to him in this way—but I cannot help that. I was desperate and could not stop to care about what seemed coarse and what seemed fine. After I understood how to make him do as I wished, it mattered to me not at all to do as he wished. It cost me but little.

Toward the afternoon of the day, I could not keep my mind from

THE WET NURSE'S TALE

thoughts of my little baby, my Davey, and my bosom became right soaked. He looked down at me and saw the stain and his eyes popped.

"Why, missy, your shirt is all over drenched."

"It's me leaking," said I to him, just so he'd close his mouth.

He wrinkled his brow and then understood "You have a babe, then?" said he. "Is it dead?"

"No," I said and then I began to cry. "He is not dead. He was took right away from me and I'm on my way to get him back. Can you not hurry your horses, dammit?"

"Who took him then?"

"A woman took him." I was weary of him.

"I shall speed them, then," said he, and he whipped them up so they ran faster than before. "A little babe belongs with its mother, don't it," I heard him mumble, "not with no stranger."

We reached Longbourne Village while the sun was still high.

"We've made right good time," said he all smiles, "and ain't it been a enjoyment!" He helped me down like I was a fine lady and showed me into the inn, where he sat me right down and found me an ale and a pasty. As I ate, he inquired about the night coach. He came back from the bursar very pleased with himself.

"Well, missy, and this will suit you very well!" said Jim, sitting himself down on the bench next to me. "The coach for London will leave in one hour and as the man's my cousin, I'll get you a good rate!"

I gave him the money he asked for and off he went again. I used the outhouse and tried to ease myself of some of the milk in my dugs, as I knew the coach ride would not allow for such. But I felt too wild and nervous for the milk to come down and thus it was not successful. I was quite dazed with lack of sleep and with sorrow: I thought to myself that if only God would look after me, though I was a bad girl, then I would keep my milk and not come on with the milk fever like I did at the Holcombs' in Aubrey that once. I feared milk fever very much, for the pain of it, and the trouble.

Jim waited for me to get on the coach. "Good-bye, missy," said he. "I hope you find your baby." I left him standing on the road, waving to me like I might have been his old granny, on my way home after a lovely visit. I was fagged almost to death. I did not wave back.

And then I had a piece of the most lovely luck in the world. Reader: you will not be surprised that I was overjoyed at my situation. For there in the carriage with me sat a woman with two little babies! Two of them! One was a little lad of about a year, sweet and plump, and the other a tiny mite of a squally thing, just born. The woman's only help was a small girl, of perhaps four years old, who made to hold the older of the babes as the mother rocked the smaller. The single other passenger was an old parson, who looked like a scare-the-crow in a field. He seemed quite deaf, which was a lucky thing for him, as the babies were quite restless and uncomfortable.

I wasted no time.

"Missus," said I, "do let me hold the little one, for I can see that the bigger one needs you now."

"That would be most kind," said the lady, who looked as tired as I felt myself to be, "for little Mary here must sleep herself, mustn't you, dear." She smiled at the little girl, who gave her the bigger baby and I took the smaller.

"Are you bound for London as I am?" said I.

"Yeth," said the little girl, answering for her mother, "we are going to thee Papa. He hath a houthe for us there and I am to have thugar candy every day."

Her mother and I laughed together. I felt my milk come in just to hold the small baby, whose own cries had begun to strengthen. The mother had already undone her shift to nurse the older babe, who was eyeing the smaller one at the noise it was making. "Oh," said the mother, "look how he looks at his little sister. He's a selfish one, this one is, and resents to share me. But you must, you know, Samuel," she said, talking to the baby at her breast, who looked up at her into her eyes as he suckled away, "because your sister needs me too."

"Ma'am," said I, trying not to sound as desperate as I felt, "I can help you and you can help me." She looked alarmed, so I hurried up a bit. "I have a baby not six weeks old, only as you see, he is not with me now. But I am full to the brim and would ask you please if I might feed this little one here." She opened her eyes a bit wide.

"Do not fear," said I. "I am quite clean and healthy and indeed, wet nursing is my trade. But as you would be doing me a favor, a big favor, I would not think to charge you. That is not why I ask. I ask only because I fear that I will dry up before I get to my baby again, and then I will have nothing for him. That is all." I thought I must tell her the whole story quick, before she wondered what sort of witchcraft I was up to.

"Well," she said, considering, and at that moment the little girl squalled as if I'd stuck a pin in her which Lord knows I did not. Her cry woke the parson, who sat up and looked at the babies with pursed lips.

"Harrumph," the man said loudly, "should you not be in your own homes, women, with these babies? What does it mean that you cart them about? It cannot be good for them, surely." He thrust his head back as he looked at the both of us, down his nose, and didn't it make me angry. Men believe that it is they who are the passionate, they who are above the beasts and above women too, but I have never yet seen a man who could both juggle a baby and get on with whatever needs doing. My father certainly could not. The few times my mother asked him to pick up a baby and jiggle it a bit to keep it happy, he could neither walk nor speak nor even find the door; holding the mite took all he had. And I believe all men are such. The minute I find a man who can at once hold a baby and hand round the bread and cheese, that's the man I'll fall in love with.

"No, sir," said I before I thought what I was doing, "babies are much happier cooped up in coaches, did you not know it? We had the choice, sir, of staying home with our own kith and kin or sitting in this little shaking box with its smell like old men and their farts, but reason with her as I might, my sister here would not agree. She would drag the babies onto the coach and no two ways about it!"

Well, of course he glared at me and I glared right back, and at that moment, the little lad laid a giant shite into his nappie and then grinned as wide as a cheese. Twas really funny and between us women laughing at that, and the old man huffing, and the small baby squalling, the mother looked at me and nodded that I should nurse and so I did. Aah, the relief of it was tremendous, and I nursed that baby til she was drunk with it all. I nursed her three times more before our ride was over and I swear if it didn't save me my milk.

MRS. CANTY'S REASON

I have practiced medicine since 1821 and I may say that my record
of cure is as good as any surgeon's in Aubrey. Indeed, my knowledge of my trade came from my apprenticeship to Mr. Callum in
Durham, who, as you may know, has a most sterling reputation and
who did not scrimp in the knowledge that he passed along to me.
It has been a satisfactory living for me and my family and I have
been mostly kept interested. Had I more elegant custom, I am sure
that my house would be larger and my carriage better, but I believe
that I would have soon tired of treating the gout and dyspepsia that
seemed to afflict the better classes. My wife understood me well and
has been my constant friend and advisor during my years as a medi-
cal man.

Indeed, it is due to that good lady, my wife, Mrs. Drake, that the
tale I wish to relate here reached a happy conclusion.

Twas the middle of the night (as it is so often) when I was shaken
awake by Mrs. Drake to attend to a pounding on our door. I opened
it to find a small boy shivering on the doorstep. He told me that his
mother was suffering much in the childbed and that the midwife
could do no more for her. He begged that I come immediately. I am
used to such midnight calls and quickly donned the breeches that
Mrs. Drake had for me. I noticed that she had dressed herself and
when I wondered at it, she said, "Mr. Drake, I will attend you this
night for I believe I know of the woman you will treat."

As I whipped up the horses, she told me that she knew Mrs.
Canty as a seamstress who had six children already who could ill

afford to lose their mother. "I know of no child who can, my dear," said I and she agreed.

The night was a long one. Mrs. Canty suffered as much as any woman I had seen who yet lived. I feared for the worst. Her labor had lasted more than a day already and the midwife, a crone with hands not altogether clean, had done her best. Twas a breech, just as I feared. The midwife had been able to turn the baby, but this had exhausted Mrs. Canty beyond what was necessary for the work yet to be done. That lady lay in a pale faint and could do little more than groan at each contraction.

My wife surveyed the situation—the poor woman on her back, the blood already spilt, the miserable husband and children huddled in the front room—and rolled up her sleeves. "Mr. Drake," she said, "I was raised on a farm and have seen many a cow and a horse give birth and have always wondered why it is that we, who are no less God's creatures than they, choose to do it on our backs. Help me lift her."

With the help of Mr. Canty and his eldest daughter and the midwife, all holding the suffering woman upright, my good wife urged that poor lady on through each pain so that finally the baby was born and Mrs. Drake catched it quick. With the baby came a copious amount of blood, so much that the daughter shrieked and must be hurried out of the room.

I did not think the woman would live for loss of blood. Indeed, she did not rise from her faint for four days altogether after the birth, but instead lay in fever and delirium due, no doubt, to some infection. I urged Mr. Canty to quickly take the baby, who was quite healthy, to Mrs. Rose, a wet nurse in Leighton, lest he have two deaths to deal with instead of just his wife's one. She was reliable, I told Mr. Canty, and would do the job. He charged his daughter with bringing the baby there so that he could stay with his wife, which was as it should have been.

Indeed, Mrs. Canty recovered. I believe—and Mrs. Drake concurs—that her good health may well have been one of my deepest victories, for she was in dire straits indeed when she was at her lowest. A combination of physic and bleeding and rest was the tonic the lady needed, though she must stay in bed for some six weeks before I would approve her rising from it. She was lucky, I think, in her daughter who was able to care for the children in her place. I heard that the little baby grew up simple, but I am not surprised. Such a terribly hard birth must have some effect in the end.

Ten

London was right astonishing. Twas so noisome and it stank so! The people rushed hither and yon with no thought to whether they had stept on your shoe or poked you with their elbow. I helped Jeannie down from the coach with the babies and stood by for her reunion with her husband, who was a broad man with a mustache. He seemed very glad to see her and gave her and little Mary a kiss and then he looked at me in a kind way so that I was not afraid to say my name to him and how I had met his wife on the coach.

"And oh, Michael, Susan helped me ever so much with the babies on our journey," said Jeannie.

"How de do," said he and tipped his hat very friendly, but did he make to take the sleeping baby from me? No, he did not. Jeannie gave him a nudge with her shoulder, but he did not see what she was about until she told him to take his son. Then he understood and made a big show of accepting the child from my arms, while Jeannie and I made faces and rolled our eyes to each other where he could not see it.

ERICA EISDORFER

"Will you have a bite of dinner with us then, Susan Rose?" said Jeannie, but I said that I would not, for I had no time to lose and must get me to where my son was being kept. We hugged each other, and she wrote her address in a quaint little notebook that she had and tore out the slip and handed it to me. I put it in my parcel for safekeeping. I did not tell her that I did not have my letters; instead I said that I had no home, so far, but when I did I would be sure to write to her. It sent a chill up my spine to think that for the first time I had no firm roof over my head, but I could not tarry to think on it and instead, I bid her and her family Godspeed.

I had in my mind but three words: Norval and Hampstead and then Street. Those three words I had recited over and over to myself for the whole of my journey. They had been the words that the wheels of the cart beat out whilst I sat with the nice old carter who drove so slow; they was the words I heard in the soft sobs of the poor girl in the carriage to Mansfield; they was the words I chanted in my head as Jim banged away at me on our way to Longbourne Village; those was the words I felt all through me as Jeannie's babies suckled through the night. Norval and Hampstead and Street. And so I made to find them as quick as I could.

Twas not difficult, not compared to the journey I had been on. There was a stand of cabs waiting for fares right there where the coach left off, and I spied them out to see which of the cabbies had just put his horse's bag on its nose and that's the one I chose to talk to for that's the one as had a minute. He told me what I wanted to hear the most, that Hampstead was but a short walk up the hill and he pointed east. I had to ask only twice more before I found the very street I wanted, and then I walked along and waited for a servant to come out with a shopping basket, which did occur very soon as I knew it would, for it was still morning. Of her I asked in my politest way if she might know which home was Mrs. Norval's, and though the snit sniffed at me through her nose, she pointed to the house and there I was.

But where was I, to be sure? I did not know what to do next. All that time in the coaches, I had imagined that the moment I stood before the house where my baby was being kept, I would know just what to do to get him back. Now I saw how it was not true, and I felt a flame of fear and my heart burned me where it was under my breast. I knew that I could not simply stand in front of the house, for it would look very odd and someone would spy me who should not. I must act with stealth and with patience. But oh, it was very hard to do! I walked up the street in front of the house and then back down again, but I saw no movement behind the curtains. My own sense told me not to knock at the back door.

I loathed to spend a farthing, but I thought to myself that I must have a place to stay the night. It came to me to walk back down to where the coach had left off and there to find a cheap room in a cheap inn, just for to have a place to land my bundle and also, if truth be told, to have a place to piss. So I took one more turn up the street and then back down, and just as I was passing the front stoop, look if the front door to the house did not open and a lady did not come out! She was very slender, like bones only, and she had the arm of a gentleman with a top hat. He looked down upon her head like she would break, but not quite as if it would pain him if she did. As the door was closing behind them, the lady quick turned and leaving off her grip on her companion's arm, she pushed it back open a bit.

"I hear it, James," I heard her say, "it will never be quiet, you know. I think it must drive me mad."

"And that is why we walk, Jane," said the gentleman as if he was trying for patience but would rather have acted like my old dad and blacked the lady's eye for her. Indeed, she shrank back from his tone and let the door close behind her. I did not wonder what they spoke of for I thought to myself that I knew quite well: twas but Davey's crying for his mother. I felt again as if I might scream if I did not work fast, but patience was ever my tool and I must use it well.

The couple turned toward me as I stood there watching them. I stepped back several steps and made as if to retie my bonnet and move my bundle-basket, as if I had just paused on the street. I knew that if they spied me with any interest, it would be hard to place me: I had the look of a servant but not the uniform, and thus made a strange piece to the puzzle. But I was relieved; they walked right past me with nary a look which shows that if you're servant enough, you can shrink into the shadows, even in the bright morning sun and even if you're large enough to often block it.

I followed them, natural enough. I wondered who the gentleman might be, for I knew the lady's husband stayed in India and that there had not been enough time passed for him to have come to her, if what Cousin Anne at the Great House had told me was the truth. I followed them into a park where they walked. They did not speak much. Sometimes the gentleman would bend to address her a word; she answered him but little. I could not hear what it was they said to each other, but I saw how it was between them. His jaw was set; she did not look much at him. Twas a lovely mid-morning, before luncheon and thus there was quite a throng in the park, for which I thanked God. I hoped to seem like a servant on her half-day, taking the air.

Soon enough the lady seemed to tire and the gentleman led her to a bench. Another bench stood next to theirs, but it was occupied by two nursemaids, each minding a pram, so I could not sit near enough to hear the lady and her companion speak. I found a seat across from them, and though it was too far for me to hear any words they might speak to each other, I could see them well enough. The gentleman spoke to the lady, but again she did not answer overmuch and at length he drew out from his pocket a newspaper, which he opened and began to read. I thought to myself that it was rude of him to do so but I saw how often he would read to her from the print so as to make it seem less of an affront.

She did not listen to him read though, for I could see that she was overmuch interested in the prams next to her. But, Reader, she did not look into the prams to see the little faces and to smile at them. Instead, she looked as if there was some insect in the carriages, something that gave her fright and repelled her. Twas unnatural! I could hear nothing for the crowd around me, but one of the babes must have begun to wail, for I saw the nurse bend down over her little charge and talk to him or jiggle him or try one of those tricks that we know to try. And as she did, the lady's hand went to her throat, her chest in its tight bodice rose and fell faster than a bird's breast, which I could see even from where I sat across the walkway.

It seemed that the nurse could not quiet the baby by sitting, as is often the case, is it not, so she stood up from the bench and her friend did as well and off they strolled. Quick, but not too quick, I crossed the walk and took their seat. I put my back to the lady and looked through my basket as if for a purse or paper, for I did not want her eyes on mine. When I felt that her interest had shifted, I turned slow around so that I was sitting on the bench, very quiet, not like you'd even know I was there at all.

"My goodness, Jane, hear this if you will," I heard the gentleman say to her, "it's quite horrible!" He read, "'Elias Lucas and Mary Reader, who were indicted for the willful murder of Susan Lucas'—that was his wife, I suppose—'were hanged, just yesterday in front of the County Gaol at Cambridge for murder by arsenic poisoning.' Why, we have seen that very place a dozen times! Recall if you will—it is just across from the eating house where we supped with Gerald when we saw him but a month ago, do you remember it?"

"Oh, James," said the lady, "how horrible."

"Yes," said he, "I shall read more . . ."

"Brother, no," said she, "do not, as I hate to hear such things."

He read on as if she had said nothing. "They write of the trial here," and he read, "'It will scarcely be believed that hardened man, as he saw his innocent and unsuspecting victim eating the deadly poison, and expressing a disgust at the taste, the food being thoroughly seasoned with arsenic, brutally exclaimed to her complaint, "O dall it, mistress, I'll eat mine if it kills me."'" Here, the lady's brother gave a great loud laugh which made her blush and shush him.

"My God, what a rake," said James. "He certainly deserved a hanging. Oh, and listen. Mr. Martin, the surgeon of Haverhill, made a statement which they have here: 'I went up to the body and it was warm,'" read James, disregarding his sister's discomfort. "'I observed that she died in a state of collapse and that her fingers were clenched as if,' oh, do listen, Jane, this is awful, 'as if in a bird's claw.' Can you not see it? What a terrible death!"

At this he put down his paper to look at his sister. Despite his ill manners toward her, I do not think he meant to distress her quite as much as he did, for he seemed to feel some shame when he saw her face.

"Oh, Jane, you are so pale! I did not mean to upset you so! Come, cheer up now! Why, I recall as youngsters that your stomach was iron. Look how dainty you've become. Let me help you home. I do apologize," and with that, brother helped sister up off the bench and they made their way back, I suppose, to Hampstead Street.

I did not rise. I was thinking very hard and desired to continue. I was thinking of a plan.

❧

After a little while, I felt hungry. I had long finished the loaf that I had bought when the coachman took a stop to water the horses. I recalled a pub just by the big square where we'd all left the coach and where I'd said my good-byes to Jeannie, and because I knew the way—indeed that was the only bit of London that I did know—I headed toward it.

I ate a pasty at the pub and then inquired about a room to stay in for the night. The hussy behind the bar asked if I wanted to share or not, and I said I didn't mind, for I had little money and needed yet to spend a bit that very day. She showed me to a room up two flights, and I paid her my farthing and asked for a pitcher of water. She said I might have it if I pumped it myself, which I was glad to do as it gave me a chance to rinse the pitcher, which was none too clean. I went up to the room and closed the door and emptied my dugs into the chamber pot, for there was nothing else and I had to drain. I wept as I milked to think of little Davey in that house which was yet one half hour from where I there stood wasting his own milk into that wretched pot. When I finished, I bathed my bosoms with the water from the pitcher til they was as clean as I could make them. I had no bit of soap to help, which I wish I had done.

Back in the pub, I asked the girl for directions and then I asked her if, by chance, she knew where the foundling hospital was. I thought that if it passed that I could not get to Davey quick, then I would need some employment and the hospital was most likely to give it to me. She looked at me odd and at my stomach, but I shook my head and said that no, I was a nurse bound there for work. I did not care to tell her more than she needed to know. She admitted then that she did not know its whereabouts and that she "'oped Oi neever nade it," is how it sounded to me, but I knew well enough what she meant.

My first errand took me several blocks toward the town where the barristers had their chambers, which I knew from a man in the pub who said he'd been one once, before the drink got him. I did not need a lawyer, more my luck, for I had not nearly enough money for one. What I was after was a scribe and there I found one, right on a street corner, as I knew I should. Where there's lawyers, there's papers with writing.

I asked how much and was told, and I asked about the stamp and the mailing and was told. The scribe was an old man, which I chose though there were many younger, both men and some women too. I chose the old one for I thought in his long life, he'd have heard much and be surprised by little. Here is the letter—I have memorized it.

> *Dear Madam,*
>
> *Please forgive my intrusion but it is my Christian duty to warn you of a worm lurking in your very household. I do so hope that you will see me later this very afternoon so that I may explain—before it is too late.*
>
> *I remain very sincerely yours,*
>
> *Anna Caraway*

I will tell you, Reader, where I got the name Anna Caraway: from off a gravestone in a small churchyard in a little village on the way to London. When the coach stopped—I cannot even tell you the name of the town for it was in the dark of the night and I never heard it—I found I had to piss so, that I could not wait for the outhouse, for there was a line what with Jeannie and the coachmen and others needing it too. I stepped over to the churchyard and knelt right there, for the dead do not know what we do here on earth, even right above their heads.

I was a little frightened, but not too much for I was much relieved with my pissing, but as my eyes could see better in the dark, I saw that I was making my water very nearly on top of a brand-new grave, so new twas not yet sunk. There was a gravestone but I could not read it. Back at the inn, I asked the stable boy who it was that was buried there in that new grave and he told me her name which was Anna Caraway. He said she had died in the birthbed just a fortnight past, but when I asked him if the child had lived or died he could not tell me.

Once my letter had been posted, I asked the scribe for a used-clothes seller and he pointed me the way. I recalled to myself the Hebrew section of Aubrey, where I had got my sprigged that I was wearing even now, and I thought upon Harry Abrams and what he might be about. London was so vast that there was no telling where Hebrews lived there, not that I had the need to know; I needed only a used-clothes seller and they come in many faiths. I found the stalls soon enough and saw right away what I needed. I bought a black veil, and though it cost me dear and I did not want to spend the money, I bought a black bonnet to go with it. My purse was shrinking, which gave me a chill.

Back in my room, I lay on the bed and slept for a time, for I was much exhausted from the journey as well as the thinking and walking. I kept my bundle under my head as a pillow, for I did not know who shared this room with me. That I did not see any item of theirs I took as a cue for myself to leave none of my own. It was but a room with a bed and a basin, and that was all.

When I woke, I found that I had cried in my sleep, for my cheeks were wet. In my dream, I had seen the face of a girl I remembered, no more than thirteen she was, and she'd brought us a baby, for her mother had been took too ill with childbed fever to nurse it herself. The girl's face had stayed in my memory, though I was but eight or nine when she left off her charge. She was pale with worry, she was, and not able to take the porridge my mother pressed on her. She said her stomach felt too knotted up to eat it. She had not tarried, but had left the babe and gone back to her mother.

It did not surprise me that my own dream was an unhappy one. I felt despair, Reader, and there's no other way to put it. Though it seems to me now there's two kinds of it: the sort that causes a person to surrender and then the sort I had which made me take risks and make plans. Considering it all, I was glad to have the second sort for I do believe it kept me alive through those horrid days.

I fell to my preparations. First, I went down to the pub, where I bought a meal of bread and cheese and oatmeal with a glass of beer. Then I fetched a pitcher of water full to the brim. Back in my room, I again milked myself like a cow, though this time I did not cry, for my mind was too full. Then I took a rag and washed my body: my face and my breasts very well and my armpits and then my crotch. I had a comb and I combed my hair as best I could and arranged it in a way that I did not like and that did not favor me at all: pulled back very tight. From my bundle I took my weeds that I had not worn in so long and put them on. The dress was tight but not so much that I could not do it up. At last I donned the ugly black bonnet and veil. There was no looking glass in my room.

I crept down the stairs to the pub and waited til I saw the girl who tended the bar go into the back room, and then I walked quickly out of the door onto the street. After a minute, I walked back into the pub. She looked up at me and nodded, quite polite.

"May I get you anything, then?" she asked me, and I could see by her face that she did not recognize me. That had been my aim, so I asked her some slight question about the coach which she answered easily, and then I thanked her and went out. I did not even change my voice much when I spoke to her, but as she did not know me at all, I knew that my disguise had done its duty.

Twas mid-afternoon which, as I knew from my work in Aubrey, is the time that gentlemen and ladies go a'visiting each other. I knew that I did not resemble a lady, but I thought that my letter along with my weeds might gain me entrance into that house. I did not worry that the lady's brother James would be at the house any longer, for I had heard him tell her that he would visit her again the following week as they rose from their bench in the park. I felt that I could make myself understood to Mrs. Norval for I had learned to mimic a higher kind of accent when I lived with the Chandlers; indeed, I used to make the maids laugh with imitating Mrs. C. asking for this or that. I thought of the lady who let me go from nursing for not being able to understand me and shrugged; if I'd thought to learn her accent then, I could've kept my place and only God above knew how different my life would be. For my present chore here I did not need high speaking, just high enough to make myself clear.

I walked up to the front door of the house on Hampstead Street. I had never knocked at a front door of a fine house before. Even with my fist ready, I remembered in time that a bell would ring if you pulled the rope outside, so I did that instead of knock. The blood drummed in my ears. The door opened. The maid, I could see, did not know exactly what I was. So I quickly asked to see Mrs. Norval.

"She may be expecting me," said I quite calmly. "My name is Mrs. Caraway." The maid went off. I stood very still and waited for her. My baby was in that house! He was in that very house, my own baby, who I carried in my belly and who I birthed and who I nursed and who I loved. He was just up the stairs, perhaps, with some woman who did not love him like I loved him, be she as mild as she may. I wished again to cry and to shriek, but I counseled myself thus: Remember yourself, Susan, remember how it is when you're a'nursing and you must be patient til the babe had drunk its full. Remember that and act with that patience now and you will get your Davey back. And so I took my deepest breath and I waited for the maid to return.

"Please come this way," she said when she came back to get me, when she could have left off the "please" or she could have just said, "Follow me." It seemed that the maid did not know what to make of me and thought to play it safe with manners. This was just as I wished. I began to understand that if I was to make myself believed, I had to half believe my own story, or act like I did. I tried to imagine as if there was an actress on a stage with my face and I myself was sitting on the benches looking up at her doing her playing. It somehow made me calmer and better able to tell my fibs to think on it this way.

The maid took me into the drawing room and there was Mrs. Norval sitting on a settee. She had my letter in her hand. I bobbed a curtsy to her, for I had seen plain country people bob to higher folks and thought that it would make me seem real.

"You are Mrs. Caraway, I think?" said Mrs. Norval in a tight voice.

"Yes, if you please, ma'am, I am," said I.

"Will you sit?"

I sat.

"You see I have had your letter this afternoon," said Mrs. Norval. She was quite pale and so thin that her arms seemed scarcely able to hold her hands, they were that much like sticks. Could she not eat? I wondered. Did she never feel hungry?

"Perhaps, Mrs. Caraway," she said, "you will illuminate me as to the meaning of this letter."

"I beg your pardon, ma'am?" said I though I thought I knew what she was about.

She sighed and fretted. "Do tell me the meaning behind your letter, won't you?" said Mrs. Norval. "It has worried me very much."

"As well it should," said I, confidential-like, "but I shall be as plain with you as I know how. But first I must ask you one question, if you will allow it."

She nodded and fixed her eyes on me to listen.

"I know that you have recently brought a baby into your household?" Again she nodded. "My question is this," said I. "Will you please tell me the name of the baby's nurse?" I whispered this last part as if to draw a curtain over the very name I was to learn myself.

"Why, it is Sara, Sara Moore," said Mrs. Norval. "Why?"

"Does the poor little mite cry very often?" said I, "or is Sara Moore able to quiet him readily?"

"Oh," said the lady very fast, "he does cry ever so much! It does indeed make my head throb to hear him. But what of it? What do you know, Mrs. Caraway?"

I sighed, though I wished I could kill her for having him when he was mine. "Surely you have heard, Mrs. Norval, that a nurse's milk may turn if her actions are evil, if her heart is impure? It will turn, Mrs. Norval, if she is not the Christian she ought to be, and can you imagine that milk in an innocent baby's tiny stomach? How it must burn him!"

Mrs. Norval sat on the couch as if in horror, her eyes wide and her hand to her mouth. "But what makes you think it, Mrs. Caraway? What is it that makes you think that Sara's milk is impure? What is it of which you accuse her?"

"I will tell you," said I. I drew a breath. "Sara Moore and I are from the same part of the country, indeed, we are cousins far removed. She was not a good girl, Mrs. Norval, though I am sad to say it. I am sure that she told you that she was married?"

Mrs. Norval nodded. "Yes. She is recently widowed, I believe."

"That is true enough. She was married to John Moore, and a more decent man you could not hope to find. But while he loved her, she did not love him no more than a stone loves the wind."

As I told my story, I made my voice low. When I had told stories of goblins and witches to my brothers and sisters, I had done the same, and the hush around us would scare them so that they could not sleep for it. I saw the same thing in Mrs. Norval now, which was just as I'd wished it when I had earlier thought of how I would say what I knew I would say.

"The worst of the story is this," said I to her, our eyes locked together. "She would have his brother! And it was not for true love, no, it was for matters of the flesh that they were drawn together. Twas like a devil was in them. Twas the talk of the town. Indeed, the brother lived in their very house with them and so they were thrown together, overmuch, and the consequence was as wicked as it could be."

Mrs. Norval's knuckles were white where her one hand clutched the other and her brow drawn up.

"Go on," said she.

"One morning, John Moore was found dead in his kitchen. Sara had found him, she said, and had run for the doctor, but the talk was that she had not run, not run at all, no indeed. Rather, it was said that she and the brother, whose name was Tom, sat down to their breakfast as the poor man lay dying on the floor from poison!"

"Aah," Mrs. Norval gave a gasp, "but this is so like the story in the paper just recently, from out Cambridge way. Did you happen to hear of it? The man and his wife's sister murdered her with arsenic!"

"What?" said I, stunned-like, "but that is exactly what they thought John Moore to have died of! Only they could never find the poison itself! They searched the house, but not a trace did they see."

"And was there a trial?"

"No," I shook my head, "no trial for lack of evidence."

We were quiet for a moment.

"You know," I said as if I were thinking deep and not really conversing no more, "you know, they said poor John Moore ate the poison in a mess of bread and water that she gave him . . ." I shot Mrs. Norval a horrified look and met her own. "Oh, ma'am," said I, pretending my best, "you have never seen Sara eat a mess of bread and water, have you, ma'am?"

"Dear God," said the lady, shaking, "I believe I have seen it. With my own eyes. Oh, Mrs. Caraway!"

I wondered if I had not perhaps gone too far. Mrs Norval trembled and gasped, and looked so pale that I thought she might faint.

"Ma'am," said I, moving next to her on the couch, "are you well? I am sorry to bear these tidings. I am indeed. I thought it was best you should hear them."

Suddenly, she quit her shaking and sat up straight and gave me a look I had not seen from her yet but had thought that I might. "May I ask," she said very stiff and stern, "may I ask what business this is of yours, after all? Why do you travel here to tell me such things? What have you to gain from it?"

I had indeed wondered if she would think to ask that question. It had given me pause to wonder what I would answer if she did, for what could I say that would make her trust me, as I needed her to do? I had not solved the matter before I'd gone into her house; I had simply hoped that she would not ask me what I was about, for I had not thought out an answer that seemed as if it would satisfy. Whatever would, after all, make a woman journey to tell such an awful tale as I had told? I looked at my hands where they were folded in my lap and I prayed to the good Lord to help me.

And then, Reader, He did. Through the open door of the parlor, from away up the stairs of that fine house, I heard my own baby cry. I recognized him just as if his little face was right in front of me, just as if I held him in my own arms. He was so close to me, his little body, his little mouth needing my breast, his sweet dark hair, his eyes, his little hands. Oh, I was overcome. As if I lay in my own coffin and the dirt had been shoveled over my grave, I was that covered up with misery, and I fell to weeping.

"Why, Mrs. Caraway," said Mrs. Norval, surprised-like, "whatever can it be? What has occurred to cause you to weep so?"

"Oh my, oh my," said I, choking out the words, "it is my brother, you see. My poor brother. Oh, I am forlorn without him."

"I am sorry," said Mrs. Norval, "but why do you think of him now?"

"It's just that I heard the babe," said I, weeping afresh, "and I thought to myself how happy his own little baby would have made him if ever he had been able to see it. But he was not. He was a soldier, you see, and was far away from his wife when she gave birth. He had only just had word of his fine little son when the fever took him. They have such fevers out there, you know. Such terrible fevers as we have not here. Tis for him that I wear these weeds."

"And where was he, your brother, when he died?" she said, very quiet.

"India. He was stationed in India and a more dangerous and horrible land there is not on this earth, what with the snakes and heathens and terrible fevers that make good decent Englishmen sweat blood. Oh, I am sorry, ma'am. I do just hate the place, with a passion."

She did not answer. I turned toward her, slowly, as slowly as I could, and saw her, drawn back on the back of the couch, with her hand on her heart.

"But my husband," said she, so calm it seemed strange, "that is where my husband is even now. He is there even as we speak and I have not heard from him in a very long time."

I said nothing and just looked at her, my eyes still full. I could feel the tears running trails down my cheeks but I did not sob; it was as if the sobs had worn themselves out.

"Tis a terrible thing to have in common," said I after a moment. "I am sorry for you, ma'am." And then, praying that my game would work, I made myself say, "Well, I have told you what I know and now it is time for me to leave you with it. I am sorry to have brought you this news but I thought it best." I reached up to arrange my veil and then I rose.

For a moment, two moments, I thought I might die but then she said, "Do stop a moment, Mrs. Caraway," and I felt a wash of warmth flood through me like as if I had drunk a glass of rum.

I sat again. "Yes, of course," said I, all concern. "What may I do for you?"

"It is clear," said Mrs. Norval stiffly, "that I must get rid of Sara Moore immediately. Only," and here her voice grew small, "how shall I find a nurse for the babe so soon? I do not know if it can be done, yet I cannot bear to have that woman under my roof."

"Yes," I said, my heart beating so hard I thought she'd see it thumping under my dress, "that is a fix." I pretended to think. "But wait," said I, "I think I may have it! I have a friend who lives just outside London. The poor thing lost her baby not a week ago. I just came from her house where I stayed over on my way here to see you. She will help you, I think. She is a fine girl and you will like her. I am sure she can be here by tomorrow afternoon, and the baby can be hand-fed til then, can he not?"

"Oh, Mrs. Caraway, that is excellent. Even if this girl . . . what is her name?"

"Her name is Susan Rose."

"Even if Susan Rose cannot stay, she will at least do for a temporary nurse, I believe. And she may care to stay. You may tell her that I will pay her a pound a month, if you like. Can you go to her now?"

"Yes, miss," said I, "only . . ."

"Only what?"

"Well," said I, "perhaps you should wait til morning to tell Sara Moore that you no longer need her. It might not do to have her angry with you in the night." I had thought, just in time, of Davey and how he would suffer, the poor baby, without a nurse. If Sara Moore were to lose her position after all, she might as well give my baby suck one night more.

"Oh, yes. To be sure!" said Mrs. Norval, her eyes wide. "I shall not sleep a wink tonight. Do hurry and send your friend."

"Yes, ma'am," said I. "She shall come by public coach for the thrift of it, but she shall come."

"Oh no, the coach will take very much too long," said Mrs. Norval, going to a dainty desk and removing a small purse from a drawer. "Please give her this. And tell her to take the train."

And that is how I came to be employed as a wet nurse for my own child. I did not feel happy about poor bewildered Sara Moore's plight, but I could not think on it overmuch as my own need loomed so large. That night, I went to the old-clothes seller and sold the bonnet and the veil, and I took a part of that money and bought myself a good hearty supper and two glasses of ale. I had all the cause in the world to celebrate. I was to be like Moses' mother, a new Jochebed, gone to hire to nurse my own little son.

MRS. SMITH'S REASON

I am called Bess Smith as was Bess Taylor. I married my Bob in the springtime. In truth I will admit that at the time of our marriage I was already somewhat gone with child. Twas nothing so terrible, for we had meant to wed for some time. When I knew of the state that I was in, I cried to Bob and he told me to post the banns right away which I did, so no one was the wiser. Only my gramma shook her finger at me and told me that I had been up to no good. She is old, though, and not much listened to.

Indeed the baby was born not eight months after the wedding, very healthy. Indeed, I could have wished that she had not been quite so hearty, but when I told that to Bob he shushed me and told me to bite my very tongue. He does dote on Maggie.

The baby nursed very nice for the first two months of her life, but then she began to fret at the breast and I did not know why. She would suck away with all her might but she could not be satisfied. When I would try to draw the milk forth myself, with my own hands, I did notice that there was less than there had been and I did wonder at it. At this same time, I began again to feel my breakfast tumble in my gut, just as it had when I carried Maggie. And then I understood why Maggie fretted so. It is a well-known fact that a woman's milk will dry up when she is pregnant. And so it was with me. It is no wonder really, for Bob is like a billy goat himself, as I joke with him, and will have me every night if he can. It was a hardship to him to leave off for a fortnight after Maggie was born, but as he loves me, he let me be for that little while.

I did try to feed Maggie by hand, of goat's milk, both with a rag dipped in the stuff and a spoon. But being so very small, she could not drink it well and it did drain from the side of her mouth. Bob worried very much that the baby would take sick from hunger as well as from the weather—twas the coldest winter I can ever remember.

Bob recalled that he had an auntie, who was wife to his mother's brother—a Mrs. Rose—that wet nursed and that he would ask her if she could take Maggie for less than her usual fee, seeing as we was family. She agreed to do it if we might give her a goat if we had one born. We expected several kids in the spring and told her that we would save her one and thus our deal was struck.

Eleven

The next morning I dressed and broke my fast and did my hair in my old way and went, much earlier than I needed, to the house on Hampstead Street. I walked the street, up and down I went, for perhaps an hour til I saw a young woman leave from the servants' entrance. As she carried a bundle and her face was swelled with crying, I made up my mind as it was Mrs. Moore. I turned away from her so that our eyes would never meet. There was a word I heard Freddie say once, in connection with something naughty, but I thought it might fit here as well and that word was "avid." I thought I might have a look like that on my face and I did not want the chance that anyone might see it.

When I could be sure that she was gone on her way, I made myself go into the little park where I'd spied on Mrs. Norval and her brother. There, I sat on a bench and waited. The weather had turned chilly and I was not comfortable but I waited, nonetheless. I had a pasty in my bundle which I ate up to pass the time. I did not feel overmuch hungry for I had breakfasted well; it was the unease that made me nibble away at what I'd meant to save.

The bells chimed noon and soon I saw a shopgirl or two come hurriedly into the park, eat their cheese and apples, and then scurry off. I felt my own stomach gnaw and pinched my own fat gut which could not hold off from eating my meal too early.

At length, I decided that I had sat long enough. I wanted Mrs. Norval to be glad to see me, which is why I had made her wait for me. I wanted her to worry that perhaps Mrs. Caraway had taken her coin and lied about her friend Susan Rose. But I could no longer bear to be further from my Davey than there was need to be. Now it was time. I felt as excited as if I was to see the circus-men. We saw them once when I was little, and my father spent a penny to take us and we looked at the fire-eater and the rope-walker and the dancing bear. They even had a lion in a cage, though to be sure, the beast looked more like a rug than anything else.

Thinking of that time made me remember my father: his blue eyes, the leathern vest he wore always. I remembered his laugh which was rare but something we loved to hear, so loud it was, and deep. Perhaps it was yet fear again that made me weep just then to think how much I hated him whose own blood flowed in my very veins. If I thought I could go uncaught, I would love to stick a knife into him and twist it into his heart. Oh me, I thought to myself, am I as bad as he? Am I past redemption? It came over me as I made to leave the bench and head straight for what I'd worked so hard to get to: can it be that I am too evil to have back the innocent mite who I love so much? Had God been keeping us apart for Davey's own sake?

Ah! What was I about? Here I was, so close to what I needed and what needed me and I was stopping my own self with my weakness. What a fool I was! I shook my head, very hard, as does a horse bothered by flies or a dog who has dipped its head too far in the bucket.

Two young girls, sitting on a bench opposite, saw me and giggled but I did not care much. I stood up, straightened my back like a soldier and made for Mrs. Norval's house.

I used the servants' entrance and knocked at the door. A sassy little scullery answered, and when I told her what I was about, she allowed as how I had been expected and shewed me into the kitchen. It surprised me greatly to see what was in front of me, which was the cook and her girl sitting at the table and eating cake, along with another girl who looked like the upstairs maid. Was it tea already? I did not think that it could possibly be so late. What were they about that they were sitting so? I could not understand it.

"You're the new nurse, are you?" said the cook. "She'll be right glad to see you, I expect, then. The old one left in such a hurry. Lydia, show her up, do."

Lydia, who was the upstairs maid, brushed off her apron and shewed me the way up. I waited while she knocked very proper at the same door of the same room I'd seen Mrs. Norval at before. I could have wished it another room so as it wouldn't remind Mrs. Norval of one of my bulk and stature in that very chamber just one day earlier. But I could only hold my breath and pray as the door opened.

Mrs. Norval stood near the window looking out. She whirled when Lydia showed me in and I bobbed to her and waited.

"You are Susan Rose, are you?" was what she said, and I said that yes, I was.

"I think your friend Mrs. Caraway told you about our situation here?"

"Yes, ma'am."

"And you can nurse a child?"

"Yes, ma'am."

"Have you a reference?"

"No, ma'am. I have not done this work before." I thought best to keep my answers short. I did not want her to recognize my voice.

"No. But you lost a child, I believe?"

She did not know how true her words were. I winced to hear them and she took it as a sign of my grief, which in a way, is what it was. "Yes," I said very low, "my little Joey. I lost him not long after he was born."

"A pity," said she. She did not seem without a heart, but distracted-like, so that I did not hate her for her cold words. She turned away from me and again peered out the window. She seemed to forget that I stayed there and did not turn back around.

I did not know what she was thinking but thought I must hasten the matter at hand. I cleared my throat and she turned back.

"And so, ma'am, you need a nurse?" I said, to remind her, like.

"Yes," said she. "Very direly. The baby has no nurse at present and cries very much."

"I can nurse him," said I, for I thought that I must gently prod her. She seemed strangely quiet. My mother had an expression for it, this lost look. "Have the fairies got you, then?" she'd say when one of us was just staring and not doing. "Get to your mending, or they shall," she'd say and it would knock us out of our daydream. Mrs. Norval looked up at my words and her eyes grew sharp and she came all over brisk.

"Good. Is there any reason that you should be unable to perform your duties in this regard?"

"No, ma'am, I cannot fathom a thing," said I. "I have no one at home, as my husband and my little one both were taken from me. I have naught to keep me from what's here. I have plenty of milk for the baby and can begin as soon as ever you might need."

"And are you healthy?"

"Yes, ma'am."

She paused as if judging my possibilities, but I thought it might just be for show. Quite quick enough she told me I should do and she named my wage. I bowed my head to her and thanked her. She seemed quite relieved to have the business of it out of the way.

"I shall take you to him myself," she said.

The thought that I would see his face in a moment almost broke me down and made me wail. I could hardly bear to walk up the stairs; I would rather have been able to take them by twos or threes. I did not know what to do with myself, and yet I must remain quiet and calm. I was quite wild and could hardly attend to the words that Mrs. Norval spoke as we climbed.

"His name is David. You shall sleep in the nursery with him as there is no spare room for you in the servants' quarter. You must make him be quiet if you can. He is a good baby but I am afraid that the previous nurse's milk may have disturbed him somehow." Her voice trembled as she said this last and I thought to soothe her.

"Aah," said I very serious, "it is a well-known fact that even bad milk does not make a lasting mark on an innocent baby if it is raised in a good home."

Mrs. Norval stopped on the stair and turned around to look at me. Her eyes were wide and her mouth quite pinched. "Then he may not be permanently marked?" she gasped. "Is this truly the case?"

"Oh yes, ma'am," said I. "'Tis certain."

She brightened and smiled a bit. "Well, that's a great relief to me," said she. "Mrs. Caraway may have told you that the previous nurse was not all that she should have been. I had quite worried myself to death to think how it had affected the babe."

"I am sure," I ventured, "that with fresh milk he will take no lasting harm."

And then she opened the door and there he was, lying asleep in the cradle: an angel, a darling, my own bright little star, my own dearest love. His little mouth worked as he slept, his lashes feathered his little cheeks. A great sob welled up in me which I could not hold back, and my mouth opened like a guppy and out it came. The tears coursed down.

Mrs. Norval peered at me in surprise. I did not want her to think that her new nurse was strange so I dug my fingernails into my palm hard to calm myself. "Well," said I just to say something, "he is lovely, isn't he."

I yearned to snatch him up from his cradle and smell his hair and kiss his sweet eyes. I yearned to pet the soft little back and to rub my hand over the down on his head. I could not wait to check his little body for rash or bite, to look in his ears, to remove the lint I knew was clutched in his tight fists. I yearned to change his nappies and his binding cloth and to listen to him breathe as I held him with his head near my ear. But most of all, I craved to nurse him and to feel that pull on my poor dugs that I had battered so over the course of this week, as I kept them full for him.

He opened his eyes and my milk let down at once. He let out a wail and I made to pick him up, and then I thought I'd better ask first, to show that I did not assume higher than my place. But when I glanced at Mrs. Norval to see if she did approve, she seemed struck as if by a panic. Her eyes were wide and she had flattened her palms over her ears. "Oh," said she, "oh, do make it stop."

I quickly picked up little Davey and patted his back, and he stopped his crying just as fast as ever you could like. But still Mrs. Norval was the picture of horror, so I took one of her arms and gently drew it down so that it was next to her side and no longer near her face. She did not move the other hand the way you might have thought she would, but kept it instead where it had been, close over her ear. She seemed like a little child with the night worries. I had never seen anything like it in my days before. I wished to slap her and send her out of the room so that I could fondle my baby and kiss him and love him, but

I could tell that she was the more in need than even he and that never would I be able to attend to him as I wished til I had to her.

"Come, Mrs. Norval," said I in my gentlest voice, "come and lie down for a moment. You look pale and tired, you do."

"Yes," said she in a wandering voice, "I do not sleep well, it is true. I slept hardly at all the last night, what with that woman in the house."

I felt a pang for the lives I'd mucked about with, but shook it away.

"Do come," said I, leading her into the hall. "Now, which is your chamber? This way? Come, I shall help you."

Still holding my little son, I led her down the hall and into the room she pointed at. I was shocked, Reader, at the sight I saw there. The bedclothes had not yet been put to rights, though the day was nearly done, and the grate was filthy. The curtains were still drawn and there were underclothes on the floor. I saw more than one breakfast tray balanced upon a little table, rimes of toast still on the plates.

"Come, miss," said I, thinking that the "miss" might be comforting to her like as if she were a little lass being tended. "Shall I help you with your stays?"

"No," said she. "No thank you. They are not so very tight. I think I shall just lie down for a moment and rest my eyes. Suddenly, I am overcome."

She lay herself down and I covered her over with her bedclothes. "There now," said I when she looked more comfortable, "is this somewhat better?"

She looked up at me. "Oh," said she, "you still carry him!"

"Yes, ma'am," said I, smiling, "I can do as much with one hand, as most can with two; I am that used to holding a babe."

She nodded but then wrinkled her brow. "My impression," she said, "was that you had only the one child whom you lost. And yet you seem to know much about little babies."

"Ah," said I, "my mother, you see, was a wet nurse, and I grew up watching her."

"I see," said she. "Thank you, Susan. I shall rest now."

I left her room and closed the door quietly. And then, as quick as if I were stealing a gold piece, I ran to the nursery and closed the door behind us. There was a bed in the room and I sat on it and put Davey on my lap and gazed at him, just as much as I had craved to do since he had been taken from me. I kissed his sweet face and his mouth, just like a bud it was, and his little shoulders. His nappy was wet and when I took it off, it was as I feared: his bum was red and raw. I took a soft cloth that was hanging near his cradle and dipped it in the basin and breathed on it to warm it and dabbed him and then rubbed the lard on him to soothe the rash. I smelled his neck and nuzzled him and kissed him many times. My tears washed his little hair and ran down into the folds of his neck, and he looked up at me with his big eyes.

Finally, he whimpered and so I unbuttoned my frock and he nursed very sweet. He put his two little hands on my dug, as if helping to hold it, and he gazed at me as he drank. He looked very thoughtful as he nursed, and I imagined that he was remembering me from when I carried him in my belly and when he was born and indeed, from just four days ago—though it seemed a lifetime—when he had been taken from me. Twas a very sweet hour. Is it foolish of me to think that he knew his mother, a baby that small? And yet I believe he did.

Soon he slept, and I felt hungry and thought to go look for some dinner. I put him gently into his cradle and made sure that he was full asleep before I left the room, for I did not know the tricks of the house—whether the door would creak when I opened it, whether the window rattled in the wind. I wished for nothing to waken him. I was nervous that he might rouse Mrs. Norval if he cried and that if he did, she might dismiss me for not keeping my duties as I ought. But as all seemed well, I left him in his cradle and gently walked out of the room.

On my way to the back stairs, I passed the lady's room and listened at her door but there was only silence. I wondered about the state of the room. Would she let no servants enter? I thought perhaps that was it; I remembered that Mrs. Chandler, who was mother to the twins, acted thus for a week once. In her case, it was a pout that made her do it. I wondered if Mrs. Norval was a pouter as well.

There was no one in the kitchen when I entered, and though I was very hungry, I did not like to take without permission. I called and received no answer which I thought was quite odd, as it was time for tea. There was no kettle over the fire, nor cake to be sliced, nor bread to be toasted. Did Mrs. Norval not take a regular tea? Did she nap through teatime every day as she did today? Perhaps the servants were used to such behavior and had no thought about it.

I was not used to such. Tea is quite the best meal of the day, in my mind, and what separates us Englishmen from those heathens in Italy and suchlike. Not that I had ever had much time for more than a quick cup, but still, whenever I was needed to serve, I would like to very much, so as to see the dishes and the sandwiches and cakes. They always used the prettiest plates for tea. And if ever there was cake left over, we servants would sometimes have a treat.

At any rate, I found the larder easy enough and a loaf. And I stirred the fire so's it would heat the kettle and then must look for the tea leaves which were there in a tin, just as in other houses. As I spooned leaves into a plain teapot, I heard an odd sound coming from behind a door off the kitchen. Twas a thump, thump. I could not tell what it might be, but as my kettle began to sing, I thought no more about it for a minute until another sound gave it away, and that was a groan and then I put the thumps and the groans together, and then I knew what I was hearing.

I could not imagine what happened in this house: no tea in the afternoon but this instead? Twas utmost strange to me, but as I wanted to be with my baby more than feast my wonder, I quick made my tea and took my cup and my slices and started out of the room. And then the door opened and out came the cook herself, and a working man whom I had never seen, and we all stopped and stared at each other. They had been laughing but when they saw my face they ceased off. The man tipped his head at me and then at the cook and fairly ran out the door.

"Good afternoon," said I, making to go up the stairs, but she stopped me.

"No need to spy around," said she in a nasty way that I did not care for at all. She was a strange-looking cook, to begin with, for she was not nearly as fat as I nor was she much older. I thought there might be a story to how she came to have her position, but I thought I'd like to get it from the maid instead of the cook herself, for then I'd perhaps get the truth. I wondered if it had to do with the absent Mr. Norval and if the cook's position in the kitchen had anything to do with her positions in the bedroom.

"I was not spying," said I as mildly as I could. "I came for my tea but as there was none, I made it myself."

"Humph," said the cook. "Well, you needn't tell the missus about Teddy. What she don't know won't kill her, as they say."

"That's sure," I said, relaxing a bit, "but should I not bring the lady a cup?"

"If you must," said she. "Go ahead and make it."

She showed me Mrs. Norval's teapot and a tray and such, and I made it all up which was not at all my job, and went with it up the stairs and knocked very soft on Mrs. Norval's door. She answered it, and I went into her room and set it on the floor as I could see no room for it on the table near the bed. Quick as I could, I cleaned the table and then I poured her a cup. "Now," said I, "drink this right up and here's a nice cake for you as well." She sat in her bed like a little child and sipped at the tea. "Can I get you anything more?" said I, "before I check on the baby?"

She looked at me odd, but then she murmured, "No thank you," and so I went back to Davey with my own tea, which I had left outside her door and which was still warm.

❧

That night, I slept with him in my arms and at my breast. I wept with the joy of it and could not think of a moment when I had been as happy. A beloved baby is like an arm or a heart; the wrenching away of it is terrible. To have him back with me was as good as heaven, and when he awoke in the night, which he did right often, I soothed him and nursed him and kissed him til he slept again.

Once in the night I was awakened by the door of our chamber opening very wide. I looked to see who might want me but there was no one there. When I went to close back the door, I could see nothing at all in the hallway, but of a sudden, the gaslight glinted on a puddle on the floor just outside my room. Tea perhaps? Water? Piss? I did not know what it might be, so I closed the door and went back to my bed.

In the morning, Davey awoke very early. I cooed at him and changed him and he looked at me very serious the way a tiny baby does and waved around his fists. The soft dark hair on his head grew in a swirl like the shell on a snail and one of the tops of his little ears was still folded from his sojourn inside my belly.

I looked out the window to see the weather and knew that the day would be fine. Twas autumn and very gold. I wondered about a pram and thought that it would be lovely to take Davey for a walk in the little park around the corner. He was wide awake, and I knew that he would fuss if I left him, but as I had had no dinner and not much in the way of tea, I was half-starved and wanted my breakfast. So, I swaddled him tight and carried him down the back stairs into the kitchen.

Nothing! No one up, no one getting the fire in the stove, no maid with a blacking can, no one washing last night's dishes in the sink. Well, someone had eaten for there to be such dishes as there were, but it was not me and I did not think it was Mrs. Norval either, for the dishes were plain and very greasy with pork fat—not at all what a lady like Mrs. Norval would take in any event.

"Well, Davey," said I quite loud, "what is this house about? Who does the work of it, is what I'd like to know?"

I bustled around, with my baby on my shoulder, getting a meal together. I laid him in a basket of soiled table linens and put that with him in it on the table so I could see him and he could see me. Then I lit the fire in the stove and then took him up out of the basket again. It felt just right to hold him as I did my work and as I could, I did. I made myself some eggs and found a piece of sausage which being very rough, I knew was not for the lady, so I took it for myself.

"First as comes is first as served, right, Davey?" said I as I fried it up. I sat at the table and ate my breakfast with him watching me from the laundry basket. I drank two glasses of ale for I was exceeding dry. Davey watched me down it. "Nursing's a thirsty business," I said and then I laughed for that's what my mother would say every day when she drank her own mugful. I wondered for a minute what my father had done to her when he returned and found that I'd gone off to the Great House. Would he find out that I'd got as far as Mrs. Bonney? I did not know and neither did I care, but for her sake. I hoped again that he'd die and leave her finally in peace. When I recalled myself back to the present time, I saw that Davey was still watching me with his serious eyes and I laughed. I do not think that babies that small can see well enough to tell a pleasant thought on a face from a grim, but if they could, I would not disturb him for an instant with my own sour look.

"You are a darling, you are," I said to him and blew him a kiss. A piece of gas or a wing of a fairy—again my mother's voice in me—made his eyes open quite wide just as I tossed him off his kiss and that made me laugh all the more. I finished my meal with several slices of bread and butter, and then, for good measure and because there was no one there to stop me, I cut two more slices and buttered and sugared them and put them into my pocket. As I was cleaning up after myself, into the kitchen came the two maids I had seen yesterday, tying their aprons behind them. They started back when they saw me.

"What are you doing in here?" said the one named Lydia.

"I am the new nurse if you recall," said I, still tidying up.

"You're up early then, aren't you?" said the scullery. "We're just up ourselves."

"Is it that early?" said I, for I thought that indeed it was not. "I have no clock and must use him as my timepiece." I nodded over to the baby in the basket.

Well, didn't they coo. "Isn't he lovely this morning," said Lydia.

"You brought him to the kitchen?" said the scullery, which seemed so obvious to me that I refrained from answering.

"If we're to work together," said I, "we should have each other's names. Mine is Susan Rose." Lydia told me hers, which I knew, and then the scullery told me hers, which was Carrie.

"Short for Caroline?" said I, and when she told me yes, I allowed as how my mother, who'd been a nurse herself, had once had a fancy baby called that very name. The scullery liked to hear "fancy" and her name together, and the rest of them liked to hear that piece about my past, as I'd thought they would, for it shewed them that I was not a secret-keeper, or so they thought. We became friendly right off.

Carrie thanked me for lighting the stove and Lydia asked me if I had breakfasted, which I said I had but would not say no to another piece of toast. She cut several slices and I toasted them for all of us til Davey started to whimper. I picked him out of his basket and gave him to nurse which he did very hungrily.

"Did the other nurse never bring him downstairs then?" I asked.

"No," said Carrie, her eyes very wide. "We thought she was just shy but it turns out she was really a murderer!"

"My goodness," I said, eyeing Lydia to see what she thought, as she was the sharper of the two. "How did you come to find out?"

"Mrs. Norval found it out! Oh, twas horrible! She had poisoned . . ."

Here, Lydia interrupted. "Now, now, Carrie," she said, "no point in telling tales that might be true but mayn't be." And here she dropped her voice. "Mrs. Norval can think some strange things now and again." She did not look at me as she said it.

As Carrie began to wash the dishes, and Lydia put together Mrs. Norval's tray, the door to the cook's room opened and in she came looking very mussed indeed. When she passed me on her way to the larder, I thought she smelled of brandy, but I pretended not to notice though it seemed right early for such a thing, unless she used it to wash her face in of a morning.

"Ready then?" said the cook to Lydia.

"I'd as soon get it over with," said the maid. She looked a bit forlorn as she picked up Mrs. Norval's tray.

"Shall I do it for you, then?" I said before I thought.

Lydia and Mrs. McCullough, as was the cook's name, looked quick at each other. Mrs. McCullough quick stepped forward and took the tray from Lydia and gave it to me. Lydia thanked me very nicely and turned back to the baby.

"I'll watch him for you," she said. She picked him up and he smiled at her very broad, like indeed he did know her, so I felt that he was quite safe enough for the moment.

I wondered at Lydia and Mrs. McCullough as I climbed the stairs with Mrs. Norval's tray. The mistress must be a right monster for them to act thus, but I had not seen it myself. Twas strange. The tray I carried had almost nothing on it, I saw: just a piece of toast and a cup of tea. No jam, nor even butter. I quick took one of the buttered sugared slices I'd taken for myself and put it on the plate and knocked on her door. At her answer, I walked in.

The lady was sitting in her bed when I carried in the tray. She made no mention that I was not Lydia but neither did she greet me. I set down the tray over her lap and poured her a cup. She picked it up and held it in her hands and then looked at the sugar-bread.

"What might this be?" she asked.

"That's a treat for you," said I.

"Did Cook prepare it?"

Wait a bit, I said to myself before I answered. What if she despised it for some reason and scolded the cook for my error? That would not do, for I was hard at work that the cook might take me into the circle and make me welcome.

"Begging your pardon, ma'am," said I. "But I put it there. I thought perhaps you could do with a sweetie."

She tilted her head at me like a bird and began to eat in very small nips. I bobbed her a curtsy and made to leave the room but then I stopped.

"Shall I send Lydia to make the fire?"

"No indeed," said Mrs. Norval, glaring somewhat but still chewing, "it is far too warm a day as it is."

Twas not warm, twas chilly. I bobbed and turned to leave but stopped once again. "Miss," I said, "if you wouldn't mind . . ."

"Yes?"

"Shall I just pick up a few of these things then?"

Mrs. Norval looked around her like as if her eyes had just been put into her head and she could finally see. She seemed surprised at the mess. "Why, yes," she said, "thank you."

I quick picked up the clothes from the floor and the chairs and the table and piled them onto a bench. Then I gathered the old trays and brought them into the hall. I could not imagine how many trays the house had; it seemed to me that Cook would have run out of cups and pots before now. Last, I tied back the curtains around the bed as the laces had come undone on one side and had loosened on the other.

I left her room and piled up as many of the trays as I could to take downstairs. When I brought them into the kitchen, I saw the cook and Lydia exchange a glance.

"You're . . . all right then?" said Mrs. McCullough.

"Yes and why not?"

"She didna' bark at you then?" said Carrie from the sink. "Once, when I brought her in her tray, she reached up and scratched my cheek til it . . ."

"Shush," hissed Mrs. McCullough, "and back to your work."

I wondered at their mystery, but just then Davey awoke with a wail, his face red as an apple. "How's my little man?" said I and reached my finger down into his nappy. It was wet. The more he drinks, as my mother would say, the more he'll piddle, and that's a great thing for a little one, to make sure his innards are working proper. "Oh now," I said to him, "let's get you dry. Then we'll see about a snack and that walk we were planning." I nodded to them that was in the kitchen and took him back upstairs.

YOUNG GIRL'S REASON

Reader, I died. I was too young, and very slender, and my hips couldn't stretch enough to let the baby out. It was, I daresay, as painful a death as could be. Twas a sea of pain, which I say though I've never seen the ocean. I had a brother as went to sea, but as he couldn't write and none of us could read, we never did hear from him again. He may be dead and at the bottom resting with the fishes. I cannot say where I am, but it is pleasant enough—neither too warm, nor too cool, and I'm never hungry the way I was sometimes when I lived my days on earth. I was taken by a horrid man in a filthy alley in Leeds that smelled like piss and shit, and when I went to my mother and cried, she cried too and told me that the same had happened to her and that's how she got me.

When the baby was being born, I shrieked for three days before I died. At the end, I felt as if I floated above my own cot and I could hear the strength of my screams weaken. It made me sad to think that I'd never see my mother again. I died with the baby still alive inside me and the midwife took her knife and slit my belly and took it out. I looked down and saw the top of the baby's head: bruised almost black with the banging against those bones like they were a door fast shut and its head was knuckles.

After I died, my mother took it to the church and left it as she certainly had no love for it for having killed me. I wanted to follow her home and watch her while she wept for me, but somehow I could not leave the baby, though I cared nothing for it. I watched the reverend take it to a woman as already had a cradle in her kitchen and then I watched as that woman brought it, by public coach, to a woman she called Mrs. Rose.

The woman gave Mrs. Rose some coins, though not many, and then left the baby. Mrs. Rose seemed too old to me but as soon as the woman left, she sat in a chair and opened her shirt. I watched her suckle the babe a bit, but as it mattered little to me what happened to it, I left as soon as I was able and returned to my own mother.

Twelve

As I settled into a routine at Hampstead Street, two things became clear to me. The first was that Mrs. Norval was mad and the second was that I was trapped.

Here's the second first. I had only planned as far as getting myself back to my baby, which I had done. Indeed, it made me proud that I had been able to do it, despite my terrible journey. Having done what I set myself to do made me feel like that Judith in the old book, like I would not shrink from any horrid thing at all in my mission. But now that I had my darling, I saw that I had acted in haste and left the next steps unconsidered.

I could not simply take Davey away from the house on Hampstead Street. Where would we go? We could not go home to my father's house; no, not until I heard that my father was mouldering in his grave could we go home to Leighton. I had no friends anywhere in London to go to and not the money to set up for ourselves. I let the thought of Harry Abrams's dark face wander into my head and then I shook it away. There was no point in wishing for a thing that was impossible and so I would not wish for it.

And even if I did have a place to go, Davey was not, as far as those in that place knew, mine to take. Who would the police believe: me, a penniless country girl who had told lies to get her place, or Mrs. Norval, who, while she cut a strange figure, was a rich London lady with proper talking and money to spend? I did not think that it would help Davey much if his mother were to hang for kidnapping him.

And what's more is that I liked the money. Indeed, twas hard to forget that Mrs. Norval was paying me handsomely for nursing my own babe. Who would not want such a position as I had?

Twas dangerous though and I knew it. As the days skipped by, I remembered Mrs. Chandler, the mother of the twins, who cast me out without so much as a by-your-leave when she was ready for her babies to wean. I could hope that here I would be allowed to stay on as my son's dry nurse, but there was no guarantee. Now that I had him back, I could not entertain the idea of losing him once again. It was necessary for me to make a plan in my head but I could not fathom what it was to be.

And thus it was that I was as trapped as a pig in a pond. I could not leave; I hoped only to stay. I aimed my every thought at how I should try to make the mistress think that she could not live without her Susan Rose, as it was that she called me, like as if I had two Christian names instead of one. My task seemed simple, for Mrs. Norval seemed as lost as the little girl in the wood. But what I realized soon enough was that though it might be easy enough to make her fond of me, the greater trick was to keep her sound.

One morning when I was playing with Davey in our room—he had just learned to laugh, and it was my joy to hear his deep baby chuckle as I bounced him—I heard a shriek as if we were all a'trapped in a fire. I put him in his cradle, which I can assure you he did not like overmuch, and I ran toward the shriek which was coming from Mrs. Norval's bed-chamber. The noise came from her bath closet and when I snatched the door open, there stood the lady herself accompanied by Lily, her dull little maid. As I looked at what was before me, I heard the others come pounding up the stairs; there came Carrie and Lydia looking over my shoulders at the sight and a strange sight it was.

Lily had backed herself against the wall, and she was crying with her hand on her cheek and her hair all out of its cap, like someone had pulled it hard. And there was Mrs. Norval screeching like the monkey I once saw on a chain. She had taken off her underclothes and was shredding them like they was paper. She had her bodice on but wore nothing on her legs. We saw her hair: twas so thin I could see the slit of her privates. I saw that she had her monthly and that she was bleeding very much so that it fell to the floor in drops.

"I do detest it," she screamed over and over as she shredded, "I do detest it," as if she could end it with a tantrum. She did not seem to see us. Instead, she whirled and her view lighted on her tub all full to the brim with water. She took hold of it and began to pitch it back and forth, and I could see that she meant to spill it over. I marveled at her strength for all that she was a reedy little thing.

I felt a nudge and looked behind me to see Carrie pleading to me with her look. Twas she that would have to sop it up were it to spill out. I stepped forward.

"Why, missy," said I, "you have got yourself a little dirty, have you not?"

I had learned that the lady seemed to like it best when she was treated like as if she was small and so that is what I thought to do. Indeed she stopped her screeching for a second but then started it again.

I tried once more. "I shall help you to tidy up," said I very loudly so she could hear me over her own noise. "And then you shall have a nice cup of chocolate and some toast. Will you like that?"

She turned to look at me.

"Chocolate?" said she in a baby voice.

"Yes," I said and shot a look at Lydia, who ran to fetch it. "Carrie," I muttered, "do peep at Davey."

"What?" said Carrie, still gaping. I thought to myself that if there were ever a real panic in the house, Carrie would be like a dragging anchor and I would have to leave her to burn up in it.

"Please check on the baby," I hissed, my head turned full away from Mrs. Norval. I thought it best, in such a situation, to avoid reminding her of the baby in the house.

After I had got Mrs. Norval calmed down, she seemed to come back into herself a bit, and then she came all over with tiredness though she'd just risen from her bed not long before. She let me put the rags in her underclothes just like I'd changed Davey's nappies that very morn. She let me take her elbow and draw her to her bed and brush her hair, which she liked, and she drank the chocolate that Lydia brought to her. Lydia was smart and left it outside the bedchamber rather than entering. Twas all I could do to get dull Lily to leave the room but when she finally did, Mrs. Norval did not seem to note it at all. At last, she slept so that I could go back to Davey, who had been good for Carrie but was happy to see his own mother.

❧

When I first came to Hampstead Street, I found it very odd that the servants seemed to do little and eat much. Indeed, I thought to myself that the situation was nothing more than a weak mistress with a staff of servants who cared only to take advantage of all they could. But as my stay in Mrs. Norval's house grew longer, I began to see that this was not exactly the case.

After all, the rooms in the house other than Mrs. Norval's bedchamber were clean enough. And the servants were polite to their mistress, and did not talk about her overmuch behind her back. It is true that the schedule of the house seemed odd, but as the lady had few visitors and never any tea, the servants did what they must and the house ran as well as can be expected with a strange lady to guide it.

That Mrs. Norval had taken to me as she had, and so soon, was a blessing to me but odd. She called for me often and I helped her with little things. She began to allow only myself to bring her her breakfast tray at which I thought Lydia would take offense but that was not so.

"Oh no indeed, Susan," said Lydia to me when I told her that I meant not to take her place. I did not want to cause bad feeling with the servants; I knew that was the quickest way to get the boot from a house. "No indeed, you go take the tray, if she likes it so. She scares me, she does, for her peculiar ways and I am pleased to have someone else do it."

I was glad that Mrs. Norval liked me of course, but I wondered at it. Was it my novelty? Did she recall her own nurse to look at me? But then one day, I understood.

One morning, earlier than Mrs. Norval was awake, I was taking my breakfast in the kitchen with the other servants before our day began afull. I had learned to sleep quite late—often past seven o'clock—so as to keep the schedule of the house, and wasn't it a luxury! This morning, as I finished my bread and butter, I saw Carrie standing with the blacking bucket and Lydia with her dusting cloths and the cook with her knives and the cook's girl at the sink. And a thought came upon me.

"Why, look," said I, "I'm as different from the rest of you as if I was the short thumb with the long fingers!"

They laughed and Carrie, who was the best tempered of them, said, "Oh pshaw, Susan," but anyone with two eyes could see it was true. Mrs. McCullough had lovely yellow hair and Lydia's nose was as elegant as if she was a lady and Carrie had skin as smooth as Davey's and the cook's girl had teeth that shone very white. But what was hardest to miss was their figures. To a girl they was slim and tall with a nice high bosom.

"And I suppose you've all been with the family long?" I inquired, for I looked to prove my point to myself.

"Yes," said Lydia, hunting for more dusting cloths. "Now where's that polish gone to? Before Mr. Norval went away to India, we was all hired. Cook's been here the longest."

"Oh?" said I to Mrs. McCullough, but she was whipping some eggs and did not answer me.

"Oh, she's been here ever so long," said Carrie, giggling at the look which the cook threw her. "Mr. Norval hired her himself, same as he did me and Lydia, to save the missus the trouble."

I saw Lydia wince. The cook's girl looked around, but when she saw me looking back at her, she turned fast back to her washing up. Mrs. McCullough sighed.

"Mr. Norval likes to handle the servants himself," she said, and then she glared when Carrie burst out into laughter.

"Oh come," said Carrie to the rest of them, "he wasn't so bad, though he was handsy. And he's gone now, anyhow."

And then Davey woke up hungry and Lydia took her cloths and polish and our day began. While I nursed the little mite, I thought that I knew why Mrs. Norval liked me best. Twas my lumpy figure and my potato nose and my rough hair she liked, I think, as much as my skill as a nurse. I was nought to worry about, was I. Not like the other servants, the ones her husband had got.

So, now I knew that while the husband might have been a rascal, the servants themselves were not. On the whole, they seemed a fair bunch of girls. And so why did they avoid their work? Quite soon, I saw that it was all for keeping Mrs. Norval calm. If she could not abide one of the pretty servants in the bedroom she had shared with her husband, well, they would not go in, though the room might fall to shambles. If she preferred to nap her tea away—a time when once a comely upstairs maid might have catched her husband's eye—well then, they would let her sleep through it. After all, they were as anxious to keep their positions as I was mine. They were paid well—Mr. Norval had seen to that—and if they were to have to find another place, and without a reference from the lady of the house—it would go poorly for them. I knew that Lydia sent money home and I knew that the cook might be secretly wedded—I had seen the same man leave her bedroom two or three times now.

And thus my position seemed secure. I made up my mind that if I could fix her attachment to me very firm, without provoking the servants, that I would do just that. Thus, I cleaned her room and made her comfortable and treated her like a little lass, what with bringing her treats from my pocket. Indeed, when Lily with her open mouth did not think to do it for the lady, I suggested a bath and then soaped her back myself. Or perhaps I would show her the day and pack her off for a walk in the little park. She was like a child: she would do what I told her but if I did not tell her to do a thing, she would stand by the parlor window and look out at the street for a full hour at a stretch. If another lady came to tea, which did not much happen, Mrs. Norval could sit and listen to the lady and pour the tea and then say a pretty good-bye, but this was as much as she could do by herself.

I had my hands full, what with the baby and Mrs. Norval, especially because the lady did not like me to hold the baby while I tended to her, though I had proven that I could. And so, I had to very much be thinking of when to do a thing: would the baby sleep while Mrs. Norval watched me tidy her room as she liked to do? Would Mrs. Norval drink a cup of tea like a good girl so that I could nurse my Davey? Would Carrie have done with the silver so that she could look in at

Davey while I persuaded Mrs. Norval to answer her husband's letter, so that I could play This Is the Way the Lady Rides with my Davey? Ah—it was all as tight as a knot. Indeed, it made my guts curl to worry it so and all that helped was bread to eat, so that I did eat it very much and Carrie teased me for it.

~❧~

After I had lived in the house for a little longer than a fortnight, Mrs. Norval received a letter from her husband and whatever there had been of her right mind left her. Twas a shame. By then I had come to pity her for her strangeness which we lived with and had all got used to somewhat.

Her habits were odd, it's true, but no danger to us nor to anyone and so we did not fear them overmuch. She complained of the heat constantly, like as if she had a fever, but she did not, and her clothes stank of her sweating. It was full winter by then and we servants shivered upstairs for she would allow no fire in any hearth. Twas all the cook could do to explain to her that there'd be no cooking without a fire in the stove at least.

"Oh me," said Carrie one evening as we sat in the kitchen before bed, "I'd do any amount of blacking if only for a bit of warmth. I'd black all day."

"Yes," said Leah, the cook's girl, clutching her shawl around her, "it's as cold here as in my mam's house. They all told me it would be warmer in the city when I come up."

At night, I would take Davey in my bed with me and we were warm enough, but during the day, I kept him wrapped. Even so, he had a cold and twas hard for him to nurse with his nose that plugged, poor thing.

Another strangeness was her dress. She had begun to demand that

Lily put her good gowns on her even though it was early morning. Lily, who had felt her slap oftener than us others, was too afraid to cross her. Thus there came Mrs. Norval walking down the stairs at ten o'clock in the morning dressed in lace with a train or deep velvet with the huge crinoline just in fashion. Often, because she sweated so, Mrs. Norval would make Lily leave the buttons undone and the dresses would gape open in the back. Indeed, she was bony enough that they hung on her even when she did them up.

"She must have had more bosom at some time," said I, after seeing her in the lace one and Lydia agreed. The mirror was not big enough for the lady to see her whole form, so she would call to me or to Lydia to tell her how she looked. We always promised, of course, that she was a vision for we were servants and knew our places.

As to the baby, more and more she did not want to see him or to hear him. She never said a word about it, but only winced when she came into a room and he was in it. It did not happen often, for I kept him cloistered like a little monk so that she would not be bothered. She seemed to have forgotten about him most times, and then when she saw him it would be as it surprised her that such a thing was in her house. Once, when she came into the kitchen, she saw me nursing him and seemed ashamed, like as if she had never thought such a thing possible. For two days after, she did not ask for me once but shunned me, but then she suddenly seemed to forget that the thing had happened at all and required me to bring her a cup of clear broth which she did not drink.

One December morning, Mrs. Norval sat at her desk in her morning room when the post came as usual. Lydia said that she brought it up on the salver, as she always did, and that she believed that one of the letters was from Mr. Norval. Lydia could not read but had delivered the mail often enough that she could tell the difference by the stamps.

Twas hardly ten minutes later that Lydia came up to my room to ask me to attend Mrs. Norval and to bring the baby with me. We looked at each other in surprise.

"What does she want with him, do you imagine?" I said as I retied his little bonnet and gave him another jacket; twas an especially blustery day.

Lydia shrugged and so down I went carrying Davey, who looked like an angel: his eyes were round as nuts and he smiled as if we were on an outing.

I knocked and went in. There was Mrs. Norval in her fancy dress with the back open, a'pacing, with her arms wrapped around her bony frame like as if she was in her own embrace. The letter, clutched in her hand, was behind her, for her girth was so slight that her hands nearly met behind her back. She did not unwrap her arms but took a step toward me when Davey and I entered the room.

"Ah, Susan Rose," said she, "you have brought the little baby."

"Yes, ma'am," said I.

"And how does he do?"

"He does very well, ma'am. You may see for yourself how fat he's got."

She wrinkled her brow. "Yes," said she. "He is very fat indeed. Is that all from . . . just . . . from what you give him?"

"Why, yes," said I. "But very soon, ma'am, if you think it proper, I believe it will be time for a bit of porridge."

I could have bit my tongue to say it for what if I had put the idea of weaning into her head. But she was not thinking on that. Instead, she looked alarmed. "Porridge?" she said in a high voice. "Why do you ask me? How am I to know? How am I to guess whether he will choke on it? He must not choke, Susan Rose! Is he very healthy, do you think? Will he live without porridge? Is it too soon? How am I to know?"

Her face had paled and her lips pinched, which I knew for signs of one of her fits. I thought to distract her if I could.

"Now, miss," said I firmly, "this little man will certainly not choke. I shall watch him as if he were my own and give him the tiniest bites possible. He is as healthy as a plum. Shall you like to watch him eat? It may help you feel less afraid to see him like a bite of cereal very much. It has always made me laugh to see a baby eating porridge for the first time for they make the strangest faces you could care to see."

"Watch?" she said. "Shall I?"

So, we went down into the kitchen, and Mrs. McCullough made her to understand that the stove would need to be hot enough to heat the water, and then she watched him eat his bit of porridge which he did love very much. I wondered at the situation for it was so strange: he was my baby, I would have liked to have this time for myself, but I had invited her in for pity of her. She seemed to have few people of her own, save her brother James, who would come and visit her on a Sunday.

The letter she had received that December morning became a matter of curiosity between us servants because we could all see the difference in the lady after she'd got it. The day after she received it, she refused to get out of her bed at all. When I brought her her tray, she turned her face away. I felt her forehead and she did not seem feverish though she stank very much of sweating. She asked me about the baby and whether he was well and I told her that he was. When later in the day I suggested that we call in the surgeon, she sat up and asked for a big dinner of beef and salad, but Lily told us that she lost it in a bucket right after.

"I saw her put her fingers in her throat so she'd retch," giggled Lily, who is a twit.

"Well, is it still there?" asked Carrie.

"It's not mine to remove," said Lily, eating an apple. "Disgusting, is what it is."

"I'll get it," said I. "Just watch the baby, for he'll wake soon."

The day after, she got out of her bed and told Lily to put out her walking clothes though it was very cold—as cold as when I was a girl and John brought a rook into the house and said it had fallen, frozen, out of the sky. Then, though it was still early morning, Mrs. Norval told me to prepare Davey for a stroll.

"Oh, but, miss," said I, "it is so cold outside! And it is so early in the day. Will you perhaps prefer to wait til it clears a bit?"

"I have heard that exercise is the best thing for a baby," she said, taking up her gloves and hat. I followed her down the stairs. "He will enjoy the walk very much."

"But, miss," said I.

She would have nothing but the stroll. I took out the pram and quick got my coat and hat for she was most impatient. Then I wrapped my baby in blankets and buntings, as much as I could to keep him warm, and put him in the pram and we went out into the street, with me pushing and Mrs. Norval walking in front of us.

"We will go to the park," she said, though she had to raise her voice to be heard over the wind. We saw very few people on the street for the weather was not fit for a dog. There was a constable standing miserable on a corner and he looked at us exceeding strange.

She had her walk. We turned into the park and walked along the path, which made a loop. At first, Davey was quite warm though Mrs. Norval allowed as how she thought he'd suffocate in all the clothes I'd put on him. But as the stroll progressed and the wind howled yet more, he began to feel the cold and cry. His little cheeks was getting raw.

"Miss," said I, filled with the worrying of it, "missy, I believe the baby's cold."

"Nonsense," she said. "I have heard exercise is the best thing for a baby," she continued, just as she'd told me earlier, in the same way. It gave me a chill, how she said it, more than did the weather itself, for it was like as if a tin soldier said it or some wood figure, without no heart in it. By this time the baby was crying full out with the cold of it and my blouse was wet with the milk that I let down to hear him cry. I did not know what to do and thought that soon she would turn back, if she had any sense left at all. Indeed she did not. She walked like we was in an army, so brisk and so hard, I had almost to run to keep up with her as I pushed the pram.

As we rounded the path and came up to the Hampstead Street gate, she did not turn out of the park as I had wished she would but instead began another turn. By this time the baby's wail was so loud that I thought she'd put her hands on her ears that way I'd seen her do, but though she looked distressed at the sound, she would not stop her tread. We took another turn and then another.

I thought of a train and how it's kept to its tracks by its nature and how it cannot move from them unless it is turned over and wrecked. I thought I might have to slap her to change her mind but I did not dare to do it. I prayed to God to help me and then I thought of what to do.

"Miss," said I, running to catch up with her and talking very loud, "miss, the lady down the street who has a baby—and they all say she's such an excellent mother, that's Mrs. Stone? Do you know her?" (There was no such lady. She was a figment of my mind.) "Mrs. Stone lays much stock in walking the baby, just as you have said, missy, but only thrice around the park or else it's too much for its constitution and it will cry all the night through. Missy, you know how he keeps you up if he cries so you must let us go back to the house now."

I said it very firm and very loud and also I stood up on my tiptoes and very near her so that she would have to look up at me. This, I had noticed, served as a way to call her back to herself. It did not work so well this time as it had before—she did not drop her strange look.

"Mrs. Stone?" she said. "I do not know a Mrs. Stone."

"Yes, you do, ma'am. Do you not recall? She lives just down the street, and you have told me several times that she is a most excellent mother." (More lies, may God forgive me, but I was desperate.)

She looked confused but then nodded at me. "I shall walk."

I could no longer wait for her permission. I thought to myself that I would simply leave her there by herself and suffer what consequences I must when she returned to the house.

"Jane," called a voice.

I turned and saw Mr. Brooks, the brother of Mrs. Norval who she called by James. He came hurrying across the park to us, holding his hat on his head with one hand and his coat closed around his neck with the other.

"Look, miss, here's Mr. Brooks," I called out, but Mrs. Norval would not stop.

"Jane, I say," said Mr. Brooks, huffing as he came up. He looked at me in wonderment as we followed close after Mrs. Norval.

"Sir, I must take the baby in, he is froze."

"What has happened?" said he.

"I beg your pardon, sir, but I must take the baby in, if you please, sir."

"Yes, yes," he said and ran to catch up with the lady. Still she would not stop until he caught her by the arm. "Jane, did you not hear me? What brings you out in this weather? With the little baby? Oh, Jane!"

"I have heard that exercise is the best thing for a baby," I heard Mrs. Norval say to her brother in that same strange way she said it to me.

❧

I waited to hear no more, but ran home and snatched the baby out of the pram. His little hands was icy and his lips were blue. I tore off his clothes and ripped open my bodice and put his little body right onto my warm breast. I wrapped a blanket around the both of us and allowed my body to warm his. He was so cold, Reader, that I wept over him and feared he would not warm up, but that was just a mother's terror. At first, he was too frozen to suckle, but soon he became more lively and sucked away very fierce, as if he was quite furious with what had occurred.

When he was all warm and sleepy, I put him in his cradle and crept down the stairs to the kitchen. There I found Carrie and Mrs. McCullough and Lily. Lydia was upstairs with tea for Mrs Norval and Mr. Brooks which he had ordered when he had brought her home.

They asked me what had happened and I told them, and I admit that I burst into crying which I normally would not do. Carrie came to put her arm around my shoulder and Mrs. McCullough gave me a cup of tea while I recovered myself.

"I was afraid the baby would die, I was," I sniffled.

"Ah, but it's all right now," said Carrie, comforting me. "I wonder what it is she wants with the baby, though, so sudden-like. For ever so long, she never seemed to know he was here at all, bless him."

Lydia, who had come back into the room, said, "It's something to do with that last letter, mark my words."

"Yes," said Mrs. McCullough, "it must be. Her husband's letters affect her very strong. After the last, she took to her bed for the longest time until Mr. Brooks came to get her out of it."

"But what could this one have said?" I wondered. "I have seen it lying on her writing desk in her room but I cannot make out any words of it."

Lydia said, "Well, it may have nothing at all to do with what's in the letter. It is hard to know with her, she is so strange."

We were quiet for a moment and then Lily said, "No, it is the letter."

We all looked at her. "How do you know, girl?" said Mrs. McCullough. "Are you able to read it?"

"Yes, I can read," she said. "I read it the day she got it."

We all looked at each other. I wished to slap her very hard which I think Carrie could see. "Lily," said Carrie, "will you tell us what it said, then, for we are most curious."

"Oh," said the stupid girl, looking down her snub nose at us. I made up my mind there and then: if a girl as stupid as that could learn how to read, then I could too. "It was from her husband, you know."

"And what did it say?" repeated Carrie with more patience than I will ever have.

"Mr. Norval said that he would return in July and that he yearned to see his dear wife holding a sweet baby. He said—I remember these words because they were so pretty—he expected she was the perfect picture of motherhood. Is that not pretty?" Lily smiled at us and took a sip of her tea. I had watched her sugar it: there were four spoons of sugar in that one cup.

"Is that all?" asked Mrs. McCullough.

"The whole letter was like that," said Lily. "All about how he wished only to see Madam and the baby together and how darling he thought it would be. It was all like that."

We were all of us quiet for a minute til Mrs. McCullough's girl said, "Strange is as strange does," and then we all laughed. But I pondered on it. That's why the lady was wanting more to do with Davey. She was preparing to be her husband's mother-wife, just as dear as ever he could have wished.

❦

I had returned to Davey's room to watch him when I heard steps in the hall and then a knock at my door. "Susan," said Lydia, putting her head in the door. Her eyes were wide. "Mr. Brooks wants you. He sits in the parlor." My heart beat in my chest. Would he let me go for having taken the baby out in such weather? Would he let me explain or would he just dismiss me?

I knocked on the parlor door and walked in. We were alone, he and I.

"It is Susan Rose, I believe?" he said when I walked in.

"Susan, sir," said I. "Mrs. Norval prefers to use both my names as if it was one."

"Ah." He looked friendly enough. "Do sit down, Susan. To be honest, this is delicate, what I have to say to you."

"Yes, sir," I said, and then, "Begging your pardon, sir, but the lady?"

"My sister is fine," he said. "Her maid has brought her upstairs to rest."

"Yes, sir."

"May we speak plainly, Susan?" said Mr. Brooks. "This is, as I said, a delicate thing."

"As you like, sir."

"I fear that Mrs. Norval may not be . . . altogether well. She suffers a great deal from nerves, as I am sure you know."

"Yes, sir. She is . . ." Then I thought to stop speaking.

"Do go ahead, please," said he and when I looked up at him I saw that he was indeed worried and that he desired what counsel he could come by, even if it were from a servant.

"If you please, sir," I said, "Mrs. Norval is nervous, to be sure, but mainly we here, we servants, can make her quite . . . comfortable." I catched his eye as I said it and saw that he and I knew what the other was about. It was not her comfort, not entirely, that he worried on. He hoped that she was presentable, as much as comfortable, and I knew it.

I did not think that Mr. Brooks was in any way a bad man. He did not seem to me to be one of those who would like their relative to be locked away in a place. He did desire her to have as pleasant a life as she could, I reckoned. But he was as anyone would be in his shoes: afraid for what she might do, afraid for how she might seem when she walked out in public. He required us servants to do much for him. He needed us to do what he could not do for himself.

"You needn't worry overmuch, sir," said I, "for we do our best for Mrs. Norval and generally, she is glad at home."

"But today!" he exclaimed. "The baby must have suffered."

"Yes," I said, "it was quite a fright. But most times I can control her so that she is happy enough."

"Control her," he repeated. I closed my eyes with what I had just said to him, for I could think of nothing else to do.

"Is she that bad then?" he said in such a small voice that I opened my eyes back up and looked at him again. He was shrunk into his chair and so sad that I leaned forward in my own.

"Sir?" said I.

"It's just that she was so lively as a girl. I hate to see her this way."

I said nothing.

"How bad is it then?" he said.

"It's not so very bad," I said as gently as I could. "She is like a little girl, very often, and likes to have her way, but it is nothing too terrible. Between us servants we see to her. She does not perhaps eat as much as she should, but that is not," I said quickly, "because Mrs. McCullough's cooking has anything wrong with it, no indeed, sir."

"No, I know, Susan, and you needn't worry. I am grateful to you for . . . seeing to her."

"She is a good lady," I said. "And we all think so."

"What of today, then?" he said, worried.

"Twas my fault," I said for I felt that it was. "I should have been firmer with her. But I would not have let anything happen to the child. I had just made up my mind to disobey her, if you please, sir, when you came into the park. I would not have let anything happen to him for I love him as if he were my own."

"Yes, I can see that," he said. "He is fortunate to have a nurse such as you."

He stood up and walked around behind the sofa. I thought it seemed as if now we had got to the important part of the conversation. I kept very quiet.

"Jane has taken to you, I think. She mentioned your name several times as I brought her home and seemed eager to see you when we arrived home. Twas just by wheedling that I managed her into Lily's care without your attendance."

"Sir, I would have come!"

"Yes, but I thought you would be with the baby and I did not like to disturb your work." He looked at me kindly as he said it.

"Yes, sir," I said slowly, for in truth I was still suffering with the upset of it. "He did need a warming up, but I feel sure there wasn't no permanent harm done to him."

"Thank God for it," he said.

We were both quiet for a minute. Suddenly, he took his head in his hands. "Louisa Bonney is a stupid, meddlesome woman," I heard him say under his breath. "After what happened before, she should have known better than . . . I believe I will bring her here to see what she's done."

"Sir?" I said. "I don't understand." I was right astonished to have heard my old mistress's name though I realized that of course she was his relative, same as she was Mrs. Norval's, and he would know that the baby had come through her arrangements.

He shook his head at my confusion and smiled a bit. "It is nothing, Susan. Here. I will out with it. I should like to thank you for looking after my sister so well."

"You needn't, sir," I said.

"Please, Susan. I rest easier knowing that she is being well cared for and that the baby is safe."

I looked at him more sharply than I meant to at that word "safe," and he stiffened just a bit. I wondered about it but quick looked back down at my hands.

"And, Susan," said he very low, "I should like to ask you to continue, if you would, to look after my sister. I know that you were not hired to do this work, and so it seems right that you are recompensed for your labors in this regard." Reader: he handed me a sovereign!

"I will do my very best, sir," said I, taking the gold piece.

He thanked me again and then I excused myself and went back to my room. Davey was still asleep in his cot. I took him up and brought him to bed with me and he did not waken fully, but settled in to suckle. I worried for a time about Mrs. Norval and whether we could make her be good and what sort of place it was that Davey had been brought to, and then I fell asleep and we both slept til the afternoon.

MISS GARDNER'S REASON

Here I relate a circumstance that occurred so long ago, truly I cannot say that I remember all of it exactly. I will try to recall it as precisely as possible and to be as truthful as I can, though it may cast me in a poor light.

My mother having died in the childbed with me, I was taken by her cousin Lord W___, and raised as a companion to his own daughters. Whilst I was given the same education as those young ladies, yet I was made to wear their castoffs and denied many of the pleasures they enjoyed.

"Laura does not care for picnics. Laura does not care to primp for a party. Laura does not enjoy to ride" was their mantra, and thus I spent many a dull day inside with an even duller book. In truth, I owe them thanks. Without that I was envious, I may never have found the strength to seek what it was I desired—which was all they had that I did not!

I say here, and though it may sound a boast, indeed it is not: I was the most beautiful young woman for many miles. I know it is true for I saw the others. Against their flaxen blandness, I stood alone. My hair was like flame, my eyes large and dark, my nose elegant and aquiline, and my figure slender and tall. It may sound odd to you to hear someone talk thus about their own attributes with what seems like little humility. But I tell you now that I have had a long experience in the field and that I speak from a seat of judgment.

One day when I was about fifteen, I chose to walk in the garden while the young ladies of the family were at a dinner party to which I had not been invited. I came upon a houseguest, a friend of Lord W___'s. He was an older gentleman who had shown me much kindness over the years. We fell to walking together. By the end of our walk, I was no longer a maiden. He had not forced me; I had simply agreed to his heartfelt request.

He took me home with him to London under the guise of wanting to "do something for me," and do something for me, he certainly did. Having been to the Orient, he was schooled in many exotic ways of love, all of which he taught to me. He delighted in my candor, in my enthusiasm, and indeed, in my natural abilities. He gave me gifts and took me to the theater, and on his arm, I met the great artists of the day. When he died, he left me some money, but also, something more important. He left me his set.

I decided to strike out on business for myself. Always ambitious, I had no interest in luncheons and whist; I preferred to take my fortune and make it larger. My clientele was quite the very best of England's cream. I saw Paris and Venice and Rome. I lived as I wished and worked when I liked. If I did not like, I knew that the men would wait, as a dog waits for its dinner.

When I found myself with child, I was not entirely displeased. Like many other women, I had felt the draw of motherhood. I certainly had enough money to raise a child and to give it the best of everything. If society proved a problem, I could live in France or even America. Should I later need to marry, for the child's sake, I saw no reason why that should prove difficult.

What I could not do, of course, was to suckle it. Work such as mine depends on a figure. Mine, even during pregnancy, proved an irresistible draw to whatever gentlemen I wished to see. I knew I could regain my former slimness after the baby came. But suckling a child causes a flaggy bosom which would never do. Therefore, I sought and found a wet nurse, a Mrs. Rose from Leighton who came highly recommended, and I brought my little daughter there. Caroline lived there til she was twelve months old and I found the arrangement very satisfactory.

Thirteen

I could not have loved my Davey more. Indeed, I was amazed at how my heart would beat to see him again, even if all I had done was to run to the kitchen for new nappies. I thought of all the babies I had nursed and how dear they was to me, every one, but, Reader, the difference between how I felt for them and how I felt for my own child was the difference between milk and cream. Twas all I could do to hide it, for I must hide it, from the other servants and Mrs. Norval both. There is a look as mothers have for their own children that they do not have for those they look after and that is what I could not show to any but Davey himself.

He was getting fat on mother's milk and his bit of gruel. His belly was as round as a plum and his eyes were like gray stars with lashes just as long as ever you could please. It seemed to me that his eyes would turn brown, like his father's, and I wondered if his hair would curl. Ofttimes now I would think on Harry Abrams and try to picture his face in my head. I would not allow myself to go too far, for I did not want melancholy, but I was pleased to think my dear baby was that man's son for I thought him a fine man.

When Mrs. Norval did not require me, I would spend all my time with my little son and gaze at him as much as I liked. I could not forget the horror I had felt when I had first understood that he had been taken from me. Losing my Joey had been a sadness I almost could not bear, but the hell of knowing that Davey was in the world but not with me had been worse.

For a few weeks after Mr. Brooks had talked to me about his sister, all was well. Christmas Day came and Boxing Day, and we servants had a goose to eat, as a treat from Mr. Brooks, and also some extra shillings in our pocketbooks, from him as well.

"He is a lovely man, ain't he?" sighed Carrie when he had wished us all a happy Christmas. Mrs. McCullough looked at her very severe which made us all laugh loud.

"Mrs. McCullough!" said Carrie. "I mean nothing of the naughty sort and you know it well! The idea!"

Mrs. Norval seemed to enjoy Christmas. She felt well enough to attend church with her brother and his wife and to take supper with them. Not a day went by that she did not ask to see Davey and one day she told me that she would like to give him a present. I suggested that he have a horsehair brush for his hair, which was not much on his head but which one day would be. I had always liked a horsehair brush, those that I had seen on ladies' tables, and thought that since he was but a baby and would not need it for a while, that I could use it myself and it would be no worse for the wear. Mrs. Norval was surprised that a baby might want such a thing, but I explained that while babies want nothing but their milk and a dry nappy, that Mrs. Stone, the lady who lived up the way, had a hairbrush for each of her children as a present as that was the way a good mother did it. I chuckled to myself later: I had used Mrs. Stone so often that she seemed real to me, and I had to recall myself to myself to remember that I had quite invented her.

On Christmas Eve, Mrs. Norval asked to hold Davey on her lap which she did do though only for a moment. I had to show her how to hold him around his little waist so that he did not topple over, and I begged for her to smell his head which carried the lovely yeasty scent that a baby has. She looked up at me, where I was standing over her as she held him, and she said, "Like this?" and I thought to myself, Dear Lord, this lady does not have the sense God gave a cat. She gave him back very soon; neither of them seemed overmuch comfortable with the other one.

At Twelfth Night, something turned in her head. I did not know why; none of us did. All us servants noted it; twas as if she had another letter, though Lydia swore that she had not. Twas all we talked about below-stairs, how strange she had turned, stranger than even Mrs. McCullough, who had been there the longest, had ever seen before.

Overnight, she became quite violent. She scratched Lily so hard on the cheek that the blood ran down her neck, and Lily cried that she'd be scarred for all her life. While Lily was a pudding, I did not like to see Mrs. Norval abuse her so, and so I told the girl to leave the lady entirely to me for the rest of the day. I myself attended to her and saw that her hair was done, as best as I could, and that she ate. She was docile for me, but I could not take her care all on myself what with the baby to look after, so I had to give her back to Lily the next day.

For several days, Mrs. Norval had her tantrums and her fits very often. Once, twas that her soup burned her tongue; at that, she threw the rest of the bowl to the floor and pulled the window curtains in the dining room from their rod. Another time, she screamed at Lydia when there was nothing to her liking in the post. Lydia was calm and smart and also, it seemed to me, she had seen this madness before in another place, for it did not shake her as it did the others when

Mrs. Norval shouted and made no sense. It did not shake me either, which I believe is because I kept such careful watch of her. I could not help but fret, though, for what it was she might do when she was not o'erseen.

Twas not only Davey I worried for. I had grown fond of Carrie and Lydia and the others though it is true that I had a secret from them. But who among us does not nurse a secret? And I believe that if ever they had learned that I was Davey's real mother, they would not have blamed me for my actions. But never mind. It is Carrie who suffered the most perhaps from Mrs. Norval's strangeness, as we called it to be polite, though madness cannot be hidden by pleasant words.

One morning, as Carrie stood on the front stairs polishing the banister, she came into Mrs. Norval's view as that lady went down. And without a warning, Mrs. Norval pushed. Twas very terrible, indeed. She pushed Carrie and then stood and laughed while we all came a'running to see what the noise had been. There was Carrie crumpled at the bottom of the staircase with her face very white with pain and red with blood. Her foot was broke, but what's worse is that she had hit a small table with a blue vase on it, and the vase had shattered and one of the shards had flown into her eye. Mrs. McCullough called for the surgeon very quick and he came and said it was a wonder that she did not lose the eye completely. He bandaged it but it began to seep and to cause her very much pain indeed. For a week after the bandage came off, her eye was blood-red and she could not bear that a speck should fall into it, so that Lydia and I shared her blacking chores between us and were thus very tired by the day's end. Indeed, her eye still ran with green weeks later and I cannot tell you whether it ever healed completely or not.

When Mrs. Norval pushed Carrie, we all of us turned against her. I was the biggest and she minded me the best and so I was elected to bring her her meals and to help her dress. Lily was afraid of her; Carrie would not go near her; only Lydia and I could together see to her needs and defend ourselves from her violence.

I had begun to fear for Davey very much. What seemed very bad to me is that Mrs. Norval became quite fixed on him. She asked for him every day and no excuse I could make—that he was asleep in his crib or that he was rashy—would suffice but that she should see her little angel as she had begun to call him. Indeed, it did seem that the sight of him would calm her when she was disturbed, but I did not leave her alone with him, not even for an instant, nor did I step away from them when she held him stiffly on her lap the way she would do when I handed him over. He had grown to know her and would smile at her, but she did not smile back nor did she meet his eyes and talk to him. She just held him in front of her with her arms very taut. I thought he was a heavy baby to hold the way she did, but I think now that her madness gave her strength.

When she held him she kept very quiet. At first, I would chuckle and coo and say words such as, "Oh, is he not a little man, miss? Can you see that soon he will be a great brute?" But she did not answer. It made her think of something else or some other time to hold him like she did, and she was as one in another land where she could not hear me speak. It made me glad in a way that she did not like to have a fire in her grate, because I would not have put it past her to chuck him into it like a lump of coal into a stove. She was that strange.

Imagine my surprise, then, to hear what I will tell you next. Twas a freezing afternoon in early January. We had suffered much from her temper that morning, being as how she would have her window open to the weather and she would hang out of it in plain view of the street, with only her shift to clothe her. When I tried to pull her in, she reached around as quick as a spark, to slap my cheek. I was quicker than she and grabbed her arms and held them tight. I could feel the unnatural strength in her, welling up, like there was something underneath urging her. If I was not the Christian that I am, I would think that it were witchcraft at play. Twas the first time she had ever attempted to slap me, and it worried me very much and caused me to wonder whether we ought not to dose her with laudanum to keep her just a little sane. Twas a problem, indeed.

And therefore, that afternoon when she asked for the baby, I was full ready to refuse her. We had discussed it below-stairs earlier that day, and I had given forth that I thought she ought only to be allowed to see the baby when she was good.

"Like a reward?" said Lydia. "Can we, do you think, treat her thus? We must not overstep our bounds."

"Tis true," said Mrs. McCullough. "Mr. Brooks, for all that how friendly he is to us, will have an eye out to whether we are cruel or kind, or whether we are taking advantage. She is not so mad that she cannot make him believe her yet when she tells him she wants a thing and we will not give it to her. The trouble is that he does not see that she's as mad as she is. He cannot see it, for she acts more regular when she is with him. That's the problem but there's no ending to it that we can predict."

"Yes," I said. "She's our better, though she's mad. Tis a strange way to run a household but there you are."

"Susan," said Carrie suddenly, "I worry for the baby, you know."

"Yes," said I, though twas hard for me to speak, as my words did not want to form. "Yes, I do as well."

"We must all keep careful watch," said Mrs. McCullough.

As we nodded together I had but one thought: I must get us out of this place, my Davey and me.

Thus, though I worried I might overstep myself, I had decided that I would not let her see the baby that day. I did not know how I would manage it, but I had decided to do it. I was ready for a fit of tantrum; I was ready for violence; I was ready for anything but that she should hold my son that day. I sat in my room with him on my lap and waited for her call.

It came. I walked down the stairs feeling like an uglier Bathsheba, bent on protecting her Solomon. Mrs. Norval sat in the sitting room, just as usual, in one of her fancy gowns, unlaced at the back. The sweat stood on her forehead.

"Where is the baby?" she asked as I came in. "I called for him."

I had prepared myself. "Ma'am," said I very firm, "the baby is asleep. He is a'sleeping in his crib. I am sorry, ma'am, but he is not to be wakened just at the moment."

I heard her gasp and I held my breath and clenched my fists and looked at the floor. I was ready for what she would have for me. And then I heard her let her breath out and this is what she said to me.

"Yes. Mrs. Stone told me just recently that a sleeping baby must never be waked up. I suppose you must let him sleep and I will see him again later. Thank you, Susan Rose."

I was so surprised that, Reader, I swear I almost pissed myself. Twas eerie, to be sure. I thought to ask her when she had spake to Mrs. Stone and where and how, seeing as she was not a real person, but then I recalled to myself that I had got what needed to be got and I curtsied and went back upstairs.

In the days to come, she spoke of Mrs. Stone more and more often. Between times, she seemed as confused as ever. She would take up a book and turn the pages but I could see that she was not reading but just turning. Or we would take the baby for a walk if the day were not very cold, but she would not be able to stop walking, and so I would bring the baby back and send Lydia out to fetch Mrs. Norval in. Or else she would sit on her settee and rock, though the settee was firm on the floor, and she would eat up a whole afternoon just rocking and talking to herself.

But when I let her see the baby, she would tell me how Mrs.

Stone had told her to hold the baby "like this, that his little head may lean against me" (that was I who had showed her that) or that Mrs. Stone had suggested that the baby might like a game of Pat-a-Cake (which I had showed her how to do). Once she told me a story that Mrs. Stone told her, all about a baby who had very bad colic and had died. "How terrible for his poor mother," said Mrs. Norval, shaking her head sadly.

At first, I thought it was vastly amusing that Mrs. Norval seemed to speak with Mrs. Stone so very often, because she seemed to think Mrs. Stone a sensible person and it was helpful to us all that my lady would take her good advice. But soon, the advice became strange.

One day Mrs. Norval allowed as how it was Mrs. Stone's suggestion that the baby have some bites of meat at his next meal. No contradiction was allowed, though I pointed out that the baby's teeth had not yet come in and that he would certainly choke. Mrs. Norval did not care. And so I took the meat and chewed it to thin strands, as thin and soft as ever I could, and put the tiniest taste in his mouth, for she would watch as he ate his meat. He did not like it at all and it came out in his drool. But that did not matter to her: as long as she had followed Mrs. Stone's directive, she was very happy. Another day she was quite firm that Mrs. Stone had told her not to take the baby out of doors til full summer. As he loved his outings, this made me very sad. But she did not care. If Mrs. Stone had said it, it was what she would have.

And then one day, I came back into our room from the outhouse and he was gone. My heart banged once, so hard it hurt me. I yelled very loud so that Mrs. McCullough came to the stairs to see what was wrong. She did not know where he was and neither did Lydia nor yet Carrie. My blood rushed behind my eyes with fear. I made for Mrs. Norval's room as fast as ever I could, but I ran too slow, for as I opened the door of the bedchamber, I glimpsed her face as she closed and,

Reader! locked the door of her bathing room. I had seen her eyes and seen the evil there, and it was horrible.

I was quite beside myself. I banged on the door very loud and heard her giggle and speak, and I knew that she had my Davey in there with her. All us servants were a'banging and hollering but she would not open the door. And so there was nothing for it but that I must break it down. Twas not a heavy door, but not so thin either, but it did not matter what it was made of, I must get behind it. So I started at one side of the room and ran toward it as fast as I could, with my shoulder out to take the weight. And it broke open with a burst. I fell into the room nearly on top of Mrs. Norval, who began to shriek when she saw that her plan would be thwarted.

Lydia burst in after me and I saw her, from where I scrabbled with Mrs. Norval on the floor—I saw Lydia reach down into the tub and lift my baby out of it. He was dripping but thank the good Lord, he coughed. I heard him cough. And then it was that I heard Mrs. Norval cry, "Why did you interrupt his bath? How dare you? Mrs. Stone recommends a bath and I was so careful. Do you think I would ever have let it happen again? Of course I would not. I was ever so careful."

I stood up and took the baby from Lydia's arms. I was crying very hard and Lydia could see that I could not bear to care for Mrs. Norval just then. I took the baby and sat on the settee, which being satin became very water-stained, but I did not care. I examined him and saw that he was quite well, though still coughing a bit. I heard Lydia coax Mrs. Norval, with Mrs. McCullough's help, into standing up off the floor and getting into her bed, though the lady fretted and muttered to herself.

When I looked up at her in her bed, I caught her staring at me. The look she gave me was so contrary: contrite and naughty and angry all at once. And there was something else there too and I knew right away what to call it. It was glee, Reader, and I could not bear to see her, so I turned my face away.

I saw Mrs. McCullough say a thing to Lydia in her ear and then Lydia came over to me and took me from the room and down into the kitchen. I put Davey into his basket that I kept for him in the kitchen, and then I lit as big a fire as I pleased and I rubbed him with a towel til he was nice and dry, and then I suckled him til he was asleep. I saw that Lydia was brewing tea for Mrs. Norval. I saw her go into the cook's room and when she came out she was holding a small bottle. She tipped a bit into the teapot, and then she looked at me, and then she quickly went up the stairs with the tea tray. Carrie came to sit with me from where she had been hiding in the hall outside Mrs. Norval's room, as she feared to see the lady up close anymore. We sat together and did not speak.

Soon enough, both Lydia and Mrs. McCullough came down the stairs and into the kitchen.

"Brew us all a cup, won't you, Leah," said Mrs. McCullough to her girl, who had just come in from the market and did not know what the fuss was.

"Was it poison?" asked Carrie after a moment. "Was it poison that you gave her, Lydia? I would not blame you, but I wish you would tell me."

"No, no, child," said Mrs. McCullough. "Just a drop of laudanum, just so she'll sleep and let us have a moment. That's all. No one will be poisoning someone in this house, I don't think."

I cleared my throat very hard. I had not yet said a word for I feared that I would begin again to cry if I must speak. But I wished, like Carrie, to know the truth.

"Lydia," said I, with my voice very low in my ears. "Was he under the water? Did you find his head under the water?"

Lydia nodded at me, very serious. "I do not know," she said, "whether it was so before you knocked the door down, Susan, but he had sunk low into the tub when I saw him first."

"Yes," said I. "She may have been bathing him proper. It may indeed have been I who caused him to drown."

"But, Susan," said Lydia very gentle, "he did not drown, you know. You see that he is fine."

"There's one as did," whispered Mrs. McCullough.

We all looked at her to see what she meant by that. She was holding her two hands around her cup and looking into the fire. And this is what she told us.

"When I first came here, twas because the cook before me would not stay. She told me that a baby had drowned in this house. She told me that Mrs. Norval turned her back on it for an instant and . . ."

"You must never turn your back on a baby in its bath. Everyone knows that," said Leah very loud.

Then Lydia said, "Who is Mrs. Stone? Do you know, Susan? You are much with Mrs. Norval. Have you heard before of a Mrs. Stone?"

I nodded. "Yes," said I. "But she is not flesh. She does not live except in Mrs. Norval's mind. She is from her imagination only." And we all looked at each other and drank our tea.

"I wish," said Mrs. McCullough very soft, "I wish there was a way to remove the baby from her hands. I think a baby is not safe enough in this house."

I nodded and an expression jumped into my head. I had heard it only once before, and that was when I dined with Harry Abrams and his sister and mother. His mother said it, laughing at something he had said, and I remembered it. Twas a Hebrew expression, I knew, for she had said it in her own rough language, and they had laughed and then he had explained it to me and I had liked it.

"From your mouth to God's ears," said I. Lydia looked at me and smiled and Carrie held my hand and Mrs. McCullough nodded at the fire, and then we drank our tea.

❧

I knew that Davey and I could not stay in Mrs. Norval's house any longer. I must take my baby and leave. I must have a plan as soon as it was possible. And then, the very next day, just as if God Himself had heard my prayer in the kitchen, the answer to my troubles appeared to me.

It being a Sunday, Mr. Brooks stopped by to see his sister. Mrs. Norval was calm enough; it seemed that the laudanum that Lydia had dropped in her tea had still some effect. She greeted her brother nicely and offered him tea. Lydia said that when she served it, Mr. Brooks was reading his paper while Mrs. Norval sat very calm on her sofa.

After about an hour, Mr. Brooks called for his coat and hat and Lydia brought it. I had just closed the door of the baby's room and thus happened to be in the hall, so I heard what he said to her as he buttoned his coat and put on his hat.

"Jane, I almost forgot. I have had a note from Cousin Louisa Bonney."

My heart bumped my breast to hear the name.

"Have you?" said Mrs. Norval.

"Yes. She will come to town for the season and will call upon you next Monday. I shall bring her. She writes that she will look in on the baby to see how you come along."

"Oh, James!" said Mrs. Norval very loud and very sudden. Lydia told me later that the lady's face looked very red and white, at once. "Oh, James, do not let her come! I cannot abide her. She does not care for me and . . ."

"Nonsense, Sister," said Mr. Brooks quite sternly. "She is your cousin and she likes you well enough. She has asked to come and see the baby, and I will not deny her such a simple request. What would she think!"

"Please, James, cannot you tell her . . ."

"Jane, you must stop this immediately. We will stop by on Monday week for tea. Thank you, Lydia. Good-bye."

I remembered what he had said about Mrs. Bonney being a meddlesome woman. I thought he would bring her so that he might rub her nose in what she'd done by bringing a baby to a woman who was not herself all sane. I knew that Mr. Brooks was angry with Mrs. Bonney for having worsened a sad situation. I thought he was right to make her see what she had done, for Mrs. Bonney should suffer some, as well as the rest of us, for her meddling.

And so I came upon my plan. I thought it all out as I nursed my baby, in those long hours of the night, when everyone else is asleep. The picture of it played out in my mind, like it was a skit. Once the Bonney girls had given one for their friends, and Ellen and me had hid behind a door and watched them play, these rich young ladies and their pretty friends. When I thought about what I would do, I saw it like that: what would happen first, then next, then finally.

The next morning I told Carrie that I must do an errand and that she must watch the baby. I told her to take him into her own room upstairs, for Mrs. Norval would never think to go looking for him there. "I will do your chores for you, Carrie, if you will watch him. And, Carrie, do promise me . . ."

But here she interrupted. "Susan," said she very serious, "you needn't worry. There is no one more than I who knows her madness. I would not let her get him, not for anything."

I nodded and gave her a kiss, and then I put on my hat and coat and went out of the house. I quickly walked down to the square where the cabs waited, where I had got off the coach when first I arrived in London. I asked the way to where I wanted to go and paid my fare to the cab man and was taken there. Twas across London and took upwards of twenty minutes and along the way I saw sights I had not yet seen in my weeks there. We crossed the river and I saw the Tower and the clock. I might have felt like a holiday sightseer, except for my errand which was of a gruesome nature.

The cab left me off in front of the spot I needed. From there, I could see the dead yard, which it being London, was enormous. The day had gone blustery and cold, and the trees stretched down their branches toward the stones like fingers. Twas a terrible sight. I thought of my Joey. I thought of the baby who had drowned in Mrs. Norval's house. I thought upon Mrs. Caraway, the dead woman whose name I had taken to trick myself into my position, and of Ellen, who I mourned still, and of my father, who might yet still be alive but deserved to be dead. I hoped that when he died, and it could not be too soon for me, that he would lie in a poor grave with no stone so that no one would know who it was who was buried there and his name would be lost before many of his kin yet lived and died.

I entered into the house I needed and transacted my business. Indeed, it did not take long at all though the price was higher than I could have wished. When I finished, I found another cab quite quick to take me back to Umstead Square where I had got on. I found an apothecary and went inside. Last, I went to the used-clothes district, which I knew where it was, and bought the prettiest baby cap that I could find.

"I can wrap it in a bit of paper if you like, love," said the woman and I told her yes, please, as it was to be a present for a lady. And then I walked back to Hampstead Street where I found Carrie playing nicely with the baby. When I looked in at Mrs. Norval, I found her sitting on her sofa, fiddling her fingers near her mouth like a child.

Mrs. Norval was like a cockroach in the fire for the week before Mrs. Bonney was to come and visit. She could not sit, she must pace. She could not eat. She muttered to herself quite constantly. She could not be calm though she was not violent in any way. She did not ask to see the baby though she talked about him very much.

I arranged it with Mrs. McCullough and Lydia and Carrie so that I could leave the baby in their care more than I was used to doing. I told them that Mrs. Norval was quite beside herself and needed my attention, and as they were very glad to avoid her themselves, they were grateful to me and happy to watch the baby. I wished to be in Mrs. Norval's presence very much. Twas part of my plan.

The first thing that I did, on the afternoon after my errand, was to go into the sitting room and see her. I behaved as if all was very well. I smiled greatly and acted very gay and as if nothing unusual had ever happened. I feared that she would see me different after I had broken her door, but she seemed to trust me as much as ever. I treated her just as she would like, as a little lass, all beribboned. I confess that it made me sick to do it, but twas necessary.

"And, miss, you will never imagine," I said very bright to her as she watched me tidy up the room as she liked to do, "Mrs. Stone's maid has brought by a present. She told me to give it straight to you, as her mistress would like you to have it very much. Shall I fetch it?"

Mrs. Norval was very excited to see the gift and so I quick got it and gave it to her. When I laid it in her hands, she looked up at me all smiles and I had a pang for her sometimes sweetness. She was not bad, not to the heart. She unwrapped the package carefully, so to save the paper.

"Oh, Susan Rose, do see what Mrs. Stone has given the baby," said she as she held up the pretty bonnet. "How thoughtful! Oh, it is lovely, is it not?"

"Oh yes, miss," said I, "it is. Oh, miss! Might he wear it for your cousin to see him in?"

Her face fell as she recalled the visit she dreaded and she put the cap back in its paper and put her fingers into her mouth.

"Now, missy," said I, "Mrs. Stone will want to hear how much you liked the cap. Do sit at your desk and write her a note, will you not? I shall find out her address for you, if you like."

And so she did.

Reader, every day, nay, every hour I could do it without making her suspicious, I spoke of Mrs. Stone. Most of what I said was trifling: how Mrs. Stone's hair was very thick or how Mrs. Stone had trouble with her downstairs maid or how Mrs. Stone's elder boys, Luke and John (which names I got from a pair of twins as my mother nursed), were set to go to public school in Oxfordshire. Sometimes, I would tell Mrs. Norval about things more important to good mothering: how Mrs. Stone wished her children to learn their catechism and how she would not let her children stay up past their times and how she herself brought the baby to his father for a good-night kiss.

Mrs. Norval was eager to hear about her, very eager, and asked me many questions which I answered. Sometimes, so as to make it seem like the truth, I told her I did not know the answer to the question she asked but that I would ask my friend who nursed for Mrs. Stone. And then the next day, I would tell Mrs. Norval the answer like this:

"Ma'am, do you recall that yesterday you wished to know whether Mrs. Stone will let her children eat as much toast as they like at tea? And I said I did not know?"

Mrs. Norval nodded and looked at me for the answer.

"Well, just this morning I saw my friend Jo as works for her, and I asked her that very question, and she allowed as how Mrs. Stone gives them each no more than two slices, as she says more will cause indigestion. Is that not wise?"

All week, I peppered her with Mrs. Stone this and Mrs. Stone that, til the poor lady was quite gripped. I felt in myself that all my lies were somehow evil, but I could do nothing else. All I had to use was what I had in front of me and that was Mrs. Norval's strangeness and my own wits. And I must use both to save my child and so I would not think about what the most Christian thing might be. I had not the time.

As the week waned, I was hard pressed to remove Mrs. Norval from her bed. Her nerves were very bad. I had thought that I might need to be constantly reminding her of Mrs. Bonney's visit, for I wished Mrs. Norval to be nervous about it, but I did not need to mention it. The visit was overmuch in Mrs. Norval's mind, and indeed the only comfort she had at all was talk of Mrs. Stone.

On Saturday, she wept and would not eat and on Sunday, she retched into a basin after her luncheon, while I held her hair. She was very wretched and I felt pity for her, but I had started on a course I could not depart from, and must continue on my way.

"Ma'am," said I when she was calmer and cleaned up, "missy, Jo told me that Mrs. Stone wished you the best for your visit with Mrs. Bonney."

"Oh," said Mrs. Norval, her eyes very big in her white face, "how I wish I could talk to her about it. I am sure she could advise me."

"If you please, missy," said I, my eyes lowered very respectful. "Indeed, Mrs. Stone has offered you some of her thoughts about what she would do were she in your place. Shall you like to hear them?"

"Oh, I should like nothing better," said Mrs. Norval, sitting up in her bed. "She is so very kind! But I wonder that she did not write to me! It is odd to send her messages through a servant, is it not?"

"Oh, ma'am," said I, causing myself a chuckle, "not so odd, if you were to see her great number of children and how she cares for them. She says she would have writ indeed except for that she has never the time to pick up a pencil!"

"Well, I expect not; not when you have as many children as she," agreed Mrs. Norval. "But come, Susan, what is her advice for me? What does she say?"

"Well," said I, as if I was thinking and remembering, "she says that you must have the baby in the sitting room with you during the visit. She says that she shows her babies to her visitors and will not be parted from them. She does not have the nurse near. The nurse, she says, is for the house, not for the visitor. And besides, it is the style."

"Does she?" said Mrs. Norval. "Is that really the style? Is it really?"

"It must be so, if she says it," said I gaily, "for she is a lady who knows what it is a good mother should do."

"Well, that is true," said Mrs. Norval. "Only, Susan, what if the baby cries? What shall I do? I do not know how to make him quiet. Oh, Susan! I cannot have him in the room for fear that he will cry, but if I take him out, Louisa Bonney will think I am not a good mother. What shall I do?"

She was working herself into a fit, which I could tell because her face was again red and white at once.

"Never mind, missy, never mind. I shall look after him for you. I promise to you that he shall not cry. Do not worry yourself on that account, missy."

She looked at me blank-like, but calmed down right away and I stayed with her there, sitting on her bed, til she went to sleep.

Fourteen

On the day of Mrs. Bonney's visit, I rose quite early and my own stirring woke the baby. I carried him to the kitchen to sit before the fire so that I might nurse him while I had my tea and toast. He looked at me very fond while he nursed and smiled up at me around my tit, which made me laugh loud. He was a flirt is what he was. I kissed his brow and said my prayer that what I set out to do might work as I wished. And then I drank my tea.

Mrs. Norval rang for me very early. When I brought her breakfast to her, she allowed as how she had not slept a wink with nerves.

"But, missy," said I, very bold, "what is it that ails you? Why are you afraid of your cousin so?"

"Oh me, I do not know exactly," she answered. "She does not approve of me and thinks me weak. Ah, weak, weak, weak, weak . . ." and she would have gone on and on had I not stopped her with a shush. This is how she had begun to do. She would repeat a word over and over and not stop, just like she had walked around the park that freezing day, like as if she could not stop herself, nor could she be easily thwarted by others. Twas frightening-like, for it panicked her, as well it should. I think she could hear herself and that she knew she should stop but could not make herself do it.

Mr. Brooks was to bring Mrs. Bonney by at teatime. All week, Mrs. Norval had shown very much interest in what to serve for the meal. "Mrs. Stone says chicken aspic and cakes," she told Mrs. McCullough, who curtsied and nodded but later wished aloud for Mrs. Stone to come and cook up her own bird if she was such a proper hostess.

After her breakfast, the missus began to fret about what she would dress herself in. She forced Lily to take every gown from her cupboard and then began to shriek that she had nothing at all. When I came up the stairs to look in upon her, as I had begun to do for all our safety, I saw Lily open the door of the bedchamber and dash out. We servants had begun to know: at a certain point in her madness, Mrs. Norval did not know what we did and would not remember if we disobeyed her and so we must look to our own. This was to Lily's advantage for it meant that she could leave Mrs. Norval in the worst of her ravings and yet keep her position. When I put my head in her door, Mrs. Norval was standing in her shift and crying at her reflection. I hurried to help her.

"Come now, miss," said I, "look at all the lovely frocks. Can not you choose one?"

"They're ugly, ugly, ugly, ugly . . ."

I stepped up very close to her, and it worked to calm her down. She sat very forlorn on her settee and looked at me with tears in her eyes; quite helpless, she was. And then I saw my chance, and as I picked up the frocks from the floor, which she liked to see me do and which calmed her, I said in a very low voice, but very close to her ear, "Jo told me a secret that Mrs. Stone has."

She stopped quite suddenly and looked up at me to hear what it was.

"Now, miss," I said very brisk, "you must dress yourself. Shall you choose the blue?" (It was gauze. There was sleet coming from the sky.) She knew from my tone that she must obey or I would not tell her what she wanted, so she quick put it on and let me do her up. And then she sat down again.

"Tell me the secret," she said.

I made my voice very quiet and my look very gay. "'Tis something wonderful," I said.

"Tell me!"

"I shall, then. Mrs. Stone has a present for you."

"Another present!"

"Yes, miss. And this present will be just the thing for your cousin's visit!"

Mrs. Norval gasped and smiled her poor confused smile. "Shall it help?"

"Yes, miss," said I. "It will show your cousin that you are the perfect mother. Mrs. Stone has said that she admired the sort of mother you are . . ."

"Truly? Did she truly say such?"

"Yes, miss. She did indeed. She said that her gift to you would be a sign to those who see you use it, that you have no other thought than for the child. It belonged to Mrs. Stone, and she herself has used it all these years for all her babies and they have thrived because of it. She wishes you to have the same luck with your child that she has had with hers."

I do not know how it is I knew to say words such as those, but they worked to put a light into Mrs. Norval's eye. I will tell you here that I had a pang just then, for what I was working at because I knew that it was bad. But I thought to myself that I had no choice. I knew that the home of this poor lady with her befuddled mind was not safe, no indeed. I could not risk that she would hurt Davey, meaning the best for him. I did not know the exact circumstances of what had happened to the baby who had lived in Mrs. Norval's house before my Davey came, but I was just so curious and no more than that. That baby was someone else's baby. Davey was mine.

I looked down at her where she sat on her settee in her summery frock, all wrong, it was, with her hair a'flying out from her head and her brow damp from her sweating. She looked as eager as a pup and so I smiled at her very big.

"Indeed, miss," said I, "I will tell you what it is as you are so impatient. Shall I?"

"Yes, Susan Rose, tell me, I beg you!"

"Well," said I, going around behind her and taking the pins down out of her hair, "well, I know that it is a cradle. Mrs. Stone is giving you a special cradle." I had made my voice very excited, like I have talked to my younger brothers and sisters when I wanted them to like whatever chore I had for them. The smart ones were never took in, but the others got right to it to hear me sound so excited about potatoes or the broom. Ellen used to laugh so to hear me trick them, this I recall.

"A cradle!" said Mrs. Norval, all gasps. "Her own that she used herself?"

"Yes, ma'am," said I, "and it must be lovely because Jo assures me that it is the very cradle she kept in the drawing room so her visitors— and she had so very many visitors!—could view her baby as he slept. She does so love to show off her babies, does Mrs. Stone!"

"Yes, Susan Rose," said Mrs. Norval very thoughtful, "I do recall that you said that Mrs. Stone always kept the baby in the drawing room when visitors called. I recall that you told me that. And yet, I am afraid that he may cry. And how shall I make him stop?"

"You leave it to me, miss," said I. "I shall see to it that he is as good as gold."

She mused for a while as I did her hair up. She began to mutter to herself and I heard her say the word "letter," over and over.

"Yes, miss," said I, "you must indeed write to her to thank her kindly. But," said I as if the thought had just come to me, "where will you put the cradle? I should expect the delivery quite soon. Mrs. Stone knows that Mrs. Bonney will be by in the afternoon."

And so nothing else would do but that we must go downstairs and move the furniture in the drawing room to fit the cradle in. It upset her to do it, for she did not like a change in the way things were set about, but she watched without too much fuss while I made a space for it. She grew calmer when I plumped the pillows of the settee and when I picked up a speck off the couch that was not really there; she did like to see me tidy up though I do not know why it gave her such delight. I asked her if she should like a fire and she shook her head no, but then became confused and could not decide. I counseled against it, though the house was too cool. Mrs. Norval said she would go to her room to rest for a moment, but she bade me see to the delivery when it came. I thought that really she did not rest when she was in her room and that rather she was in there rocking or chanting or such nonsense as that. But it did better to have her gone just then, so I nodded that I would keep a good eye out.

Very soon I heard the bell ring. I ran and poked my head out of the door. There were the carters bringing the delivery and I told them they might bring it in the front door. It took only one of them to do it, for they were big men in their business.

I opened the door wide and showed the man into the drawing room and pointed to the little table I had cleared of its ornaments. And he laid the thing I had ordered on the table. I gave him a penny and he tipped his hat and went on his way.

I ran down to the kitchen to check on Davey, who was having a nap. Lydia said that she had played with him and that he had been very good and happy. I kissed Davey very soft and thanked Lydia for watching him. "She's terrible off today," I said, lifting my eyes to the ceiling to mean Mrs. Norval, and Lydia nodded and thanked me back for attending to Mrs. Norval so that she might not have to do it herself.

I heard no answer when I knocked on Mrs. Norval's door. I pushed it open to just look in at her and saw her sitting on her bed and rocking, back and forth, as if she was herself in a cradle. I thought to myself that of all the places that she would like to be in the most, a cradle was it. It seemed to me that every day she seemed to grow a little younger in her mind til I wouldn't be surprised to see her one day in a blue sash and the next with her fingers in her mouth and the next so that she could not yet walk down the stairs without her two hands held.

Rocking and rocking, she was, but when I walked in she catched herself as quick as she could and stopped it.

"Miss," said I, "Mrs. Stone has sent it and it is lovely, indeed it is. Shall you come down and look at it?"

"Shall I?" she said. She did not know how to get up off the bed, so I helped her to do it. I took her down the stairs very slow and talked to her low and light, as I have heard my brother John do with horses to gentle them. She seemed like a china teacup balanced on a mantelpiece too shallow for it; she held herself very rigid as we walked.

"It is right in here, the cradle Mrs. Stone has sent," I said. "And if you put the baby in it, he will sleep as sound as a egg in a nest and Mrs. Bonney shall be most impressed, that she will. I promise you."

We went into the drawing room and I led her over to it, and though she looked puzzled, she did not cry out. She did not want to touch it but she smiled at it and allowed as yes, the baby would look an angel as he slept there. I led her into the sitting room where she felt more comfortable and left her near the window where I knew she would sit, which she did, with her fingers in her mouth, but quiet. And then I went to prepare.

Davey was up and happy to see me. I played with him and sang him songs til he began to fret and flip his whole little body off sidewards so he'd be aimed to nurse. He was so strong! I undid my bodice and gave him suck til he was satisfied. And there I began to cry. I had known that it would come, this very moment, this which might be the last time that ever I nursed my child. I knew that what would soon transpire—and there's a big word for you—would cause our little lives—Davey's and mine—to change very large. Twas, indeed, what I'd schemed for, what I'd planned for: that they'd change.

I knew that I must remove my child from that house. I have explained that I could not simply take him lest I wanted to run for our lives for the rest of our days. There was naught I could do but what I was about to do. But what it meant was that he would be taken from me. I knew that. When they who made the decisions saw what I planned for them to see, they would indeed make haste to take Davey from the house. But that house held me as well. And thus, they would part us and there was naught I could do to help it.

I had endured and suffered and lied; I had cheated and tricked and pretended—all to get to my baby and keep him. And now, for his own sake, I must give him up. He could not stay in that madwoman's house any longer, whether it meant that we could be together or whether it meant that we could not. I thought I was like Hannah, and thought how she must have felt as she sent her Samuel, who she had pined for and wept for and wanted so bad, off to the temple. She knew it was what was best for him. It was sacrifice, is what it was. I mouthed the word as I looked at my baby in his eyes. Mine own filled up, and the tears dropped on his cheeks and he stopped his suckling to feel them.

When he had had enough and was drowsy, I set him in his basket, and then I pulled a small bottle out of my pocket. I had visited the apothecary on my half-day and had boughten this little vial. I uncorked it and as carefully as the miners must measure their golden dust in California, I tipped a drop of laudanum into my baby's mouth. He tasted it and did not like it but I watched as he swallowed it down. Then I took his best little white dress and put it on him, and smoothed his fine little hair with a bit of spit. And then, Reader, I took him upstairs into the drawing room and kissed him and laid him in the place that I had fixed for him and watched while the laudanum overcame him and he slept.

Mrs. Norval was at her place in the sitting room, by the window, just as I had left her.

"Ma'am," I said very quiet, "the baby is in Mrs. Stone's cradle now. I have taken care that he will be good and not cry. He sleeps there like an angel, just as she had said he would."

She only stared.

"You ought to go to him, missy," said I, "so that he will not be alone when your guests arrive. A good mother would not let her baby alone."

"Yes, I will," said she and drifted across the hall. I saw her give the baby a glance, and then I saw her go to the window and watch for her brother and Mrs. Bonney. I felt pins were pricking me all over, that I could not be in the drawing room to see if my scheme worked. Twas sure though, that I must stay out of sight entirely. If Mrs. Bonney were to catch a sight of me, twould go very bad. I would be blamed for what they were about to see and sent away at once, if not worse than that. And everyone would forget about Mrs. Norval and her madness, and Davey would be left there in that house with her. I must hide myself away.

I went up to my room. Twas not big enough for me to pace in. I sat on my bed and tried to be still but have never been very good at that except when there's a babe at my breast. And then I heard the ring. I quick snatched up my bonnet to shield my face, for I could not resist but to go out of my room to see. I crept toward the front stairway where I could peep down over the rail.

I watched as Lydia opened up the front door. There she was, the bitch herself, with Mr. Brooks behind her. She did not look changed at all. She was dressed warm with a coat with fur over very wide skirts. She handed her muff to Lydia and her gloves but kept her hat. I saw that she gave the house a sharp glance as she waited for Mr. Brooks to give up his stick. I heard her say that Mrs. Norval kept the house quite cool, did she not.

They waited for Lydia to put their things on the table so that she could show them into the drawing room as was proper, but suddenly the door of that room opened and out came Mrs. Norval. Perhaps she had heard them come in and her nerves would not let her wait for them. Perhaps she thought that she should greet them heartily. Whatever it is that she thought, it is certain that she did not understand how she looked in her gauze. Twas right pathetic to see her alongside Mrs. Bonney, who was dressed so elegant.

I saw Mrs. Bonney start to see Mrs. Norval looking such and then get herself over it and go and give her a kiss. I fancied I saw her draw back at the smell of sweat; twas indeed not close enough for me to see it if she did, but I had smelled it enough to know how bad that sourness was. I know that I did see Mr. Brooks look alarmed at his sister's appearance and then cast a angry look at Mrs. Bonney, who catched it but pretended she did not.

"My dear cousin Jane," said Mrs. Bonney with a false, high voice, "how good it is to see you! My word, are you not chilled in such a light dress? I admit that I am nearly froze."

Mrs. Norval stepped back and gave herself an embrace, as was her practice, with her arms curled tight around her. She said something very soft.

"You do not feel it? I wish I had your constitution, indeed I do," laughed Mrs. Bonney. "I shiver all throughout the winter months, and I must have several shawls at once."

Mrs. Norval did not say anything back and did not look up. Mrs. Bonney too said nothing. I could see her face and it wore its usual proud look though I could see worry on it too. When she catched Mr. Brooks's eye, she turned her head away and shrugged like it was no concern of hers. I thought to myself that if I were Mr. Brooks I should like very much to shake her to death. He had brought her to see what she had done by putting an innocent child in the hands of an ill woman, and the lady, though she could see that indeed the woman was ill, pretended that all was well enough. She acted as if there was nothing there that would keep her awake past the watchman's call.

"Jane," said Mr. Brooks, going to her and putting his arm around her, "how do you do? Are you quite well?"

I could not hear her answer.

"Perhaps we should walk into the drawing room," he said. "And then I am sure that Lydia will bring us some tea." He looked at Lydia, who curtsied and waited for them to pass.

Mrs. Bonney stepped through the door first, followed by Mrs. Norval and then Mr. Brooks. I held my breath but I did not have to wait long. There was a cry that I knew came from Mrs. Bonney, and then I heard Mr. Brooks yell something that I could not make out. Lydia wrenched back open the door that she had not yet entirely closed and ran into the room.

A laugh came up, or perhaps a shriek, repeated over and over, "Dead, dead, dead." Of course twas Mrs. Norval. I leaned full over the banister and tried to see into the doorway but could not. There was a crash and I heard Mrs. Bonney cry, "Cousin James!"

I could see nothing—just once I saw a flash of blue gauze swift by the open door. Lydia ran out of the room and down the stairs to the kitchen. I heard the sound of sobs and then shrieking, over and over. I could see nothing at all, and therefore twas only my own imagination that supplied the questions which beat me as violent around my head as ever my dad did hit.

Who, I wondered, had picked up the baby to make sure he yet lived? Had Mrs. Bonney fainted? Did Lydia attend her? Had the physician been sent for? Had Mrs. Norval thrown a vase? Who held Davey now? Was he safe? Did Mr. Brooks see to his safety?

Lydia pounded back up the kitchen stairs and into the drawing room with Mrs. McCullough in tow. Mrs. Norval shrieked again and again from inside the room. Mrs. Bonney ran from the room and stood panting in the foyer, with her hand over her heart, heaving and watching the door of the drawing room with horror. Mrs. McCullough ran up the stairs no doubt to come get me that I might soothe Mrs. Norval, but I quick stepped into a closet when I saw her coming so she might not find me.

The doorbell rang and I watched Mrs. Bonney be too stupid to open it up. Lydia had to come and do it. The physician came in and went toward the screams in the drawing room. He must have dosed Mrs. Norval; it wasn't long before there was finally some quiet. After a while, I watched as Mr. Brooks and the physician helped Mrs. Norval up the front stairs and into her room. They walked right past the closet I had hid in. When they had gone into her bedchamber, I ran quickly back into my room and waited. Mrs. McCullough brought me the baby, still hard asleep, gave him to me and sat heavily in my chair.

"Where have you been?" she said when she could speak.

"Why," said I, very innocent, "I was in the outhouse with a cramp. Was I wanted?"

"My God," said Mrs. McCullough, undoing the top button of her dress, "this is a madhouse. You cannot guess what she did."

"Mrs. Norval?" said I, tucking the coverlet around the baby. "Whatever can she have done? She did nothing to the baby, I think, for he looks as sound as ever."

"Nothing, you say," snorted Mrs. McCullough. "Nothing! Do you call it nothing to put a living baby in a coffin for its nap? Is that nothing?"

"A what?" I made myself gasp.

"That's right, my girl. That woman put this baby in a white coffin, all satin and ribbons, and set it right in the drawing room to look at, like a display down at the market."

"She never did," said I.

"Yes, and that bitch Mrs. Bonney nearly shat herself to see it, is what Lydia said. And poor Mr. Brooks is in a state. The doctor gave the missus something to make her sleep, and Lydia is with her for I could not find you to do it. But mark my words if the two of them—Mr. Brooks and Mrs. Bonney, I mean—don't get that baby out of here as quick as you could blink. If I was you, my girl, I'd be thinking about another position for I don't expect they'll be needing a wet nurse around here very much longer. I am sorry, for you're a good girl."

And with that, Mrs. McCullough stood herself up and went out of the room.

My plan had worked as well as ever I could have wished. I sat and watched the baby as he slept.

❧

Soon, Carrie came upstairs to sit with me a bit. Carrie told me that Mrs. Bonney had gone away, but that before she had, she and Mr. Brooks had drunk a glass of sherry in the sitting room.

"The door was not closed proper," said Carrie, "and I had gone to

252

see the" —here she shivered— "the coffin, isn't that awful, Susan, and so I heard a bit of what they said."

"And?"

"Mr. Brooks was quite hard on Mrs. Bonney for giving Mrs Norval the baby without it being her business. He said, 'For God's sake, Louisa, it is a child, not a puppet. You know what happened before; how could you have meddled so,' and she said back, very huffy, 'My intentions were the best, James,' and so he said, 'Your intentions were to meddle. You cannot treat a baby like a black slave in America,' and she said . . ."

"Did you hear what's to happen?"

Carrie's face fell. "Oh, Susan," said she, "I am so unhappy for you. They will take the baby away and you'll have no charge here. I heard him say to her that she made the mess and she ought to fix it and then I heard her say that she would send someone for the baby later today. Then she came out of the sitting room and told me to find her a cab and off she went."

I wished that my heart would break but I am that strong, Reader, that it did not.

❧

I knew that Mrs. Bonney was gone, and so I thought to walk downstairs and find myself some bread, as my stomach was rotten with nerves. I walked down the front stairway and looked into the drawing room as I felt curious to see the state of it. Twas a horror of a mess—a broken vase on the floor, the drapes pulled down, the little coffin shining strangely—and I thought to myself that I would help Lydia clean it before I left the house on the morrow. I could scarcely walk for worry of what I would do next.

I peeped into the sitting room as well and saw Mr. Brooks sitting with his head in his hands.

"Sir," said I, "shall I bring you a cup?"

He looked up. "Susan," he said. "Susan, do sit down. I'm afraid I have some unpleasant news for you."

He needed to talk, is what, and I have found that it don't really matter if you're brought up fine or rough, but that it helps to have someone to spill your sorrows to. I was just a servant in his sister's house, but my thought is that he reckoned I deserved to know what had happened, for I was shortly to be sacked. Or maybe he thought that my lowness made me the right one to hear the tale, as he could not tell his own set for fear of scandal. Or perhaps there was something about my size and shape that reminded him of his mother, who he might have talked to about his troubles when he was a lad.

He told me things that I already knew but should not have, and he told me things that I had not known at all but that made the story clearer. Some of what he told me made me put my fist in my mouth.

He told me that there had been a baby in that house before my Davey but that it had died. He did not tell me how, but he told me it had not been Mrs. Norval's baby but instead had belonged to a pretty housemaid who had lost her life in having it. He did not say who its father was but I wagered I knew. And he told me that Mrs. Norval had tried to care for it but that there had been an accident. That is how he said it: an accident. And so Captain Norval, who was in the Orient the whole time, never even knowed the first thing about it all, not even that it had been born. Only Mrs. Bonney and Mr. Brooks knew the story. And they had kept it quiet until Mrs. Bonney taked it right upon herself to award Mrs. Norval—like my Davey was a bauble—with another baby, even after what had happened with the first one. Here he shook his head. "I blame that woman for my sister's current state," he said through his teeth. "I cannot conceive what may have led her to do such a thing as give a baby—a foundling, to be sure, but still a human baby after all—to my poor sister."

I can conceive of it, I told myself. Mrs. Bonney had a baby and wanted to be rid of it and knew the way to do it. I thought back to when I was in her house begging her to give me my child and she had refused me, and how I had thought that it might be out of love for her own son that she wanted mine. But that was stupid of me. 'Twas only that when she got it she wanted it gone, by hook or by crook. By hook would have the baby in this house, safe enough. By crook would have it in this house, not safe at all. It was all one to her.

When I looked up, I saw that Mr. Brooks was looking at me quite strange. He had a look on his face as if he wanted to jump on me and kiss me or kill me. I started back, but then I held myself firm. I felt sick of this house and its strangeness.

"Susan," said he, "my cousin is sending for the baby."

I nodded, for I could not speak.

"I shall not let her have him," said he, quite strong.

"Sir?" I said.

"I cannot trust her to take care of this mess properly, though justice says she should. I shall have to do it myself." He fell quiet for a moment and then, "Susan?"

"Yes, sir?"

"You once told me that you love the baby. Is it true?"

My breaths began to come very fast.

"Like my own," I whispered.

"Will you take him?" he said quite fast. "Can you take him away from here? Would you do it, though he is but a foundling? Do you have a place to go to where you can live together?"

"I will find a place, sir," I said. I tried to sound calm but I do not think I succeeded.

"I will give you plenty of money for your trouble," said he. He took out his wallet and began to empty it onto the table. There was fifteen pounds there, Reader, fifteen pounds.

"Take this," said he, "and quickly pack your things. Take whatever you need for the baby. I shall call a carriage to take you to the train station. Can you do it?"

I nodded and started to thank him.

"No time," he said, "just hurry so that it will all be done with by the time my sister awakens. I must remove that horrid thing from the front room. Oh, one last thing, Susan. I must know this: Mrs. Stone—she is not real, is she? She is a figment, is she not?"

I shook my head slowly. "No, sir," I said very gently. "She is not real."

"Oh," said Mr. Brooks, his head back in his hands, "my poor sister." And that is how I left him.

❧

And so, Reader, I took my baby and we went to Aubrey by rail. It took many hours, but was quite comfortable after all. I had money enough to buy food and beer and felt quite excited to see the land fly by me as if I was a stork winging off north. When the baby awoke, very groggy from the laudanum, I nursed him and cuddled him and kissed him and he fell back asleep. I closed my eyes, though I wished to see the countryside go by, but I squeezed them tight to thank the Lord for my good fortune. Twas hard to believe how it had turned in the end.

I might have sobbed with happiness, but something kept me from it, and that was dread, still lingering around me. I had been afraid for so long that I could not stop my body from remembering its feeling. Let time pass, I whispered into Davey's head like as if I was talking to him, instead of to myself, as it was in fact. Let time pass, and the fear will melt away like butter in a pan.

Aubrey was bright and sunny and cold. We took a hansom to the place I knew best in the city, which was the Hebrew district. Ah, it looked like home to me!

You may not be surprised, Reader, that it was to this part of the city that I went with my baby. You may have guessed that this was the plan in my head all the time I was a'plotting and a'scheming there in Mrs. Norval's house: that if it turned out that I was able to run with my babe, I would head here, where I would never be found if one day all the truth came out about what I had done. For who would think to look for me here, after all? No one, is who. Those that do not think large enough, and that is mostly everyone, would not imagine that I had taken my baby and Mr. Brooks's fifteen pounds and gone to live with the Hebrews.

As I stood on the street and adjusted my bundles and my baby—not so much weight after all for a strong girl like me, but just enough to hold happiness—I thought a thought that made me smile to myself. And that was that as I stood there on that street in that neighborhood and looked at the familiar shops and stalls, I felt as if I was a'laying my head upon a soft bosom. Is that not funny? A town compared to a bosom! And yet that was how it was with me—twas as if I myself was a babe and had found a place of comfort. For that, Reader, is a good part of nursing right there, is it not. Tis nourishment, to be sure, but the comfort part's as important, and those of us as does it for our livings know it.

What did I hope for just then? I am a regular lass, after all, and I hoped for whatever we girls do. I hoped for safety and I hoped for a laugh and I hoped for a home. And it goes almost without saying that I hoped for love. And if it came my way in the shape of a man with curly hair and a bright brown eye, why, I thought I would catch it up and not let it go.

I asked the first passerby for the hospital and the lady smiled down at Davey in my arms and pointed to a building but a block from where we stood. There, we waited for a doctor to speak to. He was very obliging, and for a shilling or two, he told me of a lady who wanted a wet nurse and would take a one who had a baby already at the breast. There were those who would, if they seemed like they could do it, which is how I seemed. Plus, we came cheaper.

When I met Mrs. Golden, which was my new lady's name, I told her that I was a widow. I told her that I had wet nursed for many a year, from having lost a baby a long time ago. When she asked me, I told her the same lie that I had told before: that I was a Jewess but that I had been raised in a Christian home, being a orphan, and that I yearned to know more about the ways of my people. She liked to hear that, and told me that she would help me to learn. I was very happy, for indeed I much remembered my visit to their place of worship and wondered what it would be like to know more about the small customs of their lives. As I wished to make my home in the Hebrew district for a very long time, I thought it was best that I understand their ways. Though I have broken my share of rules, to be sure, I have always been glad to do as I ought, and was pleased to think that Mrs. Golden would teach me all that I needed to know.

"I shall show you our prayers and how we eat," she said, very excited and proud, "and you will feel most comfortable amongst us after a very little while."

"Ah," said I, "I am very glad to be here and would be entirely easy, ma'am, if . . ."

"If what, my dear?" said Mrs. Golden, very concerned-like.

"Oh," said I, contrite, "I did not mean to worry you, not at all. It's nothing, just a ache in my tooth, not even a ache, really, but . . ."

"Aah," she interrupted, smiling very broad, "as to a bad tooth, you mustn't worry! We have here the most excellent dentist and he will make short shrift of your tooth."

"Well," said I, very pleased and surprised-like, but wanting just a bit more, "I have always approved of a good dentist. It seems to me a most honorable way for a man to make a living for his family, or so I have always thought."

"Yes," she sighed just exactly as I had hoped she would, "but poor thing, he was widowed some time ago and never remarried. His chambers are just by here, quite near to the temple. Well, I shall point you to him tomorrow. And now, let me show you my fat little baby. Walk this way, Susan, do."

Mrs. Golden's baby was a fine boy named Samuel. He was very like Davey, with dark hair and bright eyes, but smaller, being younger. It seemed to me, and I said as much to Mrs. Golden, who kissed me to hear it, that nursing her boy would be like nursing my son's brother. She showed me to my room. It was a very pleasant room, with a chair and a good bed and a rug on the floor. And, Reader! There was a window in it!

ACKNOWLEDGMENTS

My sincerest thanks go to Alexandra Machinist, my literary agent. Every piece of her advice proved perfect. Rachel Kahan, my editor at Putnam, is a person of taste and passion and knowledge, and I am obliged to her. Thanks to Rachel Holtzman for her attention to detail and to Allison Hargraves for her editorial skill.

Allan Gurganus—genius suffused with kindness—continues to show me what an artist looks like. Rebecca Ashburn, my good friend, inspires and instructs.

I found soul food at the table of Edith Feffer. Thanks go to Vicky Dickson, Gina Devine, and Betsy Granda for wit and wisdom. Thanks to Lisa Rubenstein for wisdom and wit. Thanks to Carl and Susan Eisdorfer and Bob and Mary Deming for their support. Thanks also to Barack Obama for just being.

Thank you to my colleagues at the Bull's Head Bookshop at the University of North Carolina at Chapel Hill, especially to Stacie Smith and Mary Stone. I am indebted to the mighty Walter Royal Davis Library, also at UNC, where I found *Wet Nursing: A History from Antiquity to the Present* and *Breasts, Bottles and Babies: A History of Infant Feeding*, both by Valerie Fildes, rare and valuable books, each. Thank you to Michael Hanson for directing me to the ABNA, which I also thank. Thank you to Alison Robertson and Margaret Grayson for friendship and inspiration and to Barbara Bamberger Scott at A Woman's Write for a boost to my confidence when I needed it.

Thanks to Dave Deming, the most tolerant of men. And finally, with gratitude and love, thank you to Sandra Eisdorfer, editor, mentor, marvel, and mother.